The Memory Box

A Novel

Jay Caselberg

For my Constant Reader

Prologue

Every town has an identity. Whether it be a feeling, a sense of its own being wrapped up in the collective conscious minds of its inhabitants or not, it is still there. It is in the buildings and the landscape and it stalks the streets at night, wandering through shadowed laneways and painted with reminiscence and memory. Some might call it history, but it is more than that. The energy of a town lives within the walls and the gutters; it trickles through the day to day and stamps the impression of what it is behind the eyes of those who live there. If you look very hard, focus carefully, you might catch a brief glimpse of what lies behind.

People come and go, that's sure. They move, they grow old, they leave to another place or another state of being when it comes down to it. Newcomers arrive, swelling the ranks of population, but counted as a part of the greater sum, they are mere sand grains in a town's consciousness, in its memory of itself. They may add a shade here, or a burst of colour there, but the town itself goes on, heedless, until one day it may die as well, though that is rare. Somehow, they are far more adaptable than the individuals who might live within their bounds.

And sometimes, just sometimes, they might exert their own forces on the people who live there, whether they are aware of it or not. If we are not careful, the collected memories that shape the town's identity, may become our own.

-1-

Walter

The small corner store held a veritable plethora of delights. Tightly packed shelves that gave barely room to slide between them were stacked with spices and tinned goods and things that Walter could barely guess at. It was impossible to read some of the labels, but from time to time, Walter tried anyway, peering close, picking up a tin and turning it one way or the other trying to pick up a familiar script he could at least attempt to decipher. The family who ran the store worked long into the night, taking turns to stand or sit behind the counter, watching the small television up in one corner, and distractedly glancing at their intermittent customers. Pakistani, or Indian, something like that, they lived enclosed in their mercantile existence, somehow shielded from the rest of the world except for the lifeline that the tiny television provided and only really attached to the town by their sporadic interactions with their customers. Walter couldn't imagine that they had a life outside the day-to-day ritual of the shop. Except for those rare times, early in the morning, when he passed the shuttered windows, they were always open. The problem with the little store for Walter was that he was just as likely to come away from it with something completely different to what he had originally gone in search of: those times late at night when he ran out of milk or coffee, or needed some drinks to restock the refrigerator, or just simply when he'd been too lazy to shop, and he needed something quick and nasty he could nuke in the microwave to fill a hole. The place was a blessing really in that respect. He hated having to order home delivery and where they were, with the outlying nature of the town itself, the options were limited anyway. The monosyllabic interactions at his doorstep were not something he looked forward to at any time and out near the edge of civilised suburbia, delivery was never to be relied upon anyway. Resisting temptation for today, Walter moved to the front counter with the packet of ground coffee he had come in search of. He was okay for milk, he thought, so that would keep until his next proper expedition.

Walter — never Wally — had moved to the little town by the seaside nearly a year ago. His rented house atop a hillside looked out over the water, giving him an uninterrupted view of the beach on one side and looked back up to the escarpment behind, though he would need to stand on the tips of his toes to see over the side hedge at the back of the house that shielded his property from the neighbours to that one side. Woodford Park as a community suited him fine. It was small enough that you could know people if you took the effort, but if you had no such inclination, they left you pretty much to yourself. Two days a week, Walter caught the train into the city proper, a forty-minute commute, but the rest of the time, he worked from home. He lived in that conveniently engineered lifestyle where he could choose the hours he worked, as long as he produced the goods. Often, that meant he'd spend part of the day wandering along the beachfront or simply staring out over the ocean from the vantage of his front room while he waited for inspiration.

When he'd first seen the house, it was that front room that had sold him, those windows with their panoramic view of the cliffs and water. One of the first things he'd done as soon as he'd moved in was to set his studio up in that precise room to make the most of the view. His drafting table sat right in front of the central window. It didn't matter whether he was working late at night or in the middle of the day — he would always have the ocean.

Woodford Park had another advantage for Walter; two towns further down the coast and you'd be faced with tourists in high season, the family holidaymakers, or the simple day-trippers to the beach, but Woodford Park remained relatively unspoiled, a community unto itself. He thought that it was probably its position near a point on the coastline where the escarpment reached out, almost touching the sea, meaning that the beach and the town itself lost the sun earlier in the day than those places further along the coast. For that reason, it was as if the small community was off the beaten track, while being within striking distance of everything you needed. Of course, there were no cinemas or theatres and the nearest supermarket was twenty minutes away by car, but those were things he could live with. And after the breakdown of his marriage, Walter didn't need any of those things particularly. He'd been bitten, hard. Woodford Park gave him a refuge from the memories that lingered in the city itself and among people in general and it gave him the chance to come to terms with himself. There were times when he felt alone, but most of the time, he was perfectly content to live with his own company and the twice-a-week interactions that his architectural firm provided supplemented it nicely. For now, it was enough.

Having made his coffee, he sat sipping, his hands cupped around the mug, trying to prepare himself for an assault on the current project, but nothing was coming. By the time he'd finished his coffee and placed the mug back in the kitchen after rinsing it, there was still nothing there, not even a spark.

Walter looked out the window, down at the beach and along the coast road that ran along the ocean's edge, curving back and forth with the contours of the coastline. A line of trees ran along the beachfront, thick-trunked pines. They looked as if they'd been there for decades. Up to the left ran a row of houses, neatly tended gardens and the requisite rose bushes — old people's homes, he thought. He'd been playing with a ruler in one hand and chewing on his bottom lip as the thoughts of what had brought him here played through his head. That wasn't productive at all. He slid the ruler back and forth in his fingers and then gently placed it down on clean, unmarked paper. Time to go for a walk; he was getting nothing done here.

Funny, he'd never thought about it before, but Woodford Park didn't have a park. It wasn't a park. It had enough trees, and enough green spaces, but that hardly qualified it as a park. Woodford Beach, Woodford Bay, maybe something like that. But Woodford Park? Perhaps there didn't need to be a reason for the name. Maybe it was just a name after all.

He was still wondering about it as he reached for his old green coat behind the door, pulled it on, and then patted his pockets to check that his keys and wallet were in place before heading out. What he needed was a breath of fresh air and perhaps a whiff of old seaweed along the beach, the touch of iodine. Perhaps that would clear his head.

-2-

Angelica

As she lay sprawled across the bed on her stomach, her feet raised behind her kicking slowly back and forth, Angelica pored through her memory box, riffling through the collected keepsakes and correspondence that she had collected diligently over the years. Angelica often remembered, and she remembered very well. In some carefully constructed way, barely realised even by herself, she had made a particular talent of remembering. One could even say that for Angelica, remembering was somewhat more than a simple hobby, something she did on the odd occasion to pass the time; it was an essential part of what she was, a fundamental component of her being. After all, what we are, is as much what we remember we are, or what we have done. Our memories make us what we are, at least our perceptions of what we are.

She lifted a single letter, slightly crumpled with re-reading, and then a photograph, peering down at the smiling face, not quite in focus, and gave a half smile in return. She traced fingertips across the boy's picture chest. He had been so sweet, that one, her Damien. She wondered briefly where he was now.

The reactions invoked by the box's contents came quite naturally; they welled up inside her and touched her face as she lay there, the breeze stirring the curtains, parting them from time to time and allowing the world outside through the half-open, wood-framed window, a mere glimpse into that secret part of her life, the part of many hidden events and components that made her what she was. To be honest, when she was rooting around inside her memory box, Angelica really didn't care whether the world was looking in; she was somewhere else, in another place entirely, somewhere dusted by reality, but not necessarily of it.

She kept the memory box shoved under some clothes, some old knitted sweaters, in her bottom drawer, pushed right to the back, only pulling it out when she knew there was no chance she might be disturbed in her private ritual. Of course, there was always the possibility of a random visit from a friend, or the unexpected phone call, but they came rarely, but they still came all the same. Some days, she knew instinctively that she would be alone and would remain undisturbed while she indulged her ritual.

The box itself was deep and solid. It fit well into the heavy bottom drawer of the chest, painted white and decorated with small blue flowers, which stood near her bed. Cowry shells and lace designs adorned the box's lid and sides adding touches of white to the pastel blue motif. Pale blue and white, they were Angelica's colours and they matched the colouring of her room, the silken bedspread, the knotted lace strip that fanned out above the head of her bed affixed to the wall, just like the clothes she wore, all layered pastel, often offset by a knitted shawl. The incense smell that lingered in her room bore the taste of roses.

Summer had come early this year and already the breeze that tugged languorously at her curtains was heavy with warmth, full of the scent of seasonal grasses and slowly baking earth. When it was in the right direction, more usually in the afternoon or early evening, it carried the taste of salt and other hints of the nearby beach, sometimes the tang of seaweed after a heavy tide. She felt she should be out and about, doing something, perhaps going for a walk on the seafront, or wandering through the local market, picking through the stalls, looking for something new to echo the change of mood that came with the weather. Today, after all, was market day. She sighed and reluctantly closed the lid on those fragments of what she was, that jumbled stack that represented the collected pieces of her past, and she slid the box across the floor toward the large chest of drawers. It was time to be out and about. Rolling over, she propped herself on one elbow and combed her fingers through the long blond curls, dragging them through a resistant tangle on one side. Long pale fingers, always eager to touch, soft and sometimes hesitant in their explorations. Soft and fragile, somehow, like the image she held of herself.

Damien had definitely been the Sweet Boy's name. She was right about that. She frowned a little as she tried to remember exactly how they had parted. She recalled that he had moved away, but there had to have been something that had caused him to make that decision. In the photograph, he was standing in front of a waterfall, wearing baggy green shorts and little else, his tanned, sleek body dappled with the shadows of surrounding leaves, his dark eyes slightly squinting against the sun, but grinning that broad infectious grin of his. He'd liked that sort of thing — trekking, going off to seek adventure — and perhaps in the end, that was what had taken him away It was a reasonable explanation, but there was something dissatisfying about the thought that the world might present more adventure to him than she had. Still, it had been his choice, and ultimately, she thought, it had become his loss. Angelica had simply moved on now, but she liked to remember all the same. It was strange that the memory seemed to yellow and fade with age, just as the photograph had. It was right that she had moved on.

Angelica had moved on after the funeral too. Well, things had moved on and she had moved on with them. She had adjusted, just as we all adjust, changing that place where life is characterised by empty hollows by filling them with things that mattered in what was to become her new reality in the sudden unfamiliar shape of her world. She had never expected it to happen, but then you wouldn't, would you? Johan, Her Man — they used to joke about the way she called him that — Johan Her Man, brimming with life and his own special sense of adventure, Angelica's anchor, had ridden his motorcycle off the side of a cliff. He hadn't meant to do it of course. They'd told her that Johan had taken the curve too fast. Maybe that was the real explanation, or maybe it wasn't, but the result was the same anyway. He had always liked to ride the curves in slow motion, his consciousness slightly altered by one substance of another. It was "experiential," he had always said, waving away her protests. In that one act, whether conscious or not, he had left Angelica with spaces where once there had been someone *there* and *present* to fill the rough voids in what she was and how existence moved around her. That one act of consequence had been dreadfully unfair. Damn Johan anyway. He had always been so strong. Whether he was damned or not, he didn't have the right to have liberated that moment of weakness that had taken his life and hers along with it. She pursed her lips. She couldn't afford to think like that. But that was gone, and she wasn't going to think about it anymore, or about him, or about what could have been. Not today. She'd told herself the same thing countless times over the past six months. Outside, the sun was shining and really, she should be getting out and on with things again. She swung herself off the bed and stooping down, pulled out the heavy bottom drawer, lifted the layer of clothes with one hand and with the other, lifted her memory box, struggling with its weight, and then pushed it deep into the drawer's back corner. She stood, and with the side of one foot, pushed the drawer closed. There were things to do, she thought, with a brief glance out the window through the curtains, which had chosen that moment to part, just enough to let her see out, down the hill and further to the arc of ocean and cliff top she could see from her bedroom window.

-3-

Saturday

On a cliff top, overlooking Woodford Park's smaller bay, sat on old hotel, disused now for years. Once it had sat resplendent in pastel yellow, a bright white sign announcing to the coastline at large, Hotel Bellevue. Now, only one or two bulbs remained, dusty and yellowing, the rest of the sign gaping holes where the bulbs used to sit, like a mouth full of missing teeth. The remaining bulbs were grey and brown with dirt and age. The yellow of the walls themselves had faded towards grey as well, and the windows lay empty and dark. From time to time, Walter would look up at the old ruin on his trek down to the beachfront and wonder what it would take to bring the place back to its former glory, how much money and madness would be needed to restore the hulk. He hesitated to think what it might be like inside, now. What would years of humidity and damp sea air do to the interior of a place like that?

He'd never broached the subject with any of the longer-term locals, but he would have guessed that the hotel had its heyday somewhere back in the fifties or perhaps even earlier. He could imagine the well-to-do resort set standing out on the terrace sipping cocktails or dining in their formal evening suits behind long, draped white curtains in the panoramic dining room. It was an era long past, but one that he fantasised about, polite society, what it would be like to have been a member of that set. In comparison, modern life was all that more mundane when set against those fantasies. Looking back up at the hotel though, he could see what might inevitably become of an imagined life like that, left to moulder and decay upon a windswept cliff top, but then was this any different? He wondered. Maybe his life had become the same thing — slowly bleaching to dried remembrance by the seaside.

But Saturday was market day. It drew the locals, certainly, but also people from nearby towns and the local crafty community seemed to emerge from their burrows as well, so there was always something entertaining to look at, sometimes in a kind of car-crash sort of way, but enough to keep Walter vaguely amused, though still sufficiently detached from it all. The stallholders, local and itinerant both would set up their displays in the local school grounds, close to the small local shopping centre and the beach, including the contingent from the local church with their home-made preserves and chutney's in bottles sealed with diagonally checked waxed-paper and elastic bands, their labels painstakingly hand lettered in curling script. He would wander amongst the stalls, looking at the people more than the wares. Woodford Park also maintained a local artist's community, and inevitably, there would be the ranks of tastefully brushed pastel watercolours depicting either beach scenes or simple sea and skyscapes. Nice enough if you liked that sort of thing, but he always thought that you could have only so many of them. Every beach front resort town boasted its seascapes and the boats upon the water, either in the distance or from a much closer perspective, although to be honest, Walter had never actually seen a boat on the small town's water, only those far off down the coast. All Woodford Park was missing really was the lighthouse which would, of course, have spawned endless series of tasteful watercolours — gulls over the lighthouse, sunrise behind the lighthouse, lighthouse and the beach, and so on. Even the inevitable non-present yacht would have appeared, no doubt. Claims about the light being special in the bay were nothing more than propaganda, he thought, spread by the artists themselves to help justify their own lifestyle choice. Without the self-promoting community, he wondered how many of them would have remained as little more than hobbyists and how many of them really were anything more anyway? Then, of course, there were the potters, the woodworkers (all using either found driftwood or local timber), the intricate bead and feather work, the macramé, the knitted shawls. His favourite, he thought, was the local church, always there in the same spot, with their homemade preserves and knitted tea-cosies and the floral-dressed ladies with their tightly permed white or purple-rinsed hair. It was all very much a far cry from what Walter imagined life in Woodford Park must have been when the resort set were in their prime. No dinner jackets and cocktail dresses in this lot.

He spent some time picking his way through the stalls. The weather was good, not too warm and a slight breeze blowing off the ocean and for a few minutes he stood in the centre of the market just breathing deeply of the smells. It was so removed from the life that he'd escaped by moving down here. The city, the social obligations, the restaurants and the clubs, the competition and the noise, all those belonged to someone else now. In a way, they belonged to her; they had become a part of the divorce settlement. Thank god, they had chosen never to have more than one kid…not that it had really been a choice; it had just sort of worked out that way. Until the separation, they had both been too busy in their own ways, and then after, well, they were busy in different ways.

His thoughts were interrupted by an explosion of loud, female laughter from a stall at the end of the nearby row and he looked in that direction. Whoever it was, was making her presence felt. He took a slight step to one side to get a better view. Oh, talk about a car crash. She was standing next to one of the hippie stalls, second-hand clothing and black and purple velvets, in an animated conversation, with much hand waving involved. Walter clasped his fingers behind his back, just standing there and watching. Yet another burst of laughter, and the woman tossed back her head with it, as if she were simply laughing at the sky. Funny, her dress was almost an exact match for that sky, even down to the faint white pattern, echoing the vague brushstrokes of high cirrus far above, reminiscent even of the ever-present watercolours dotting the stalls around them. He guessed she was about forty, but she was trying too damned hard. The blonde hair was heaped in a profusion of curls and the grand gestures showed the sparkle of chunky silver rings on both hands and silver bracelets on each wrist. She leaned in closer to the stallholder, a goth woman, heavy eye makeup, draped in black velvet, as if they were sharing a secret together, and then tossed her head back again with another loud laugh. Walter shook his head slightly and then looked away. God, what a disaster.

There seemed to be nothing to hold him in the market today and the woman's laughter was still grating on him, so he decided he'd head down for a stroll along the beach, watch the water for a while, and then make his way back home, perhaps pick up a couple of things at the corner store on the way back. The beach looked empty, apart from an old couple walking a dog, a scrappy brown and white thing that kept lunging at the waves and barking. It, at least, seemed to be having fun. Looking at the old couple, he wondered. Had they been together for thirty or forty years? Was it a generational thing? Or maybe they had found each other late in life, drawn together for the solace and the companionship they could provide to each other. No, he thought, it was better not to think about that at all. I would just make him maudlin.

He had turned his attention to making a list of things he might possibly need to supplement his dwindling supplies back at the house in his head when again that laugh interrupted his chain of thought, carrying all the way out of the school grounds and down the street even above the faint noise of the market itself.

Her laugh continued, following him all the way down to the beach and into his memory later that evening.

-4-

Angelica

She had grown up in the country, the closed-community, little town environment had kept her apart initially. Though she had wanted to belong, to fit in, the town's population raised its invisible unspoken, but somehow mutually-agreed barriers. She had felt betrayed, abandoned after her father's disappearance, and desperately she had wanted a sense of family, of belonging. That was at first. In a small town environment like that, especially a few thousand souls separated from the masses by distance or geography, everyone knows everyone else or at least seems to.

Angelica had gone to live with her grandparents in Sandton shortly after her parent's separation and divorce. Her mother was forced to take a job in the city to make ends meet, as her father was nowhere to be found. He had simply disappeared, and Angelica wondered, from time to time, whether her mother had suspected or had an inkling of what he had been planning. There was a time, a period of uncertainty, and then her mother had decided what would be best for her. In the woman's mind, it was the safe and stable environment of Sandton. Safe and stable for her mother, it might have been, but she, Angelica, was a newcomer, something to be wary of, and as a fresh arrival, she had not yet shown where she belonged as far as the town's collective shared subconscious perceptions were concerned. Sandton narrowed its eyes at her, and she felt it.

The town boasted a single main street, shops, a couple of hotels, with the traditional working men's bars and a network of families that extended through the community like clans. There were the Stevens and the Blacks, and they were related somehow to the Franklins. On the other side were the Billings tribe, who were in turn connected to the Carmanolas by some curious quirk of marriage. The Carmanolas were a broad network, all fruit growers, of hardy immigrant stock that had been in Sandton for several generations, so they had proved many years ago that they were a part of everything that made Sandton what it was. Despite the name, they very much belonged. Their rambling orchards and vineyards provided summer jobs for the local kids, picking or packing, wherever the need lay. Angelica herself had spent time in the large echoing green shed with its conveyor belts and stacks of boxes while the heat beat against the metal walls, broad doors pushed open at either end to give a cross breeze and some release from the sweltering heat. That experiment had been short lived. Her grandfather, a conservative country lawyer, blanched slightly and became very quiet when Angelica had returned one day and asked him, in all innocence, what a particular word had meant. He had glanced at her grandmother and then away, not saying a further word. It was more than enough for him, and it was enough to put an end to Angelica's association with the Carmanolas packing shed.

Of course, her grandfather's actions set her even further apart from the rest of the tribe, enforcing, in their minds, an unwarranted removal from the normal yearly rituals of Sandton life. It was clear that she thought she was better than the rest of them and they didn't much like that. Afterwards, she had missed it though. Although the work had been repetitive, and she had spent most of the time slick with sweat, they had called her Angel, and she had liked that.

The rest of the close-knit community was ordinary, uncomplicated. Many of them were farmers, though another section of the population toiled in the local mine. There were, of course, the local shopkeepers, and the people who also worked at the single small department store that sat right in the middle of Main Street flanked by a pharmacy on one side and a small bakery that specialised in frosted cupcakes. At the edge of the town clustered a small community of truckers, somehow related to the Blacks, and also boasting a few of the local miners. Of course, they had kids in the local schools, but she wasn't supposed to mix with them. In her grandfather's eyes, they were undesirable. Angelica never quite understood why. Was it what they did? Was it beneath them, the right living Coopers? Or maybe it was some dark secret that her grandfather knew because of forbidden knowledge granted him by the dealings of his profession. Maybe, it was as simple as the fact that they were Catholic, and in her grandfather's eyes, Catholics as a whole were an inferior part of the community, unlike the clean-living Protestants that they were.

During her time in Sandton, she saw her mother roughly once every two weeks, on the weekends. Her mother would make the journey down from the city late on a Friday night after work to spend time with her daughter and her parents. Angelica would accompany her grandfather in the old green Volvo he favoured, to the train station to pick her up. If she was lucky, he might splash out and buy her an ice cream at the small station kiosk while they waited in the tiny wood-panelled waiting room, the station clock above the ticket office window ticking away the minutes to her mother's arrival. Angelica would sit there in the slatted wooden bench, kicking her legs back and forth, in a nice, clean floral-print dress with her hair in braids and ribbons. Typically, her grandfather would say nothing, but then, he was a man of few words, and really, he had very little to talk about with a young girl, though he dutifully held her hand while they watched the minutes click past.

Although Angelica wasn't aware of it at first, her mother looked a little more pale and drawn with each successive visit. Holding down the job in the city, teaching at a day care centre, and keeping her modest apartment were taking their toll. Also, of course, the fact that her husband had abandoned her, and she, now a single mother, was the subject of sidelong glances and the moral judgement that came with the values belonging to the time, regardless of where the fault lay. It didn't matter that she was a divorcee; her mother had become a single parent. In a sense, it was guilt by association, and somehow, some way, of course, her mother was to blame. Looking back, Angelica could see the change that grew in her mother's demeanour, and the unspoken looks that passed between her and her grandfather with each new visit. Typically, Angelica would leap from the bench and run to the platform at the first sound of the train's approach, and then stand there, scanning the passing carriage windows for her mother's face. Her mother would emerge from one or other of the carriages, struggling with the small powder blue leather suitcase she carried on such trips and Angelica would race along the platform to throw her arms around her mother's waist. Her mother would drop the case, place one hand on Angelica's back and with the other, stroke her hair as she held her close. Over time, the stroking grew less frequent, the pressure of her hand on Angelica's back less firm, but these were not things that Angelica noticed, at least not consciously. Towards the end of that period, the case remained clutched in her mother's grip, and the stroking of the hair become an absent-minded patting on the top of her head, like greeting a family pet when you had something else occupying your thoughts, as thing of familiar ritual rather than consciously directed action.

During that period, the Sandton period, of her father she heard nothing. He had simply vanished into thin air.

Sometimes, late at night on the weekends when her mother was in town, she could catch snatches of furtive conversations where her father's name was mentioned, but she either could not hear enough, or she didn't understand what they were saying. Little by little, her father became little more than a collection of disembodied images, like pieces of torn-up photographs, scattered on the wind. After a time, even his face became an indistinct blur, an image she could almost make out on the passing breeze as it fluttered past her face. Funny that the clearest image she had was of his hands. They were firm and solid, almost tangible in her mind.

It soon became clear to Angelica that there were very few individuals she wanted to be associated with in Sandton town, so rather than fighting her exclusion, she embraced it. At school, she was surly and tended to one word answers, never one to raise her hand in class. She sat alone, at the back of the classroom and scribbled in the margins and across the front of her notebook. She doodled on her pencil case with markers. As a result, her performance was less than stellar, and in later months it was to become a topic of conversation between her grandfather and her mother. In her maths class, however, the story was different. Over by the window (they all had their regular seats) sat a boy that interested her. He was something of an outsider too, a swarthy, good looking boy with longer curly dark hair. She knew, from snatches of overheard conversation, that he belonged to a family that lived about a mile outside of town, an extended network of children and faceless parents and relatives. She knew also, that somehow, the family was related to the Carmanolas, and hence they received a kind of grudging acceptance in the town, though they clearly chose to set themselves apart. The name, Minovic belonged to that clan, and Rudy was the boy by the window. There were other Minovics in the school, scattered throughout the various grades, girls and boys both.

You could tell them from the similarly dark and curly look they bore. But it was Rudy that held her interest. For some reason, she thought he looked deep, mysterious and in some ways, he was a little aloof and she could appreciate that.

In her Maths class, Angelica did well. Rudy was one of the top performers in her class, and Angelica made a point of trying to compete. It seemed to her that this was the best way to get his attention. Rudy would lazily lift his hand to answer a question, but Angelica's would be there before his. What was the teacher, Mr Banks going to do, pick Angelica or Rudy? The answer was clear and ingrained in the behavioural patterns that belonged with the town. It wasn't long before the glances started coming her way, at first with narrowed eyes and then, something else as she boldly returned his looks, making it very clear that she was looking back.

It was not long after that first couple of weeks that the pair of them started hanging out together after a hesitant introduction. Angelica could not remember particularly the first real words they exchanged, nor what they talked about during their many breaks and lunches, or walking to the bus stop after school — Rudy would always walk her to the bus stop, wheeling his bicycle along beside them — but it must have been something. There was a small cafe on Main Street, and they could be found there, huddled in a booth over milkshakes or cokes, talking about school, perhaps, or people in their class, or something that had been on television the night before, though Rudy didn't seem to watch a lot of television. The closest thing they had to a cinema was a drive in movie theatre about ten miles out of town, so that was a major expedition, and certainly not something Angelica's grandfather would have initiated, so it was unlikely that it was the latest movies they discussed. Perhaps it was simply that Rudy had stood out as different and so, to Angelica, was something of the same thing she was. Perhaps that alone was enough to keep them in each other's company during those couple of years that she thought of as the Sandton period.

Of her grandmother, Angelica remembered very little at all. She was there, ever present, but a blurry shadow in the background, always the dutiful silent wife. Her grandmother, a slight pale woman with nervous hands and angled glasses seemed not to have opinions of her own, just those received from her husband. Everything she did seemed to be driven by duty in one way or another. Dutifully, she attended Church each Sunday and dutifully she cooked the meat and two vegetables every evening. Dutifully, she nodded her agreement when her grandfather was loudly reviling something they had just watched together on television, usually some news story or another. Angelica, however, was her grandmother's precious little doll, but for all that and the behaviour that went with it, she left only minor marks upon Angelica's life. She remembered her sitting at the kitchen table, telling Angelica slightly off-colour jokes in secret, and getting a mischievous look on her face, as if she revelled in being 'naughty,' just like the cigarettes that she smoked whilst sitting at that kitchen table. Of the latter, her grandfather must have known, but he turned a blind eye to it, and it was something that only happened before he arrived home from his office in the centre of town. The strongest memory of her grandmother was when she had returned home one day from school and announced that she wanted to get her ears pierced. Rudy had an earring; Angelica thought it would be cool if she could have one too. (She didn't mention to her grandmother that she only wanted a single piercing, not two.) Her grandmother had hit the roof, even shouting at her, as if the mere suggestion upset the natural order. How dare she suggest such a thing? Was she mad? Did she want to look cheap? What would her grandfather think? And that was the root of it...what would her grandfather think? Her grandfather's conservatism ruled her life, even by proxy through the little bird woman that sneaked her cigarettes in private and treated Angelica, somehow like a girlish confidant.

When the heat of her outrage had subsided, her grandmother drew her close, conspiratorially, and told her she must never speak to her grandfather about this, ever. Angelica had nodded her understanding, solemnly, but her mind had already been made up.

-5-

Walter

The Woodford Park house was probably too large for him, in truth. It boasted three bedrooms, a dining room, kitchen, lounge, a couple of bathrooms, and what Walter referred to as the 'front' room, though, in reality, it was more at the back of the house. The true front, the side that faced the street, was, in Walter's mind, the rear of the house. There sat a garage built of dark brick, obviously a later addition that now housed a stack of boxes and other remnants of what he'd been able to salvage from the divorce. He had no car for the moment, though he'd been considering replacing the family estate he'd used to drive before his grand, enforced change of lifestyle, so the garage remained unoccupied apart from those packaged reminders of what had been before. As the garage was positioned closer to the street, those memories clustered at the back of the house and therefore conveniently positioned in the back of Walter's mind.

The house was a long, low slung, wooden affair with a driveway up one side bordered by a tall hedge that shielded him from the neighbours, and in the right month, crawled with large green caterpillars that seemed never to move, though if he stopped to stare at them, he could see their little mouths moving industriously demolishing the current leaf like an old-style typewriter. Someone, he supposed, would have classified them as pests, but Walter didn't begrudge them their itinerant residency, not so unlike his own. He would pass them on his way down the driveway to the back door, the door he always used and occasionally, he'd stop along the way to peer interestedly at their industrious destruction while he felt for his keys.

Three short steps led up to the back door and every time he returned, Walter would pause for a moment and turn, staring out at the beach below and the end of the Hotel Bellevue that he could see from his position. The faded building kept its own vigil over the waves, impassive, thinking its own thoughts, though in truth, when Walter sat watching the waves, he wasn't necessarily thinking about anything in particular either. The back door led straight into the room he used as his workspace, his drafting table, his computer and his desk. He'd set up a wireless network shortly after arriving, although sometimes he wondered why, as the only computer he owned was a chunky desktop with a boxy cream-coloured tower planted beside one end of the desk. Apart from that, there was the printer, monitor, the usual set of peripherals needed for the home office. He actually used the computer probably less than he should, but it was a necessity for work, and the lifeline to the office for emails when he needed them, but that was enough. Infrequently, he'd go online and browse for nothing in particular. Though he knew his way around computers, they really didn't form a major part of his life. Even Woodford Park boasted an internet cafe, recognition of the lifeline the technology increasingly provided to the rest of the world, but it was something he had no particular need or desire to visit. He had set up his old favourite chair (another thing he'd managed to salvage from the tatters of his marriage) a large, yellow, wing-backed affair, in one corner of the room, affording a view over the beach. Pamela had hated that chair anyway, so it had been one of those few items that remained uncontested when he had labelled it as 'mine.'

The front room, as he soon started to think of it, was lined in that faux pine panelling that had been popular a couple of decades ago, and it looked completely out of place alongside the front room's old bare floorboards. He supposed the room had been carpeted in some previous phase of its life, before it had been stripped and renovated in preparation for entering the rental market. Walter took the only option and bought a large blue rug that covered most of the exposed floor and it did the job, although he had hesitated at first, counting it as another potential piece of baggage he would have to carry around if he decided to move again, though that prospect was nowhere in his mind, for now. Priding himself on his own practicality, however, Walter, of course had to take it under consideration at the time. The walls he kept unadorned. When he'd first taken possession of the house, it took merely two days before he had been forced to remove a lovely seascape with sunset that dominated one wall and carry it back to the garage, stacking it against one wall, its face turned inwards. There was no accounting for taste. Perhaps it had been placed there as an afterthought by the owners, something that was meant to add to the whole perception of 'furnished.'

Those first few days in the new house had been difficult, transitional. During the initial couple of months of the divorce proceedings he'd taken out a short lease on a small apartment right in the city proper. He'd been there longer than expected, but then the period of the separation had been longer than he'd expected too. From the cramped quarters and the constant grind of city noise, the move to the new house had taken him some weeks. The abundance of space, the silence, the sound of water against the beach and the recognition of his own solitary state was like an awakening. In the city apartment, he had been surrounded by people and noise; here it was different. He was forced to come to terms with the realisation that he was really, properly alone, that he'd made the break with his previous life and moved on to another place altogether. Pamela wanted nothing to do with him, and frankly, talking to her was the last thing on Walter's wish-list either. There was enough rancour remaining there to bubble away below the surface for years to come. Andrew, Drew, their boy, at university now, had sided with his mother, and that was that. Walter hadn't had the energy to fight any more and Drew, in his mind, became reconciled to another of those things that Pamela had won as part of the proceedings. Drew had become 'hers' rather than 'mine.' It still hurt him, but young boys were always closer to their mothers, or so it was said.

It had been a couple of months since Walter's thoughts had turned to what had taken place, what had led him to his current state, and he sighed as he looked out at the small deserted beach that lay below. At least that was one of the advantages of Woodford Park. Though it was summer, the only person he'd seen in the last few hours had been an old lady walking her dog, carrying an old piece of driftwood, as gnarled and weathered as she was, that she waved from side to side and then tossed for the small black and white terrier to charge after, kicking up a spray of sand as it took off in pursuit. He could see the dog barking in expectation of the game, and even that, he could only catch faintly through the open window. The rest was the sound of summer insects in the grass and the waves, no traffic, no cars, and from time to time, the sound of the breeze touching gentle fingers around the edges of the house and through the leaves of the hedge.

Plucking distractedly at his lower lip, he returned to the current sketch in progress, barely started on the mostly blank sheet of paper before him.

-6-

The Panorama

Hotel Bellevue had not always been the Hotel Bellevue. When it was first constructed at the height of Woodford Park's popularity as a holiday destination in the earlier years, it had been known as the Panorama Hotel. The headland overlooking the beach and the ocean to the east was broad and flat enough to accommodate the wide rambling structure and various outbuildings and the parking areas surrounded by tall pines, all shipped in and planted in neat rows especially for the purpose. The Panorama soon grew in reputation and its occupancy remained constant throughout most of the year. The winter months afforded vistas of grey, churning oceans, waves slamming against the cliffs and seagulls riding the winter winds, looking like they were stuck in place by some invisible force in the air above the waves, the only thing distinguishing them from still life, the slight adjustment of their wings against the vagaries of the shifting air. There was a kind of romantic violence that attracted people, families, older couples who were content to stroll the cliff top bundled in their woollen coats with scarves wrapped firmly around their necks and tucked within. It grew cold in the winter months, but it was more a chill than true, bitter, biting cold. Sensible clothing and a weather eye for the infrequent rain squall were sufficient to ward against the worst that the elements could throw at you in the less hospitable seasons. Of course, the occupancy was less, and the owners tended to close one entire wing of the hotel during the low season, but there were enough visitors to keep The Panorama with a steady stream of clientele and a resident staff to service their demands.

Then, for a period, business dropped off. The train down from the city bore fewer passengers, fewer stacked steamer trunks for transport down from the station in the hotel's own small bus, and The Panorama lay empty for longer and longer periods. There was still a high season and enough of a local trade visiting the restaurant or meeting for drinks at the bar. There were also the inevitable intermittent wedding parties, who sometimes chose to hold the actual ceremony in the hotel grounds, but never in the winter months. All in all, it was enough business to keep the hotel running, but barely. Finally, the owners made the reluctant decision and The Panorama closed its doors. At the time, there was no buyer, nor enough interest or trade to warrant further investment in the extravagant pile. The hotel did not sit completely dormant. The large ballroom gave a decent affordable space to local community groups to hold events, including the regular local dance, which became known as the Panorama Dance.

Cities and towns go through phases in their lives, and that fallow period between the height of the Panorama's occupancy and what was to come later was such a time. Despite the waxing and waning of interest over the years, however, unless something major happens to alter the face of such a place, the building of a factory, the influx of a different population that claims the place as their own, somewhere like Woodford Park retains the charms and character that make it popular in the first place and things inevitably move in cycles. Sometimes, the cycles are just longer than others. For Woodford Park, the fallow period, where the rest of the world had its eyes turned elsewhere for its diversion and entertainment was to last about fifteen years. The thing that helped save Woodford Park was the fact that it had never really become a seaside resort per se; it retained that local character, that local community that got on with their lives regardless of the visitors who came and went throughout the years and so in and of itself, the town survived. It was simply a nice place to live.

Sometime later, one of those transitory residents had decided that it was a pity that The Panorama, in its prime location overlooking the sea, lay empty, and that it was an ideal place to establish or, at least re-establish, a resort destination. The buildings, the facilities, were all there. They probably needed some updating, but with a little renovation and modernisation, and the appropriate level of funding, The Panorama could be revived to something like it had been in its glory days. John Abbot already had deep pockets, but he went about convincing some fellow investors that his idea was sound, even going so far as bringing them down to Woodford Park and showing them what he was talking about. One by one, they saw his dream, saw the magnificent views along the coastline, and The Panorama changed hands from the estate of the previous owners to a consortium of businessmen that shared John Abbot's enthusiasm. That enthusiasm paid off, but no longer was it to be The Panorama that reaped those rewards. The six-foot high white letters that had adorned the upper part of the red roof were painted over, and a new, tastefully lettered sign appeared over the wide reception area announcing that The Panorama had had a change of name. It had become the Bellevue Hotel, or simply, over time, The Bellevue. It was a good name for the old place; it expressed one of the major selling features of the property itself and of Woodford Park as a destination. Yes, people, it's all about the view.

Slowly, steadily, The Bellevue grew in popularity, and the investment made by Abbot and his colleagues started to pay off. To stay for a period at The Bellevue became a mark of one's social standing, of one's place in the world, and there were parties and balls and dinners, and afternoon teas all accompanied by the proper dress for the time of day. The tennis courts at the rear of the hotel were full of the thwack of balls and scurrying and lunging figures in pristine whites. Of course, there was a hotel pool, but also, there was the beach, and it thronged with sun lovers during the summer months. A small, winding path led down from the cliff top, affording access to the beach, so the hotel residents had their choice. Or they could simply sit out on the wide, paved terrace in the sun under their sun hats, sipping long drinks watching the ocean and the sails of passing yachts.

Many of the locals found jobs at The Bellevue and, for a time, Woodford Park boomed once more, The Bellevue along with it.

-7-

Bill

Bill Gundersen had gravitated to Woodford Park by accident rather than choice. He was a short, stocky, well-tanned man, prone to expansive gestures with both hands, despite the missing top two-thirds of the third finger of his right hand and the missing top joint of his little finger on the same hand. There was no shame there, and nor was there much shame about anything that Bill Gundersen turned his hand to, partially missing digit and all. He had lost the top of his third finger as a teenager in an ill-advised manual exploration to see why the lawnmower he was using at the time had stopped doing the job it was supposed to be doing. The little finger had suffered a similar fate, but in an encounter with a folding deckchair. Bill was fairly philosophical about these minor losses. They simply were as they were.

After a set of relatively short-lived stops along the way, in various scattered locations, Bill and his wife, Doris, had come to rest in Woodford Park and now he was all that the town boasted in terms of a real estate operation. He ran his office out of his house, and his big-haired and Capri-beslacked wife Doris performed secretarial and administrative duties for him, also keeping the books, for despite Bill's predilection for trade and commerce of various sorts, he actually wasn't very good with figures. Before landing in Woodford Park, he had had a stint as a car salesman, as a gas station proprietor, even as a long-haul trucker, but for now, real estate seemed to be treating him pretty well and Woodford Park along with it. Of course, there was some competition from the more formally established (and larger) offices in neighbouring towns, but that fazed Bill not at all. Naturally, he was legal—he had done a stint in a previous life working out of one of the suburban real estate offices as a salesman—but it was Doris who knew the ins and outs of contract law and the requirements, all self-taught. Bill had the nameplate, and though he wasn't ashamed of it at all, Doris had the brains.

Bill and Doris didn't have children. They couldn't. Not for want of trying, but the medical judgement had come in, and it was Doris, not Bill, who was found wanting, but Bill had never had any doubts about his manhood, in that, or any other respect. Instead, Doris had her babies. In a fenced section of their back yard, Doris raised Chihuahuas. Bill thought of them as frog-eyed, bat-eared rodents, but damned if he would ever let her know that. They brought her too much joy, and she really did love them and treat them like her own progeny. For such little dogs, they certainly could leave a lot of crap though, and that was one of Bill's least favourite tasks in life, cleaning out the dog pen, but you did what you had to do, and local ordinances ruled the world along with the weather in high summer. Doris was always happy to remind him about that little fact of life. In the meantime, especially during those summer months, on slow days, Bill and Doris would spend most of the day on the beach, soaking up the sun and improving their never-fading tans. Bill needed to do absolutely nothing to improve his never-fading garrulous bravado. It came with the territory.

Doris made up for Bill's outgoing nature, tending to keep in the background while Bill was holding forth. Not so, when she met the girls for her regular coffee mornings, but during those events, whenever it was Bill and Doris's turn to host, he would make himself scarce: There was always a new property he had to view, or some repairs on one of the rentals that he needed to check into — the gutters needed cleaning, there was a blocked drain that he had to attend to. He knew that Doris preferred it that way anyway. It was her time to take a little of centre stage. Gossiping, Bill called it, and he was always surprised at how much there was to talk about in a small community like Woodford Park. Of course, during the summer months, there were the visiting families or couples to talk about, but the coffee circle seemed far more interested in the lives of the local residents rather than anything as ephemeral as the life of a visitor or two. There was another advantage, though, to Doris's chat circle. Bill knew absolutely everything about anything that was going on in town or even hinted at, and sometimes, that knowledge came in handy. It was a kind of insider trading in a sense, but he had no qualms about that either.

The Gundersen's house lay towards the beginning of a street that ran in, straight from one of the headlands, not the Bellevue headland, but the next one along, creating a T-intersection from the main coast road that ran up and over the hill and led down on one side to the tiny cluster of shops that was Woodford Park's main shopping centre. The house was plain, white, well kept, with little to distinguish it from the other houses except for the small white sign at the front of one side that said Gundersen Realty and listed the contact numbers, telephone, fax, email. Nothing, that was, except the big letters writ large upon the roof proclaiming the same thing, except for the contact numbers, writ large like Bill Gundersen himself. If you walked down the drive and past the house, to the left side, it took you to a sloping lawn that led down to the main coast road on the other side, the beach, the local school and the shops. Because it was a longer trek to the end of the street and down, a few of the local kids would use the Gundersen's as a shortcut on their way to school, which in turn would start Doris's rats yapping at the intrusion. Doris didn't seem to mind, but Bill had been tempted on more than one occasion to grab the hose and discourage the little interlopers.

"No, leave them, Bill," Doris had said. "The babies are just excited about having visitors. And anyway, what harm are they doing? They're just kids."

She was right of course, but he had a moment's pause while he tried to work out whom she had been referring to with the last statement, whether it was the dogs or the school children. Finally, he settled on the latter. Every time the insane yapping started up, he would grit his teeth and try to think about something else. If that was the way Doris wanted it, then that was the way it was, and it was fine by him. Mostly, if it was fine by Doris, it was fine by him. He knew, deep in his heart of hearts, that if it wasn't for Doris, Bill Gundersen would hardly be where he was today, and though he would never admit it publicly, that he hadn't achieved everything on his own, the self-proclaimed, self-made man; deep down he was very aware of it. In some sort of strange way, the pair of them were symbiotic, if that was the right word. He vaguely understood the concept, having seen something about it one day on one of those nature programs that Doris was so fond of, watching while he sat in his leather recliner and drank his evening beer.

At the start of their street, at the headland end, there were mainly rentals. A couple of them had been partitioned off into a cluster of holiday apartments, and though reasonably well maintained, they were nothing special to look at. On the town side, one was a deep grey, surrounded by a high wooden fence. On the other side, a similar affair was currently painted a pastel yellow. At least it was better than the orange that it had been a couple of years previously. Bill had nothing to do with the rental or upkeep of those two places, and for the yellow one, it seemed that the owners' idea of maintenance was to change their minds about the colour scheme every couple of years. Unfortunately, that wasn't going to go away any time soon to his mind, because to change the property into anything other than what it was would take a chunk of work and it was probably providing the current owners with a healthy stream of seasonal income. They had, no doubt, inherited the place, whoever they were, because it was not necessarily the sort of thing that you would run straight out and purchase. Maybe the owners lived locally, but it was one of the few things he didn't know about the town's market, but then, it wasn't something that bothered him particularly. If he'd wanted to, he could have probably set Doris's coffee circle the task, but really, it wasn't that important. Better to save their energies for things that he could profit from directly. The yellow job (that used to be 'that orange job' and before that 'the purple job') was about the only thing that Bill would change about Lindauer Street if he could, but for now, he couldn't, and that was simply that too.

Bill liked where he was, liked the Mercedes in the garage, the covered speedboat in the space beside the garage, the tasteful pergola draped with bougainvillea above the curved pebble driveway leading directly to his office. After all, what was there not to like? He could count his blessings on the fingers of one digit-challenged hand, but he could count them, and they were good.

-8-

Angelica

It was a funny thing, but Angelica could not really remember any of the faces of people who had attended the funeral. When they had laid Johan Her Man to rest, she knew that there had been people who were there, friends and acquaintances who had come to pay their last respects and offer their support and condolences but if you had asked her, she wouldn't have been able to name a single one of them for certain. They had to have been there, hadn't they? The entire memory floated in a pale gossamer haze. She supposed that was not unusual, that a shock like that could play with your mind and your capacity to recall, but for something as important as Johan's funeral, she would have thought she would have a better grasp on what had happened. In contrast, she could remember every detail of her grandfather's funeral. Of course, living with them out there in the country for that period had left its impression, but it still didn't explain to her why the more recent, and probably more significant event of the two remained so vague.

Her grandfather's death had, of course, been significant. In the end, he had taken a gun to his head, not at the office, he was too private and reserved for that, but in the bathroom at home, in the place where Angelica herself had spent so many hours checking her face and hair, playing with her little Sandton outsider image in the mirror. No one knew where he had come by the gun, and nobody knew a reason why he did it. There was no note, no indicator as such. He had a successful practice, a good life, and he was devoted to his wife. It later came out that he had been having treatment for depression, but no one was really sure that was enough. Of course, it destroyed her grandmother. The little bird woman had stumbled into the bathroom when he had not responded to her calls and found his body, the gun still in his hands and bits and pieces of what remained of his head newly decorating the walls and the shower. She immediately went into a state of shock from which she never properly recovered. Back then, when it happened, ECT was still in vogue, and the series of 'treatments' she received to get her over the trauma, the bursts of lightning injected directly into her brain, did little to help her memory or the actual trauma itself. All it managed to do, effectively, was to change her into something which was a mere fraction of what she had been before. Somehow, the lightning remained, lying dormant, then sparking strange, unexplained twitches when she had reached her final period of decline.

Angelica had been studying at the time, Media and Communications, something she still, finally, even after school, had managed sufficiently appropriate grades to gain admission. Long gone were any ideas of medicine or law, which she'd thought about, but only really pondered like an unattainable dream. Media and Communication might lead to something she could have fun with, and it was fringe enough to provide the sort of mystique that she sought. God knows, she didn't want to end up in advertising or something similar, but film or theatre might have been an acceptable path in her mind. Something creative. As far as her grandfather was concerned, it didn't matter what she studied really, as long as she studied. After all, it was never going to lead to a career or something long-term in a meaningful way. When she had mentioned her thoughts to him in the early period of career decision making, he had merely given a semi-amused dismissive snort. She was a young woman, and for him, the path of any young woman was clear.

After she graduated, Angelica played at the edges of the city's art scene, learning very quickly the right annunciation for the term "Darling." You had to stretch that first vowel and add a touch of breath to the end. "Daaahling." Rather than film, because she soon realised that that was a long and hard road to travel, she had gravitated at first to theatre. Via that connection, she still managed to dabble in the film side of things, but the closest steps she ever took to 'true art' were a film student's first experimental short, dark and dripping with politically correct meaning, and a mindlessly stupid music video. In the end, it turned out that Angelica wasn't exactly a stellar actress, though she tried her hand at the Shakespeare and the one-acters so popular during that period. As time wore on, she found herself leaving auditions with smaller and smaller bit parts, or no part at all. Perhaps it was because she struggled with the concept of divorcing herself from 'Angelica' enough to truly live the parts she did manage to win. She turned her hand to writing. She knew the theatre; she knew stage direction; but though she tried, there was no one who was clever enough to recognise her brilliance, unless it was one or another of the young men she had taken to bedding on the side, none of whom turned out to be even semi-permanent. At least, there, she was able to take centre stage.

The news of what happened to her grandfather reached her and she was drawn back to that little country town to attend the funeral, to meet barely remembered distant relatives and struggle to put names to their faces while exchanging understanding words about how sad and how terrible it all was. Of course no one spoke of what had actually happened, the actual event. It was a performance full of slowly shaking heads and a careful skirting of the details of what had taken place, of what her grandfather unbelievably had done. Her grandmother was there too, supported on one side by a distant cousin, and on the other by her mother. She barely seemed to recognise Angelica at all as she was led into the small chapel. Her grandfather was to be cremated, but as per family tradition, it was a private service, family only. There had been discontent and grumbling in the town about that, because Angelica's grandfather had been a significant figure in Sandton and he had touched the lives of many. She learned about that later, from her mother and found it a little hard to reconcile against the stern, opinionated image of her grandfather held so clearly in her memories. She was not going to question it though; she knew better than that. There was s difference between rebellion and outright antagonism.

Her mother, along with the cousin who Angelica struggled to put a name too even to this day, seated her grandmother to the front and returned to make sure that Angelica knew where she had to be sitting.

"Don't worry about you grandmother, if she seems a little strange," her mother whispered on the way into the chapel. "It's the medication they've got her on. She might not remember things. Don't be too surprised."

She patted Angelica's arm and led her to the pew where she was to sit.

Though she saw her grandmother a couple of times after that, she never saw her in a state that was any more lucid than that day at the service with the sun beating down upon them and grasshoppers buzzing in the fields around them, a vague look on the bird woman's face as if she was wondering what she was doing there in those unfamiliar surrounds. Angelica could feel sympathy for her grandmother's state; it was odd being there amongst that extended network of family that she had never known. The great uncles and the cousins twice removed, their children, people that she had no connection with but were somehow related to her by an accident of birth and blood. Most of them came from her grandfather's side of the family and a few had travelled long distances to be there, to pay their last respects to a man, that for all she knew, had little interaction with them over the course of their lives. She had nothing in common with these people, and yet, by some quirk of fate, she did, and it lay in the smoke that circulated around the crematorium grounds and amongst this collection of strangers as they stood outside after the casket had been cranked away on its motorised platform to disappear behind the burgundy red velvet curtain and one by one, heads bowed, they had all solemnly filed outside. It was the first and last time that Angelica would see most of those faces, and yet she remembered them precisely, each and every one.

After all the relatives had departed, Angelica and her mother spent a couple of days at the old family home with her grandmother and the visiting nurse that came to see that she was okay. Angelica spent most of the time watching television or walking down in the extended back yard that ran for what seemed like miles down to a property behind where lines of grape vines extended down the hill, bare and twisted now, arms entwined, engaged in an evenly spaced carefully-trained mutual support. She had very little to talk about with her mother, and her grandmother's state did little to foster any detailed communication.

"Hello, dear." A slight frown as if struggling to remember who she was talking to. Did she know this young girl? Yes, she must. And then she was staring out the window, watching a bird picking at the orange berries on the bush outside the window. "Pests," she'd whispered harshly, her lips pressed together in a thin line.

It was with a sense of almost gratitude that Angelica had returned to the city and her studies. There was very little of Sandton that she wanted to take back with her. That had been another life, but images of the funeral stayed with her for several weeks after the event. The strongest was probably her grandmother sitting at the kitchen table and that single word. Had she been referring to the little bird outside the window, or the relatives? It was hard to know. Angelica put the thought from her though, because it was probably a little too uncharitable and she wasn't sure whether it had come from her own perspective, rather than anything in her grandmother's jumbled thoughts. Perhaps the old lady held within her a burning contempt that lay hidden from the world for most of her life, but that just didn't bear thinking about.

Back in the world of study, lectures, tutorials, critical analysis, film and theatre, Angelica soon moved on from Sandton revisited and it slipped back into a dark boxed place in her memories, only to resurface at odd times when she was not expecting it. Although she had an allowance, covering books, her accommodation and enough money to get around on, she took a part-time job at a coffee bar to help supplement what came to her every month. The course was not overly demanding, and she had enough free time that demanded a little extra disposable income. There were the parties, the cinema, the exhibitions, special dinners, though she rarely had to pay for those. Already she had started collecting her string of transitory Sweet Boys who doted on her, each in turn, for a time. The coffee bar where she worked was a hangout for the local trendy art set, close and connected to the university. Angelica, even before she had reached twenty was already voluptuous, blond, and expansive. Her close association with the theatre crowd encouraged that even more. She naturally caught the eye of a number of the pale, dark young men with their dark clothes, pallid complexions, experimental goatees and intense gazes. Angela, doing Media and Communications, fell into the acceptable category, even though her wardrobe labelled her as more of the vegetarian love child end of the spectrum. Black didn't really suit her, and she had already decided that pastels and lace where more in keeping with her look. Typically, she wore a single jade drop earring and a large silver cross, though the cross was nothing to do with any religious affiliation; she just liked the way it looked.

The first of her conquests, the first of what were to become her Sweet Boys was Al. She never knew him as anything more than Al. Pale, thin and intense, a Political Science major who carried around his convictions like a banner, had followed her around like a lost puppy, until she had relented and taken him to bed in her small studio apartment. He had looked around the one and a half room space, one by one assessing the mandala, the candlesticks, the wind chimes and the crystals, making his unspoken thoughts evident by the thin line of his mouth. He had crouched in front of her bookcase, riffling through the titles with one finger and then stood, not remarking on them at all. He paused for a moment on her large James Dean poster, but then, his attention had returned to Angelica herself and his demeanour, the implied judgement of her life simply dissolved. They never finished the bottle of cheap red wine she had purchased in honour of the event. Al had been energetic, but not particularly creative. It was intense, in the same way that everything about Al was intense. So she gave him points for enthusiasm, if not for style. When he came, he cried, and she held his dark serious head to her breasts and stroked his hair.

It soon became apparent that the act had planted a sense of ownership in Al's mind. Angelica had given herself to him, and he took that as an all-encompassing gesture. They went to bed four or five times after that, and in the meantime, Al started on his program of convincing Angelica of what she needed to be thinking and believing, what were the right causes for which she needed to wave the ideological flag. The passion of his youth overtook the passion of his desire and that was enough for Angelica. Very soon after, she dispensed with her Sweet Boy Al. She tried to do it gently, but he wept openly, finally stumbling for the street, wiping at his eyes and nose with his face downturned. It took him a lot longer to get over it than Angelica, but then she had initiated the action and for her, it had really almost been over before it had started. He lived in hope for a few weeks, and he would turn up at the cafe, sit in a corner with a group of his friends, and every time she happened to catch his eye, there would be a spark of hope, but by then, she had already drifted on. Eventually, he seemed to get the message, though, for a long time after, whenever she saw him he seemed wrapped in depression.

Angelica continued drifting, through her studies, through her succession of Sweet Boys, through various waitressing jobs and her forays into theatre. She graduated, and her mother was at the ceremony, but apart from that, there was a call every few weeks, just as much out of duty as anything else, and very little else. The opportunities for interaction with her mother became fewer and fewer. Graduation changed very little about Angelica's life. She continued to hold down her studio apartment and various jobs while she dabbled at the edges of the intellectual scene and the city arts crowd.

It was her mother who put an end to that period of her life, firmly and squarely. Her mother, who had always been there as a half-registered presence in the background ever since the Sandton period, suddenly took centre stage instead. Of course, her mother still worked, and it was for an inner city childcare program. She seemed to enjoy her work and the network of friends and people she associated with as a result. She had become quite senior in the particular organisation she worked for. Angelica was aware of at least of that much, although to some extent that was as much guesswork, because her mother spoke to Angelica rarely about her work or about a lot of her life. In fact, Angelica had no idea whether her mother even had someone she would call special in her life. She suspected, of course, but it was something that remained unsubstantiated. All that would become irrelevant when her mother's phone call finally came. That phone call would change her mother's life and Angelica's as well.

-9-

The Child

No one paid much attention to her at first, or even after. Although it was abundantly out of season for the bulk of holidaymakers in Woodford Park, a few, wiser souls, those that had been coming regularly for years, arrived at the tail end of the season and stayed the requisite couple of weeks. They could still catch that specific light as it fractured against the water sending sun glitter through the salt spray as the ocean beat itself against the rocks. On a windy day, they could catch rainbows in the spume blown from the top of curling waves that ran end to end along the beach, perhaps angling past, or rising higher over a newly-formed sandbar as the white horses charged towards the beach. Some of the more adventurous of the visitors might wade out to these sandbars to stand thigh deep and surrounded by ocean a hundred yards from shore. A lone fisherman might be seen at the edge of the rock platform that stretched out like a flattened palm, the criss-cross traceries in the rock not unlike the lines etched into a hand. Now and again, one might see, as evening approached, bracing the wind, their lengthy beach rods planted firmly in the sand or held in harnesses crafted just for the purpose, the beach fishermen, as they too stood thigh deep in the surf. But these were regulars and a familiar sight to those that had lived in the town for years. Some of them were even recognisable, had familiar faces and names.

The child was slight, a greyhound frame and tanned. Her shoulder-length hair, halfway between blond and brown streaked with traces of the sun, was pushed back from her face and held in place by ocean salt. She wore a pale, crocheted bathing suit, pastel yellow and pink in stripes. One knee bore the marks of a fresh graze, newly healing and treated by its time in the ocean. She stood on tiptoes to hand over the coins that were payment for the ice cream she had just purchased, strawberry and vanilla, two scoops. Mary, the local snack bar proprietor thought to herself that she was a pretty child and polite with it — a nice kid. She'd be a heart breaker when she got older with those pale green eyes. Mary glanced up and out of the store's front window, seeking any sign of the parents that had produced such a pretty child, but there was nobody in sight, and the beachfront lay deserted. They were probably parked around the corner, waiting for her.

"Dad, can I have an ice cream?"

"Sure, honey. Take this. We'll wait here for you. Be quick though. Quick as a flash, won't you?"

A big serious nod in response.

Mary leaned heavily on the counter on her beefy arms after the child had gone. It was mid-afternoon in the middle of the week. The video game in the corner had lain silent for a few days now and the beach had remained deserted for most of the day. Trade would pick up on the weekend, but in the meantime, she would simply wait. She had nothing better to do anyway. Already she'd read the day's papers while leaning on the counter, pausing to spend some time on the horoscopes, before flicking the page over to the sports section. There was no point even in setting up the machine to clean and slice any more potatoes. She had enough to go on with on the chance that some casual passer-by would wander in and place an order. Mary was like that though, she preferred the good old fashioned chipping machine. Do it herself rather than resort to that cheap stuff you could buy in frozen bulk. You never knew what you were getting in that stuff anyway. She had a few lone pieces sitting out in the glass heating cabinet at the end of the counter, but she had little expectation that they'd be sold before the end of the day either.

Why couldn't her own kids have looked like that She would have loved a little girl, something sweet to cherish, but her kids, both boys, took after their mother and father, solid, thick boys with brains to match. Johnny, the eldest worked as a mechanic a few towns over. His wife, Linda, was a beautician, but sometimes, with Johnny's temper, Mary was sure that she had to apply her skills to herself rather than her customers and Mary knew it was more than once. Charlie, well Charlie — Mary had just about given up hope on Charlie. Right now, Charlie was inside as far as she knew. Breaking and entering was the last one. It was no point telling herself that Charlie had simply managed to slip in with a bad crowd. The kid was just plain bad. Always had been. Ever since the day Mick, her husband had had that run in with the sixteen-wheeler in his delivery truck, Charlie had been trouble. Mick had hung on for a couple of years after the accident, bound to a chair and unable to talk. It was a mercy when he finally gave up the will to live like that. Mary hadn't had the strength or inclination to rein Charlie in. She had her hands full enough trying to manage and give Mick the care he needed, and besides, Charlie was a big boy, had been since the first years of school and he had quickly learned to use that size to his advantage. To be quite frank, Mary was afraid of Charlie. It was a pity that he didn't seem to learn anything else so quickly.

Yes, she thought, it would have been nice to have a girl, but there was no chance of that now.

She heaved herself upright, grabbing a chocolate bar from the display before pushing through the red and yellow hanging plastic strips that served as a fly screen door to the small back room and the small metal table upon which a portable television sat next to an ashtray, a packet of cigarettes and a lighter. She tore the top wrapping from the chocolate bar and took a bite as she flipped the television back on. She always turned it off before serving customers. The soap operas and daytime talk shows could wait. Her customers were what kept her sane, and that deserved a bit of respect.

Reaching over to adjust the antenna to try to minimise some of the snow they were prone to — Woodford Park was not ideally located for television reception — she gave one last hopeful look out onto the beach, but it remained as deserted as ever, so, heavily, she settled her bulk back into the single metal chair that afforded her a view of the shop and the television at the same time and peeled back some more of the chocolate wrapper with thumb and forefinger before turning her attention back to the show she had been watching before the little girl had made her welcome intrusion into Mary's day. The child had already become a memory, a shadow in a collection of past images sitting somewhere in the valleys of her mind.

-10-

Walter

Walter stared down at his drafting table at the new, modern split-level home he was working on. The problem was, it was not a new, modern split-level home; it was simply a blank sheet of paper. He didn't know where his head was today, but it certainly wasn't on the current project. It had been like this for days now. He glanced back at his computer, perhaps seeking inspiration there. Sure, there were programs he could use to assist, but Walter preferred to do things the old fashioned way. He believed his creativity flowed directly from him, through his hands to paper. To blank paper at the moment. He sighed and instead looked down at those currently not-so-magic hands, wondering not why they weren't working, but rather how fine pale hairs grew on the bottom joint of his fingers, but not on the second. He turned his hands this way and that, letting the light shine across his fingers in different ways. No inspiration there. He'd already had three cups of coffee and that was enough. Coffee as a displacement activity was no real answer anyway. It just made him jittery and even less able to concentrate.

He turned his attention to the window. Below lay the beach, deserted for the moment. From the steps, his front lawn sloped down to a small set of stone stairs that in turn led to a path that skirted the front of the properties (or the rear, depending on how you looked at it) and in turn led to the coast road and across to the beach. On the other side of the road, low, sandy dunes tufted with grass led down to the beach proper, and a small creek formed a sand delta close to the rightmost headland where it emptied into the sea, distinguishable from the rest by the brown discolouration of the sand left by the constantly trickling creek water. At the other end of the beach sat the squat headland that was home to The Bellevue, about half of which was directly visible from Walter's front window. Why not? He'd been here a few months now and had never ventured as far as The Bellevue. A walk would do something to clear his head and break this pattern of sedentary idleness. The sound of the waves was therapeutic, a meditation on its own, but along with the fresh air, the hulk of the old building might provide him some spark, or at least an interesting diversion. Modernity inspired by yesteryear. It might even work.

Giving one last accusatory look at the blank sheet of drafting paper, he stood, reached for his coat, pulled it on and patted for his keys. This beach, the smaller of the two boasted by Woodford Park was Walter's favourite. Apart from himself, the old woman who regularly walked her dog and an old beachcomber, the only people he'd seen so far had been a couple of fisherman and they had been on their way around to the rock platform at the front of the other headland. The other, main beach had a parking lot, also fronted on to the row of local shops and even had shower facilities at one end. Well-equipped enough to attract the casual visitor, it had enough to keep Walter generally away, apart from his excursions to the multi-fragrant family-run mini market on the corner or walking along its front laden with a couple of shopping bags when he'd been on one of his infrequent bus excursions to the nearest proper supermarket. This beach, Walter's beach, was far more inviting and today, he didn't need to come away from the small corner store with a mystery package; today he needed a spark, and that wasn't going to spring up out of row upon row of shelves packed with various mysterious exotica. He closed the door, locked it and then turned to stand on his back steps, considering the beach and what he could see of The Hotel Bellevue. Yes, it was a good plan or at least a plan.

Walter wandered down the path, his hands in his pockets, one eye on the old shell on the headland, but not really looking at it. Instead, he concentrated on his feet, on the old suede desert boots taking each step, and his legs within the dark green corduroy trousers, stepping, one after the other. When he reached the coast road, he glanced either way and then crossed unhurriedly, reaching the top of the low dunes and standing there for a few seconds watching the waves and the stirring of the breeze through the wispy sea grass, the slight flow of grains of sand moving across his path, and then out to the waves themselves. The tide was low, and the breaking waves ran in flatly, one after the other, a marbled pattern of white foam marking where each had been, ready for the next. A trail of footsteps marked someone's passage along the water's edge, still far enough up the beach that they would not be obliterated by the rising tide for an hour or so yet. Briefly, he wondered who had left them. He didn't remember seeing anyone down there, and yet he'd been at his window for most of the day. Perhaps it had happened when he was off making one of the succession of coffees or even before he had risen for the day.

He stood there, still watching the waves for a while before unhurriedly turning up to the headland. It must have been a magnificent building in its time, he thought. He could sense as well as see some of the old glory of the place, but it was abundantly clear that it had been several years since that glory had first started to fade. Time had done its work. Still, it was certainly worth a closer look and he wondered briefly why it had taken him so long to do it.

Though a narrow path wound up from the beach, Walter wasn't sure how safe it was. From where he stood, it looked like the path had crumbled in a couple of places and he decided it would be more prudent not to risk it without a closer inspection. The headland itself extended further out into the ocean than its neighbours and Walter could see a curved access road leading in from where the coast road curved back inland, partially obscured by the rise of the hill itself. Funny that he'd never really noticed it before, but he supposed that it was blocked from direct view from his front window. He decided he would walk the length of the beach and then cut back over the hill to the coast road again and then follow the access road up to the hotel proper. It was a good day for a walk, not too hot, and the slight breeze blowing in across the waves tempered it even more. Really, it was mild enough that he could have dispensed with his coat, but somehow he felt more comfortable having it with him. That was probably a hangover from when he used to be a smoker, always needing pockets to carry along the requisite packet of cigarettes and lighter. Anyway, if it got too hot, he could take it off and drape it over his shoulders.

The access way from the coast road turned out to be little more than a crumbling memory of the narrow road it had once been. The tar and gravel showed bald patches along its length, revealing dark brown earth beneath, broken by weeds and patches of grass. There was enough of a surface there to make the going easy, and Walter strolled casually down the small road and up again feeling more like an explorer than an interloper. The road itself led into what had once been the parking area for the hotel itself, now bare, surrounded by tall, thick-trunked pines with lines clearly marked out in sawhorse type fences made of old greying wood turned green by some sort of mossy coating. Further up, the road continued, turning into the hotel's main driveway. If there was some other route into the hotel, he could not see it. Normally, he would have expected to find a parking area positioned to the rear of a large establishment like this, rather than the front, but he guessed that the geography had given them no choice. Nor was the area paved in any way. The same dark brown earth marked the entire square, tall stands of weeds growing haphazardly across the entire area. The whole flat expanse must turn into a bog in the heavy rains when they came. The road led up and over a short rise from the lines of empty spaces to where it curved back and became the driveway. From where he now stood, Walter could see only the top of the roof and the remains of the sign with its empty sockets where once, bulbs would have sat, illuminating the front at night, and for all he knew, maybe in the daytime as well. He strolled up the rest of the rise, watching as the old hotel revealed itself to him, its tall front windows appearing gradually like slowly opening eyes, becoming aware of the world for the first time in a long time.

Hulk was a good name for what had become of The Bellevue, Walter thought. Like a large pleasure liner beached on dry land. In his mind's eye, he could see what it once would have been, in its glory days, but now, the yellowed walls, the paint having faded in uneven patches, and staining from the salt air spoke clearly of what it had become. The large front windows, looking out over the beaches and the ocean to the south were mostly intact, though a couple had large jagged chunks of glass missing and scattered in pieces on the gravel in front of them. Another bore a large crack. The remainder, were silver black with dust and age, affording no view at all of what lay inside. Watching his feet, Walter headed for the broad metallic front doors. They had probably been painted once, but for now, the paint was long gone, rusted away. The sea air had done its work. Their top halves showed an intricate pattern of wrought iron work, peacocks and grapevines. Across the two of them looped through the solid lion-headed handles, hung a thick and heavily padlocked chain, it too heavily rusted. Walter peered through the crack between the doors, but all he could see in the gloom was another pair of doors beyond, these of wood, with dusted glass in their top halves and a dusty brown and white tiled entrance. Nothing to see that way. He thought about testing the strength of chain and lock, but then decided against it. Better to see what else he could see first. Also, there was the whole question of legality. It did seem, however, that the chain had been in place and undisturbed for a long, long time.

Picking his way over the few pieces of masonry that had fallen from the upper eaves, Walter moved around to the ocean side. The aspect was north-easterly, tending more to the east then the north and more large double doors and windows gave access to a broad, paved terrace, large chunks of sandstone with the ubiquitous weeds growing up between them stretching to a spot about one hundred yards from the cliff edge. Sitting out here in the late afternoon or evening, the patrons would have had an expansive view of the darkening ocean as the sun dipped behind the mountainside behind, sending orange shafts all the way to the horizon. It wouldn't have been the same as watching a sunset, but rather the reflection of a sunset. Good enough on its own, although, at the right time of year, if you were early enough, you could probably sit out here to breakfast and watch the sun creep up over the horizon. All the doors and windows on this side had been boarded up, maybe, he thought, to offer more protection from the ocean. He could imagine tall waves battering the cliffs in winter, the wind whipping salt spray against this side of the building. A few traces of graffiti and some empty beer cans and cigarette butts scattered in front of the boarded over double doors spoke of youthful visitors, but there were surprisingly few marks. This, he thought, would have been an ideal spot for a touch of vandalism, but then maybe not. What was the point of vandalism if it couldn't be seen by anyone? "Choko, '93" in red spray can letters was about the only thing he could make out. All the rest had been rendered into illegible smudges by the gradual effects of the weather. Up here, there was a stiff breeze whipping in from the ocean and ruffling his hair, and he was suddenly grateful that he had the coat with him after all.

Moving to the rear of the building, the old hotel's true shape started to reveal itself. It was a giant U shape. Two wings ran on either side of a central courtyard, housing, Walter presumed, the main bedrooms. The area in the middle had once been a garden, the remains of dead plants, some in large pots, surrounding a pool, it too boarded over, but the boards had collapsed at some point and now lay tilted down into a dark hollow. If it had been sitting like that for years, Walter had no real desire to investigate the depths. Closer to it, he could hear the gentle murmur and buzz of insects. He could bet it was a haven for mosquitoes too. He hated mosquitoes, though they loved him with a passion. These rear sections were lower than the rest, only a single story, while the front of the hotel had two. He skirted the pool and headed for the central part of the U. He pressed his face up close to one of the small windows that stood at head height to peer through the smeared and dusty glass, hoping to get a better idea of what lay within, but he was disappointed. Behind these windows lay only a corridor, faded, stained and peeling wallpaper running the length of as much as he could see. Obviously, by the stain marks, water was getting in somewhere from above.

In comparison, the remaining side of the hotel was something of a disappointment. The wall itself was featureless except for a couple of small windows set high up towards the front. In a few places, plaster had fallen to lie in broken chunks at the foot of the wall, exposing old brickwork beneath, like reddened wounds. An old bathtub lay about halfway along, its enamel chipped, its exterior rusting. A collection of ancient metal drums formed a small headless crowd toward the rear end and just nearby lay a wooden pallet and some old bags of what Walter presumed had been cement, their usefulness long passed, and the writing on the bags long since unreadable. He turned around and faced up the coastline to the north. One more headland jutted out before the beaches gave way to tall cliffs where the escarpment met the sea proper. It was a funny place to build a hotel, he thought, cut off from the rest of the world and the city to the north by such an impressive and forbidding piece of landscape. Perhaps that was part of the attraction, an elite hideaway. He couldn't imagine that staying here would have been cheap.

A few outbuildings lay further down the back, but they held little interest for him. He circled back around the rear side of the hotel, bracing himself against the breeze that had picked up even further in the short time that he had been around the side. There were a few doors around this back side that he could try, see if he could gain access to the interior. The roof had seemed intact as far as he could see, despite the clear evidence of water damage inside, so an inner exploration might be okay. He was interested in seeing how they'd laid out the upper floor, to the front of the hotel, whether they'd been creative with their use of light in the larger public spaces that he presumed lay there, towards the front, but all that would keep for now. It was enough for today and really, he should get back and try to make a start on the project. He'd better have something to show by the time he made his next trip up to the city, just as much to give some justification to the expedition as the fact that he actually had a deadline on this contract.

-11-

Angelica

On the odd occasion, chatting with the local people, wandering along the beach front in high season, or even catching the bus to the library in Banham, a few towns over, were not enough to still some of those things that whispered quietly in her thoughts from time to time, so Angelica had a ritual. Atop the headland that overlooked the main beach sat a stone bench, placed there in memory of some long-forgotten woman, forgotten except for her name and a set of dates inscribed on a metal plaque set firmly into rough-hewn stone. It was tarnished and green from salt, but still readable, and though it appeared evident that there had been more than one attempt to prise it from its stone base, it was still intact. She had peered at it on more than one occasion, an attempt, perhaps, to conjure an image of the person that the name had belonged to. Try as she might, she had never been able to fix on one image; every time, the woman was someone different. She could have asked around, but it was probably best not to know whether the bench sat there in memory of some tragic event. Perhaps Emily Ball had thrown herself from the cliff top to dash herself to death on the rocks below, her body swept away by the hungry tide, in despair over a broken love affair, but the cliff really didn't seem high enough for that sort of dramatic conclusion. A more obvious choice would have been the scenic lookout that lay far above behind the town at the top of the escarpment. That would have provided enough of a drop to ensure the outcome. Perhaps Emily Ball had simply been a local benefactor who liked sitting at the end of the headland looking down the coast and drinking in the natural beauty. No, it was better not to know. Regardless, Ball's Point provided a place of stillness, of meditation where Angelica could seek solace from that which was troubling her.

It was perhaps ironic that this should be the chosen place of Angelica's ritual, considering the unlikely, but potential history, and in light of the fact that one of the things that continued to haunt her in such times was what had happened with Johan Her Man. She tried very hard not to make the connection. What she needed now, she thought, was another Sweet Boy to take her mind off things for a while, though right now, Sweet Boys were in short supply. Though she tried to keep herself as youthful as possible, there was a limit, and though she had retained her full-figured shape, there was a growing gap that came as much in the mind as it did in physical chronology. The more the years passed, the more she found that, although they were diversions, her Sweet Boys were starting to tend more to the Sweet Man end of the spectrum, as much by choice as by circumstance. Some of them that she looked at and considered just seemed so young these days. She tried to put those thoughts from her as she drew deeply from her cigarette and watched as the smoke of her exhalation was whipped away by the breeze. There she sat, her legs tucked beneath the bench, ankles crossed, the hand holding her cigarette propped up in the elbow of her other hand, her eyes slightly narrowed, watching, but not seeing the sun catching sparkles across the top of the water. The breeze had raised a slight chop across the water's surface, speckling the blue expanse with whitecaps.

Lately, she'd taken to dabbling with jewellery, silver and semi-precious stones, another thing to pass the time. If she could do something with it, then it would help to occupy her days and give her something more to focus on. Of course, she knew she had the flair, the appreciation of style and form that would allow her to produce such objects of desire and saleable ones at that. And not only that, it too, could become a sort of therapy. She had spoken to her friend Cara the other day about perhaps sharing some space at the local market if she made a go of it. Then she could look further afield if it turned into anything. She knew there were other local markets and Cara herself followed the calendar from town to town, setting up her stall in each location and it was a rolling calendar, not restricted to a Saturday as it was in Woodford Park. If she was feeling generous, Cara might let Angelica share some space in more than just the Woodford Park market. That was definitely something worth exploring further.

When she was here, sitting out on the edge of the headland on Emily Ball's bench, Angelica always faced south. Behind her, on the next headland, sat the remains of the old hotel, but she didn't like looking that way. It reminded her of things she would rather not think about, the passing of time, the ephemeral nature of everything that was and had been in her life. There was no such thing as permanence; she knew that very well, but it wasn't something she necessarily liked to be reminded of. Everything decayed and fell apart, some things more spectacularly than others, especially people, especially relationships. As far as Angelica was concerned, she was here for the now, and the now lasted as long as it could. She wasn't going to give it a use-by date. Her grandfather, her mother, Johan Her Man, all had shown her clearly enough that things weren't made to last, and the universe had delivered that message loud and clear, thank you very much.

Her mother's illness had taken Angelica away from her dabbling in the city artistic crowd. After her grandfather's death, and the gradual decline of her grandmother, Angelica's mother had returned to the old Sandton family home. It had become hers, after all, and the extensive estate accrued through her grandfather's many property deals, and a successful country legal practice had meant that her mother had wanted for nothing, at least nothing material. Though she and Angelica discussed such things rarely, on the few times when they were drawn into it, her mother seemed to believe that it was something owed to her by the world, this state of newly-found prosperity. She had done her penance, first with the disappearance of her husband, having to support a young girl (though she certainly had some assistance in that regard), the untimely demise of her father, and finally the months of care and attention she had spent on Angelica's grandmother. Now, since her grandmother's passing, her mother did not have a need to want. After everything had been settled, there was enough in the estate to keep her going for as long as she lived and then some. Fate, however, cruel trickster that it was, decided that the 'as long as she lived' part, wasn't going to be very long at all. That had been the first phone call:

"Angelica, sweetheart, I need you to come home. We need to talk."

Her mother's use of the term of endearment had been enough on its own to set the alarm bells ringing.

By the time it was diagnosed, her mother's cancer was well advanced and had spread throughout much of her body. When Angelica returned to that large comfortable home in Sandton, there was no hiding how much the disease had already done. Her mother was pale, shadowed and clearly in pain.

"But there must be something..."

"No, Angelica. And there is no point going down that road. You have to face the facts. I haven't got very long. I'm going to need you to be strong. I won't be able to do this without you."

Angelica had stared at her mother across the kitchen table, watching as a wave of something hit her and she grimaced in pain, trying to mask it, but not managing very successfully. Her mother sat there, not meeting her daughter's eyes, as if to do so would be an admission.

In turn, a thought took shape in Angelica's mind, and she hated herself for it. *Why now? Why is this the thing that you won't be able to do without me? It would be a first. Couldn't you have chosen something better?*

Regardless, Angelica returned to the city, packed her belongings and moved back to the country, back to Sandton, a place she believed she would never have to spend time in ever again. Watching the deterioration of her grandmother had been bad in those final stages. Seeing her mother's rapid decline was worse. True to her upbringing, her mother was determined to remain stoic. No, she wasn't going to receive any special help. No hospice. Nothing like that. This was private, and it had to remain in the family. As if, in Angelica's mind, any family truly remained. So, there were the regular visits from the doctor, the medication for the pain that brought her in and out of lucidity. Sometimes, the land that her mother inhabited during those periods seemed like a sweet and gentle place, the sort of reality that Angelica might be tempted to herself, but Angelica had no illusions that where her mother really lived was well and truly hell. Towards the end, Angelica had to arrange a private nurse to visit as well, as she was unequipped and simply unable to cope on her own. She didn't need the nurse telling her that she was being brave and strong. She wasn't.

The last thing her mother ever said to her was simple, barely heard in a breath of silence as she held her daughters hands in a grip devoid of strength.

"Angelica, sweetheart, I'm sorry," she'd whispered. She'd frowned as if a new pain had hit her, and then, finally, she was gone.

Angelica didn't know what to do then, and in the end, she'd asked for and received help from an old family friend of her grandfather's, a man whose own father had felt a debt of responsibility to her grandfather too. He knew all about Angelica, the family, everything that had happened to them, but Angelica barely even knew his name. The local doctor who had visited had suggested that he might be able to help her, that he was a good man. It seemed that her grandfather's memory extended well into the community even years after his death. She was grateful for that much, at least. Perhaps he was, after all, a good man, but Angelica had no way of truly knowing or even assessing that.

Of course, after everything was settled, Angelica was now in the position that her mother had been in for the last few years of her life. She had inherited everything built over the years by her grandfather, just minus the costs of what had to be taken care of. She stayed in the old place for a few more weeks while she worked out what she was going to do, but the memories haunted her in every room, and no matter what she did, how thoroughly she cleaned everything, there remained the ghost that she would ever associate with death. It was more than a scent, although that was part of how it manifested. Looking back, it could have been just her imagination, but it was real enough for her to spur the decision she knew she had to make. Now Angelica was a young woman of means, but she had no idea what she was going to do with it. She knew one thing though; she had time. She needed help with the next thing too, and she received that help willingly. She put the big old house on the market along with its memories and started making plans.

-12-

Doris

Doris was out in the back yard, hosing down the dog's enclosure — usually Bill's job, but for some reason he had neglected it before heading off to do his rounds — when she first saw the little girl. The child was leaning back against the chain link fence at the front of the school that separated the sports field from the road, pressing back against the fencing with the weight of her shoulders and bouncing, as if lying back on a semi-solid trampoline. She had on a pale blue sun dress and blue ribbon held back her hair in a ponytail. White sandals and white socks with a small pattern at their top border completed the picture. She was quite a pretty young thing decked out like that, would have been quite an attractive child, even dressed some other way. Two thoughts ran through Doris's head: First, she didn't recognise the child as one of the local kids; second, if she kept pressing back against the fence like that, she'd leave dirt marks all over the back of her sweet little dress. Her mother, wherever she was, was going to be pleased about that, for sure. The girl was staring out across the road and down to the beach, just rocking. Doris shook her head and stooped to give one of her babies attention. Coco, for it was Coco, jumped up and down at her side, her little pink mouth open and panting, her tiny paws scrabbling at Doris's thigh for attention. She stroked Coco's head, and then picked her up and clutched her to her bosom. The little dog wriggled and squirmed, trying to reach up to lick her face, but no kisses now. Kisses were for special. She gave Coco a little squeeze and placed her back down, playfully squirting her with the edge of the hose, so she would get out of the way and let Doris get on with what she was doing. Bill really should have done what he was supposed to before he went out, but it was okay; it gave her the chance to spend a little more time with her darlings. Hearing the noise of water splattering on the outside of his kennel, Julius came charging out, skittering across the wet concrete and then struggling to keep upright on the wet surface as she flicked the water at him. Meanwhile, Coco was still scrabbling at the back of her legs. Funny that they were all so quiet today and that it was only Julius and Coco who had ventured forth. Still, it was a warm day, and they preferred the shade of their kennels on a day like today.

When Doris looked up again, the child still hadn't moved. Was she waiting for someone? She wasn't too far from the school gates. Doris screwed the nozzle at the end of the hose shut so that the water faded to a trickle and lifted one hand to shade her eyes. The girl certainly wasn't one of the local school kids, and besides, school was in now. She should be in class, even if she was new, but Doris knew of no new families having arrived in Woodford Park and Doris should know. If the child was a school kid, she should have some bag or rucksack or something with her, but the girl's hands appeared to be crossed behind her back and empty, her fingers linked, and there was nothing on the ground by her feet.

Coco was still demanding attention, and now she had been joined by Julius. Little wet paw marks were striping the back of her jeans.

"Shush, darlings," she said, turning to look at them and holding her free hand out behind to still them. She bent down to stroke each of their heads and reassure them that they were not in trouble. "Mother's just busy for a minute, okay, my babies?"

Doris turned her attention back to the road below. The girl was still there in the same position. There was no sign of anyone else. She'd have to ask Bill when he got back later whether there was anything she didn't know about and he had forgotten to tell her, unlikely as that was. Bill told her pretty much everything, and if there was a new rental, she'd have to open a new page in the ledgers anyway. If there'd been a sale, Bill would have been crowing about it long before now. Whoever she belonged to, the child shouldn't be out there alone like that, standing by the main road, looking so sweet, anyway. Woodford Park was a safe community, but you just never knew, did you?

She was considering dropping the hose and wandering down to ask the little girl if everything was okay. The babies could keep for the moment. She was on the verge of doing just that, when the child pushed herself from the fence, and gaze never leaving the beach, she walked to the road, stood at the side for a moment or two, as if considering, and then, looking dutifully both left and right, crossed over to where the row of large pines provided shade to the parking area while people soaked up the sun. Moments later, the child had disappeared from view. Maybe her parents were down there on the beach, had a car parked at the other end out of Doris's view. Maybe they had just come down for a picnic. That would explain the child's dress...a nice day out with the family. It didn't explain what she had been doing across the road at the school though. Regardless, the child had seemed all right and Doris turned her attention back to the dogs.

"Yes, my darlings, I'm all yours now," she said, turning the nozzle back on and returning her focus to the dog yard. She would get Bill to pick up the remains of what she washed into the gutters that ran either side of the enclosure when he returned. So what if the remains would still be a little wet; it would just serve him right for forgetting in the first place.

Everyone earned their own rewards, no matter how big or how small they might be.

-13-

Walter

Walter had always been a quiet, diligent type, concentrating hard on his studies and eternally grateful that his academic discipline during high school had allowed him to meet the tight cut-off mark for entry into Architecture. He had never thought of doing anything else, really, but he'd kept Engineering in his back pocket if he had ever needed it. Thankfully, he'd never been forced to make the choice. His own, suburban, middle-class parents had been proud of their boy, although his father pushed the question of sports, from time to time. The problem was, Walter wasn't sporty. He could run, but he was never as fast as some of the other boys in his class. Long distance gave him stomach cramps, as did his father's suggestion that he devote more energy to the more physical side of life. Eventually, his father relented and came to terms with the fact that his son was not really the athletic type. No, Walter was more the chess and debating sort, things that involved a certain precision of the mind. He was a good architect. He could probably have been a great engineer, but his fascination with the dynamics and intricacies of space and light had made his path clear. Buildings simply fascinated him. Walking down a city street, or on the odd times that he had holidayed with Pamela, he would stop in the middle of a street, staring up at some structure, his mouth half open, oblivious to the rest of the people moving around him. Pamela had hated it. As it turned out in the end, it wasn't the only thing that Pamela had hated.

In the beginning, Walter had been confused and a little lost in the maze of university life. He had studied the times of his classes and their locations, the most efficient route to the library and the free slots he had to spend there. That planning gave him a solidness of purpose that meant that none of his time in tertiary education would be wasted. That was the plan, until David Whiteman. For some reason, big brash David Whiteman took a liking to Walter. They ended up sitting next to each other in one of the packed lecture halls in their first weeks. Introductory Mathematical Computing was the subject, but this bear of a boy didn't seem to Walter to need an introduction to anything. David Whitemen bore a tangle of rich dark hair, a full orange-brown beard and a large frame, with belly to match. Looking at him, Walter would have pegged him at around forty, rather than late teens, and Walter sat next to him in awe feeling slightly intimidated..

At the end of the lecture, David Whiteman had clapped him on the shoulder and said in a deep booming voice:

"Hi, that was a load of shit, wasn't it? I'm Dave. Dave Whiteman."

Walter had simply stared at him.

"Well, come on. Who the hell are you?" Dave, Dave Whiteman had continued.

"Walter Travis," Walter had responded quietly without the inefficiency of the repeated first name.

"Cool," said Dave. "Let's go and get a coffee."

Walter could have excused himself, claimed he had another class, but in some way this larger-than-life figure who had suddenly stumbled into his life fascinated him and so he quietly agreed, swept along by the simplicity of circumstance. Walter could honestly say that he had never met anyone like Dave Whitemen before in his life. On the way to the cafeteria, Dave pulled out a heavy briar pipe, tamped it a couple of times, paused while he lit it and then chuffed off in the proper direction, puffs of smoke streaming out behind like an unstoppable train.

When they reached the cafeteria, Dave bought them both coffees, after first stowing his pipe back in his jacket pocket, asked Walter if he wanted anything else, and then led them to a solitary table in the corner.

"So, what are you in for?" asked Dave once they were seated.

"I'm not sure..." said Walter, not really catching the prison reference.

Dave slapped his chest a couple of times. "Biochem, here. You?"

Okay, Walter understood what he was being asked. "Architecture." He was still somewhat in awe of this lumbering monument of a man and was struggling to find any extra words to turn this into a true conversation..

Dave nodded sagely. "Actually, it doesn't matter what I'm doing," he said. "The point of being here is being here. It's the experience, right? Work hard...hah, maybe we'll think about that. Play hard, lots. For certain." He chuckled. "Man, I'm telling you, there's a lot of living to do here. Whole new world, right?"

Dave had that much right. It was a completely new world for Walter.

"So, Walter, you show me yours, and I'll show you mine. Tell me about yourself." He peered over the rim of his disposable coffee cup with a piercing blue-eyed gaze above ruddy, full cheeks, daring Walter to try to escape, but there was no way that was a possibility. Walter was well and truly fixed in place, a moth under Dave's scrutiny.

Walter, slowly at first, and then more easily, recounted most of his life leading up to admission to university, the bland suburban existence, the ritual of high school, and eventually his hopes, what he wanted to do with this. At the end, it all sounded fairly boring, and though Walter knew that there was nothing to be ashamed of there, somehow, he did feel a little shamed by the plainness of what he'd just revealed.

Dave, in contrast, displayed no shame whatsoever. He was the only son of a wealthy carpet manufacturer and hailed from the more exclusive northern suburbs. He had a younger sister, but she was nothing much to talk about. He barely saw his old man, who was always off running factory business, and he saw little of his mother, because she was easy to escape in the vast house, pool, poolside cabanas and grounds where he lived.

"You know," confided Dave. "She's one of those needy women, always has a need to be loved and have attention."

It soon became clear to Walter that Dave Whiteman wanted for very little in his life growing up, but that his relationship with the rest of his family was somewhat distant at best. Dave paid for everything when they were together, dismissing Walter's protests with either a wave of his hand, or a simple laugh. Still, despite the discomfort, Walter found himself spending more and more time in Dave's rambunctious company. In some sort of twisted way, he was fascinated, despite himself, in the same way that you could be fascinated by a deadly spider, or a highly venomous snake; not that Dave Whiteman was dangerous in that sense, but he was something that Walter was simultaneously drawn to and yet repelled by. Clearly, the attraction firmly won out. After the whole pay-for-everything had extended beyond Walter's comfort level, he had finally summoned the courage to confront him about it. Dave's response was hardly what he expected.

They were sitting at a bench by the sports ground, just talking, killing time before their next class. Walter had cleared his throat and finally said what was on his mind, what was troubling him. Instead of waving his hand, or laughing the matter away as was his usual practice, Dave had puffed thoughtfully on his pipe for a few seconds staring out at the empty field, and then had leaned in conspiratorially.

"No need to trouble yourself with that, Walter," he'd said. "You know, Daddy has a fat wallet."

Walter frowned his lack of comprehension.

"Look, it's simple. I get a good allowance, but you know, there's those extras. Always need a bit to cover the extras." He mimed plucking something with his thumb and forefinger. "What he doesn't count, he doesn't miss. He always leaves his wallet in his jacket pocket when he's at home. A hundred here or there, well, it's nothing to him." Dave shrugged and turned his gaze back to the empty field. "So don't you go bothering yourself any more, Walter. Okay? Sharing the wealth for the common good."

Walter didn't know what to say. There was nothing he really could say, but he asked anyway. "Doesn't he suspect?"

Dave shrugged again. "Who cares? It's not as if he's really going to miss it."

Dave stood, clapped Walter on the shoulder and said, "Come on. Time for class." And that was that.

Walter thought about it for a few days after, about the fact that Dave hadn't really answered his objections, but wasn't inclined to broach the subject again. The next time he was home for the weekend, he had hovered at his parent's bedroom door, considering, but couldn't bring himself to invade that bastion of their privacy and go searching. It just wasn't in him. Feeling how that felt, Walter wondered at Dave's...bravery? No, it was something else, but Walter didn't quite know how to describe it. Though he continued to spend most of his time with Dave, the knowledge sat with him and just wouldn't go away. It made him feel slightly...unclean, as if by his mere association with Dave, he was an accessory to the crime, if it could be called a crime. Over the weeks, however, that feeling faded, as did any thought of that one-off conversation. One of the things that helped the dwindling discomfort was something else initiated by Dave in his usual style; it was Greg and Rada.

In front of the library set squarely in the centre of campus, sat a broad rectangular lawn where, on sunny days, a large segment of the student population would sit at lunch, between classes, or simply to while away the time, books and papers scattered around, or lying back, heads propped up on their bags. Broad trees lined the paved paths to either side providing some solace from the direct sunlight on particularly hot days, but regardless, most chose to sit towards the middle, either individually or in couples or groups that inevitably turned into circles. If you were looking for someone, you could stand on the library steps and scan the lawn for familiar faces or find a convenient space on the lawn to go and sit, waiting until someone else might join you, or simply to close your eyes and feel the sun. By this time, Walter had developed some other associations, but still, it was Dave who loomed large in his university life. He was hard to miss, after all, and perhaps that was one of the things that helped promote the amount of time Walter spent in his company. He was easy to pick out of a crowd. Dave's laugh also had a tendency to carry over distances, acting as another beacon to his location.

One such day, warm and clear, with the lawn crowded with people, Dave spotted Walter on the steps and waved him over. Walter picked his way through the bodies lying or sitting, and stood there at the edge of a circle looking at a collection of unfamiliar faces.

"Walter, Walter, pull up a patch of grass," said Dave, looking up at him and squinting in the light. "Come on, I can't look at you up there. Too much sun. I want you to meet these people."

Walter couldn't remember most of the people that had been sitting in that circle, but he remembered Greg and Rada.

They, the perpetual couple, were to grow as a presence in his life over the next few months. Greg was tall, well-tanned, with a thin line of dark facial hair running from the bottom of his lower lip to his chin and long pale hair tied back behind his head. Rada, much shorter, had sleek black hair and a roundness of feature that revealed dark, dark eyes watching him in a way, which to Walter, seemed mysterious. She continued watching him as Dave shifted a bit to free up a patch of lawn where Walter could sit. Introductions were made around the circle. Rada continued watching him, and Greg merely nodded. It soon became apparent to Walter that Greg and Rada were a little older than the rest of the group, and he was to learn, over time, that not only were Greg and Rada the perpetual couple, they were also perpetual students both. The thing that he noticed most, though, was the limited conversation, the economy of movement expressed by the circle as a whole. Walter's arrival had interrupted, but it seemed as if he had interrupted nothing in particular. He scanned the faces, waiting for something, not really sure what he was waiting for.

"Well, time for another," said Greg, lifting himself from where he was lying back, propped on his elbows and reaching into the mustard-coloured canvas bag that lay beside him on the grass. Dave placed a firm hand on Walter's back and peered into his face with a huge beatific grin. That particular grin, with Dave's bushy beard and ruddy cheeks would become another feature of the next few months, along with the way Dave's eyes seemed to disappear into the mass of flesh that was his face when he started into one of his giggling fits.

Next came what was to become a familiar ritual with a collection of cigarette papers all carefully glued together, pinches from a bag that filled the painstakingly constructed result, and a studied process of rolling, with Greg hunched over, calmly, concentrating on the enterprise. The result was a large, conical affair which Greg proceeded to moisten with his mouth and then light. He passed it to the person on his left and leaned back, holding the lungful he had just taken. Thankfully for Walter, Dave was before him, and Walter was able to watch while Dave went through the ritual himself, his face turning bright red as he held the breath and tried desperately to repress a threatened cough. Walter took the proffered joint, for he knew what it was, with some trepidation. Not wanting to appear like a complete neophyte, he mimicked Dave's actions, only to collapse in a fit of coughing. He could barely see, but he could see enough to recognise Dave waving at him.

"Pass it on," he hissed. "Pass it on."

Walter did just that, happy to be rid of the thing.

That first time, Walter felt nothing. He wondered perhaps if he had been doing it wrongly, that he'd made some fundamental error that he couldn't see. Dave assured him, later, that it was not unusual to feel nothing the first time, but he spent a couple of hours that afternoon watching in bemusement as the circle members became more unfocussed and giggly, laughing at things that made no sense to Walter at all or starting off into convoluted analyses that seemed to be about nothing in particular, but with the slow, meaningful nods of agreement from one or other of the circle.

It was not until his third time that Walter felt anything, and then it hit him like a steam train, rushing down upon his consciousness and sweeping everything that had been Walter away. For half an hour he sat there, convinced that he couldn't lift his arm and then crumbling into laughter about exactly that fact. Throughout it all, Rada continued watching him with that dreamy, speculative gaze. Walter simply had other things on his mind. His classes that afternoon were irrelevant. They had, in fact, disappeared from his mind entirely. Much later that afternoon, he remembered, and worked out that he had missed three complete classes that afternoon on the lawn, and for some strange reason, it didn't seem to matter at all.

-14-

Woodford Park

It is said that buildings accumulate impressions, echoes of the events and people that have lived within them. The larger the event, the greater the other-worldly shadow that permeates the walls, the floors, the very foundations. Or so they say. Some psychics make a reasonable living wandering from house to house to 'read' the energies contained in old places, and even newer ones. They even get television series out of it. These benevolent righters of historical wrongs identify presences, spirits that are seeking final rest, or even revenge from great wrongdoings enacted against their no-longer-corporeal selves. Perhaps The Bellevue would have been a candidate for such a reading, but it had never been done. Though the old hotel had its share of events that by rights, would have left their psychic stain, there had been no call to exorcise the ghosts of things that may or may not have happened there. Certainly, there had been at least one suicide, and one of the wings could claim a murder in the heat of passion, but more frequently there were the deflowerings, clandestine affairs, seductions and the ruination of more than one Jack the Lad. The Bellevue, however, had been around for years, and it was merely a venue, a repository of events that would have taken place there, or in some other location if the Bellevue had never been built. Who can say whether these actions left some sort of psychic energy that permeated the walls and rooms of the place? The only certainty is that the grand old hotel and the actions that took place within its walls and bedchambers existed side by side, cohabitants in the stream of time and history, tied to each other by the happenstance of their coexistence.

Who is to say, then, that a town is not the same, that a town or a city is nothing more than a larger collection of interconnected rooms, a house, or even a hotel on a much grander scale? Certainly, a town is a very large house and it is a shared accommodation, a student dormitory extending into the broader landscapes of life, or a large, rambling house, shared by a group of couples. Visitors come and go, perhaps even staying for a few weeks or months, or from time to time, they may become semi-permanent house guests, live-in distant relatives, or even staff. Even then, there are the long-term residents, those people who really 'live' in a place and become part of its own set of memories. With that understanding, is it so peculiar that an entire town might accumulate the energies of what takes place within its imagined walls? Part of the problem with the psychic practitioners who read those energies, perform their divinations, is that they actually do so on far too small a scale. If they moved beyond the kitchen, with its poltergeist neatly stacking the plates on the floor each night, or the attic with its ghost that is wont to leave an unexpected chill and attendant feeling of dread, or the low moaning in the still of night, if they moved beyond all that, they might discover something else entirely.

-15-

Angelica

In the end, the funds from the estate took some time to come through, and then as per her mother's wishes, a proportion of them were to be held in trust until Angelica's thirtieth birthday. That had seemed a somewhat arbitrary decision on her mother's part. Why *was* thirty any different from say twenty-five? What it meant, however, was that Angelica would have in the background a steady income that would accumulate, regardless of what she managed to do with what she did have immediate access to. Angelica tried to think back, to understand what it might have been in her mother's life at the age of thirty that decided for her, that this was the watershed of maturity and responsibility. When her mother was thirty, Angelica was only ten, and by then, anything that had happened already had taken place, or would not happen for a number of years yet, as far as she knew. Her mother had been only forty-four when she had finally made that last apology, an apology about which Angelica still had been unable to decide about, whether those last spoken words were to Angelica herself, or rather a reflection of her mother's understanding of her own life.

Whatever the case, Angelica decided very clearly that all that was over, it was gone, a thing of the past and it needed to be purged, along with the events that led up to it. With the sale of the house, she had even more resources at her disposal. She needed to have an adventure, and because there was so much that begged the subject of a proper and healthy catharsis, it needed to be a Grand Adventure. Throughout her school life, though she hadn't excelled at it, Angelica had had a passing interest in history. It was likely the romanticism and the fact that it was full of dramatic grand adventures of the type she now sought, ancient history far more so than modern. So, she decided; what better place than the Mediterranean for her first grand adventure? It could have been Italy, Rome, Venice, all of that, but somehow, she wanted to get away, to retire from the familiarity of everything she was used to. She didn't want to be just another tourist gawking at great buildings and monuments like thousands of others before her. There was no choice really; it had to be Greece. For Angelica, Greece had its own special kind of theatre, full of ancient drama, gods upon mountaintops and an endless clear blue sea. The waters plied by the Argo, those forbidding cliffs. She planned and organised with these images in mind, picking islands at random—there were so many!—and plotting a multi-site visit. Then she packed for a trip that would last a minimum of six weeks. When it got to the end of that period, she would see. If she wanted to extend the stay for a few more weeks, she could. If she wanted to go somewhere else, then she had that choice too. She was free.

The rest of the furniture and things that she didn't sell along with the house, she put into storage, and then she was at the airport, waving her hands dismissively at the claims of overweight luggage and how much she had to pay and really not caring about it at all. She was getting away. For the first time in her life, Angelica was about to have a truly grand adventure. There she was, twenty-five and in control of her own destiny with nothing to tie her to anything except the dreams she had of what she was about to embark upon and her passport. She wanted...she didn't know what she wanted. All she knew was that it had to be different.

It turned out to be completely different to everything she had imagined and different in a completely unexpected way, because the problem with Angelica's dream adventure was that it was just that, a dream based upon her fantasies of what the place should be like. The Greek islands fulfilled some of their promise, the expanses of aquamarine seas, the jagged limestone or volcanic cliffs, the rock fingers pointing upward from the water, the twisted olive groves, all were very much as Angelica had imagined from her preparatory reading of various guidebooks and web pages in the couple of weeks before she left. The caldera that was most of Santorini had to be seen to be believed, the hazy sunsets over the water hanging over a cliff and drinking cocktails. The olive groves themselves were a revelation. The ancient trees took on bizarre twisted shapes in which she could see faces, creatures, but for the most part, they reminded her of tortured bodies, lending a kind of eeriness to their presence. She decided very quickly that she didn't want to go walking through the olive groves after dark. She had no real desire to be reminded of the various failures of the human body with such referential clarity.

The small villa she had rented on her first island — self-catering, of course — was charming. Whitewashed walls and basic but adequate facilities overlooking a bay and harbour graced with old coloured Venetian style buildings, because the Italians had had their time there in the past. Wild profusions of bougainvillea and night-scented jasmine clambered over the walls and gateways. The harbour front was clustered with tavernas, bars and little shops where she could pick up anything she needed. In reality, however, she didn't need for much. On the surface, it was just as she had imagined, but her desire not to be a tourist was one that would remain unfulfilled, an impossible dream. Everyone on the island was a tourist, or served the tourists who flocked there in their numbers, or served the people who served the tourists. The waterfront bars were full of Italians, Germans, visiting Greeks from other cities and clusters of lobster-boiled British, either sitting in their yachts moored along the harbour front, or like herself, in rented villas. Most of the signs were in English, paying mere lip service to the local language with the smaller proportion having dual or triple language signs, some in Italian, some in the strangely curving Greek script and occasionally Russian. It was abundantly obvious to her though, that the primary driver and commerce within the town was British. Her naive dreams of the unspoiled Mediterranean had rapidly transformed themselves into a British holiday mecca and there was very little exotic about that. She had just missed the season where the horde of Italians popped across on their ferries and boats like a plague of locusts to career around the narrow winding streets on the motor scooters available for rent everywhere, but she saw enough of it to realise what it must be like in high season. The Italians, who had in the past, laid claim to the small island, still laid claim to it, but in a totally different manner.

It was the Britishness of everything that disturbed her the most, and it was a pattern that repeated on her second island and her third. The locals invariably spoke English, with some German and Italian thrown in. The tavernas often bore signs proclaiming proudly that full English breakfasts were available, but mostly it was the bars and the discos that quickly crumbled any remaining illusions she might have. The main difference between the islands was their accessibility and this, in turn, influenced the prominent age group of the individual island's demographic. It also seemed to dictate the number of bars and discos available and their capacity. All were full. All pumped out electronic beats, flashing lights and Europop, not caring whether the sound become a wall of intermingled noise because of their proximity to one another. In the more populous islands, the waterfronts, because there were invariably waterfronts, were little more than drunken venues for coupling, the occasional fight or displays of public behaviour that would have had her grandfather turning in his grave, none of it quiet.

Angelica believed strongly of herself, that she was nothing if not adaptable. Circumstance was always changing, and things had never quite turned out as she expected. She was used to it. Very quickly, she also got used to the program and adapted herself to it, along with her dreams. She acquired a passing parade of Sweet Boys, some of whom turned out to be not that sweet, but in the end that didn't matter really either. They were only there for a night or two, and the string of multi-coloured, umbrella cocktails served to blur the more jagged of the edges. Of the islands themselves, she saw very little. Most of her days were spent as aftermaths of the night before, essential periods of recharge, avoiding the main heat of the day, before she embarked on the next night, and the night after that. Of course, she managed to fit in the occasional excursion, or a ride in a glass-bottomed boat, even some scuba, but these she did as much out of a sense of duty rather than a conscious desire.

The six weeks were over before she really knew it, and by then, it didn't take her long to decide that the odyssey was over. The memories she would be taking with her back from the islands were hazy, a blur of faces, sound and sweaty bodies, all merging into each other into a kind of fragmented wall of images and half-remembered names. Nestled in the background of her thoughts as something she *knew* but did not particularly want to think about was the knowledge that she might just as well have been visiting — apart from the weather of course — a British holiday resort bizarrely transported to a place that was little more than a peculiarly un-British movie backdrop. It was with an unexpected half sense of relief that she packed her luggage, strangely lighter now than when she arrived, blew a parting kiss at the Greek

Islands and finally took off for home, never once feeling the urge to look back.

-16-

Bill

Bill was sitting in his leather recliner, watching the game, his second evening beer cradled between his hands and perched upon his stomach. He was allowed a couple of extra beers if a game was on, and it was Bill's quiet time, even though quiet time was somewhat of a misnomer with the volume up a few notches as it always was when there was a game on.

"You know, Bill, funny thing..." said Doris from her chair, speaking above the noise of the television.

Bill glanced over at her, frowned and then turned his attention back to the screen. She knew better that to start a conversation with him when a game was on. This was *his* time.

"Bill are you listening to me?"

This time he did more than glance. He turned fully to face her, making sure the displeasure was evident on his face.

"Yes, Doris, what? This had better be important."

"Well..." Doris hesitated. "It might be, and it might not be. I don't know. You know yesterday, when you were off doing whatever it was you were doing..."

"Mmmm," he said.

"Well, I was out cleaning the dog enclosure..."

Bill groaned and looked away. "Not that again. I told you I was sorry. I forgot, all right? That was it. I forgot."

"No, Bill, listen. That's not what I'm talking about."

Once more, he dragged his attention away from the screen and looked at her, repositioning himself and his beer so that he could sit a little straighter.

She waited until she was sure she had his full attention and then continued. "Well, I was out there, hosing out the pen, and I saw this little girl, just standing out there down by the school. She was there for quite a while. At first I thought she might be waiting for someone, but then she just took off."

Bill shrugged. "One of the local kids?"

"No, I didn't recognise her."

"Okay," he said with a little frown. "So what is that to me?"

Doris took a deep breath. "I just haven't been able to stop thinking about her. Sweet little thing. Such a pretty little dress. I wondered if you knew of anyone new in town, some new rentals maybe, someone you'd forgotten to tell me about."

Bill paused before answering, careful to keep his reply steady. "Okay, listen, you made your point, okay? I forgot. But I'm not going to forget about something like that. I'd tell you."

Doris nodded, seemingly satisfied with the answer and looked away again, back to the pages of the magazine she'd been flipping through.

"Why is it so important anyway?" Bill asked.

"I don't know. Just...something. Something about her, I guess," she said without looking up,

"Okay," said Bill, turning back to watch the rest of his game and repositioning the beer can after taking another sip. He might even have another after this one. There was still plenty of time for another. The game was only half done.

-17-

Exploration

Walter's meeting in the city had gone relatively well. His plans, so far, were more than fulfilling the client's expectations. Certainly, he had to tweak them here and there, change a couple of the internal dimensions, but they had bought his use of light and space through the main living areas. He decided he was going to reward himself with another investigative wander to the squat headland over the sea.

When he got there, the building was just as he had seen it the last time, not that he'd expected anything to change. As he stood in front, working out his plan of attack, he realised that the last time he'd been here, he had neglected the broken windows at the front. Funny, they'd completely slipped his mind. There they were, staring right at him and he'd ignored them. Though all the remaining windows were opaque, he could at least get a look through those with the chunks of missing glass. He wandered over to the one with the largest gap in it, crunching over fallen fragments, and then wary of the jagged glass edges, he leaned over to peer inside.

The shadowed space was gloomy and virtually empty. A broad tiled floor ran from end to end. From what he could see, fans of dirt, old leaves, even pieces of paper had blown in through the broken windows. Towards the rear of the rectangular space sat a solid set of desks, built into the structure, with tarnished metal signs still affixed to the walls above them. He could read the expected *Reception* and *Concierge* and *Cashier*, all dull and faded now, but recognisable. On the floor in front of the desk sat on old telephone, still with long brown cord trailing up and over the desk. In the centre at the back, sat a broad double staircase that swept back on itself about halfway up, splitting to run up to the next level on either side. Faded carpet still lay held in place by metal carpet rails on each step, set into the stone, worn through and eaten in places, but still there. It was too dim for Walter to really pick the colour, but he suspected it might once have been red. A musty smell permeated the area, old mould and mildew, and something else, perhaps rotting vegetation. Walter suddenly became aware of the large jagged sheet of glass still held in place in the window frame above him, hanging like a guillotine, and he drew back, looking once more at the windows again. That was another thing...after so much time, how was it that most of the windows were still intact? He had a brief vision of stone-throwing youths standing out in front and hurling chunks of fallen rock to watch the vast panes shatter and crash to the ground. Apparently not. What was it about the old place that discouraged such acts of vandalism? He looked back behind him at the empty beach, wondering. Without doubt, its position shielded The Bellevue from most of the town, so maybe that was it — out of sight, out of mind, but somehow, he thought, it was something more than that.

Suddenly conscious, in the back of his neck, across his shoulders, of the aging squat presence behind him, he turned back again. No, he was fuelling his own imagination now. It was just an old empty building, and it had been lucky to remain virtually whole. Okay, the windows didn't seem to provide a decent means of entry. He could hold them in reserve if a foray around the back gave no joy. With a quick look back at the beach, down the hill past the empty parking area, along the coast road, making sure that there was no one to observe, he slipped around the side of the building and headed for the back. On the way, he paused at the side to test a couple of the boarded up doors and windows, but they looked too solid. There was no way in that way.

At the rear, he had more luck. There were doors at the end of both branches of the U, but those were solid. Large round brass knobs sat on either side of thick double doors, but both sets turned out to be immovable. He turned his attention to the inner courtyard. On the left side, towards the rear, sat a smaller door, and as Walter approached, he was rewarded by a narrow crack of darkness between the door and its frame. He stepped up to the door, reached for the handle and pushed. The door gave a little, but there was something blocking it. Either that or it had just warped over time to stick in place. Not to be discouraged, he put his shoulder against it and pushed a little more. It gave a touch, shifting with his weight. He stood back and then stepped forward again, applying even more weight. With a heavy scraping sound, the door opened a fraction more, allowing enough space, this time, for Walter to insert himself between its edge and the frame and apply some leverage. With a heavy grinding and some resistance, he managed to force it about halfway open, enough space to slip through. Carefully, he slid round the edge of the door and inside proper.

Dust and other detritus coated the floor in little piles and scattered trails the length of a corridor with walls covered in the same, peeling, blotched and faded wallpaper he had spied through the windows on his last visit. Tattered cobwebs hung, blackened with dust and age from the corners of the ceilings, and made loops like rigging from the regular light fixtures along the length. On the left side, regularly spaced doors had numbers on them, counting down as they hall got nearer the front. Spaced between the doorways, between every second one, sat pictures. From what Walter could make out through the grimy glass within each of the frames, they contained old photographs — ships, construction, people on streets; that was as far as he got. If they were old photographs then...

Feeling completely like an intruder now, he had a moment of hesitation. Perhaps this was a bad idea after all. Still, he'd come this far. About a third of the way up the corridor, a couple of the doors stood open, and he headed for them. He stepped into the first room. Dim light filtered through a filthy window, affording him enough brightness to see. He didn't know what he had expected, but the room was empty. All furnishings had clearly been removed some time ago when the hotel had closed its doors. The floor was littered with dirt and scraps of something. Walter bent to look at them closer and realised that the curling, browning leaves were nothing more the pieces of wallpaper that had fallen and now lay stained and deteriorating where they had fallen. A quick look up at the walls confirmed it. He ducked his head through the other door that led to a decent sized bathroom, dim and dark, an old rectangular mirror above the sink bordered by lines of empty sockets, meant to hold bulbs at one stage. He drew back quickly. In the sink lay the corpse of a gull, blackened and twisted, but still fairly recent, feathers still in place. There was a faint smell of corruption, and he took another step back, holding his hand over his mouth and nose. The bird must have found its way in through the front window and then got stuck, unable to find its way out, flapping futilely through empty corridors until it had finally expired through starvation or dehydration. Empty sockets begetting empty sockets, he thought and grimaced. Nice. Walter withdrew from the room entirely and closed the door. He swallowed a couple of times then headed further up the corridor. After the unexpected encounter with the dead bird, he was a little uneasy now. Something creaked further inside the building and he jumped, stopping dead in his tracks and holding his breath. He waited a couple of beats. No, he thought, exhaling slowly, he was imagining things. Old building made noises. It was as simple as that. He was alone in here, alone with a bunch of old dirty photographs with faded labels and a lot of dirt and maybe a few spiders, though by the looks of things, there weren't even any of the spiders still alive. None of the webs appeared fresh.

He made his was slowly along the corridor, pausing to peer at the faded pictures as he went, not wanting to touch, but to get some sense of the faded memories. Some of the photographs had been affected by damp and mould, obscuring what lay beneath with dark stains and blotches, but he managed to see apart from the old scenes of construction and old ships, a collection of tennis players with large moustaches, a group of ladies smiling, all wearing funny hats. The old hotel, in that sense, was like an archive, old memories of times and events past spread along its walls and probably forgotten until Walter had ventured in. Did the smiling face mean anything to anyone anymore? Were there long-forgotten connections that still existed or were they merely reminders of something that had long ago faded into the past? There was no way he could really know.

The end of the long corridor turned right, leading to another, the one that Walter had seen on his last visit. Again a length of light fittings, hanging cobwebs, dirt and odd bits of unidentifiable rubbish along its length. This corridor led to another turning at the end, leading, Walter presumed to the other side of the U, the other wing. Halfway along, there was an open archway, leading, he guessed to the front. It was a strange construction if he thought about. It was almost as if the residential section of the hotel had been tacked on afterwards, added to a main building that already stood. He could see how you could do that, knock through the back wall, giving access and then add the wings, though why they would choose to do it that way rather than building two separate wings directly out from the back of either side he couldn't understand. Maybe there was some sound structural reason why they would make such a choice.

He wandered along the central corridor, considering, passing old brass signs with arrows, pointing the direction of room numbers, 1-20 and 21-35 in the other direction. The right hand side must contain the suites, the larger, more expensive rooms. Again, a strange choice. He would have expected those to be on the cliff side of the hotel, rather than facing the mountains.

The central archway did give access to the main lobby. From the rear, Walter entered, starting as a lizard scrabbled across the floor and out of sight with his appearance. It looked pretty much as he had seen it from the window, but from this end, he could see the old bar at one end, and the beams of light filtering through the front windows, dappling the dirty floor with patches of light and shade. He tried to imagine the space with the windows clean and full of furniture. He conjured cane chairs, large, overstuffed leather lounges around the central area, perhaps potted palms on either side of the doorway. Over by the bar would have been tables, wood and upholstered chairs. He could see it all in his mind's eye, waiters and hotel staff in black and white uniforms circulating amongst the guests. It would have been impressive in its day. Through the window, he could see vague shadows of the ocean beyond, and he tried to imagine the panorama through those windows, panel after panel of blue water, sparkling in the sun, topped by paler blue sky. It would have been a vision. He could appreciate what they had done. He suddenly thought how strange this really was, him standing there in the middle of this empty shell, constructing someone else's vision with his imagined pictures. It was like faded energies reaching out through time. He was sure it must have implications, though he wasn't sure what they were. He gave a slight shiver, and then turned to the central staircase.

He had to watch his footing on the decaying carpet, careful not to slip. One by one, he took the stairs and ascended into the upper gloom. The top of the staircase opened up to a landing. An old wooden chair lay propped against one wall, beneath an ancient notice board, nothing on it but a few pins. Three separate signs announced *Ballroom*, *Dining Rooms* and *Offices: Private*. He had a quick look through the double doors leading to the ballroom, but it was just a vast empty expanse of floor with a raised dais at one end and six chandeliers hanging from the ceiling, one at a crazy angle where the chain connecting it to the ceiling had dropped. A scattering of crystal droplets lay on the floor below.

The dining rooms were just rooms. Once they would have been packed with tables and chairs. Double doors led off, probably to an area where staff had disappeared to return laden with trays or plates to serve the guests. Broad windows also afforded a view of the ocean. He could imagine groups of diners, sitting here in the evening over candlelight, watching the glittering of cruise ships far out to see as they sat at the prime tables near the window. Maybe, even, those plum spots were reserved for the more important guests. Were there peacock and ostrich feathers, dinner jackets and ivory cigarette holders? He could see them all.

A quick inspection of the offices revealed a series of interconnected small rooms, just what he would have expected from offices and nothing that really interested him. But there was something missing. Where were the kitchen, the laundry? There might be place for staff in some of the scattered outbuildings he had seen to the rear, but there had to be rooms to service the dining and housekeeping needs somewhere.

He turned back to the staircase and walked back down to the ground floor. On one side of the staircase, he thought he found his answer. A small sign said *Staff Only* above a modest door. He opened it to reveal a dark space with the start of a staircase going down. There was no way he was going down there, not without more than simply a flashlight, something he didn't have anyway. The blackness was impenetrable. He closed the door and shook his head. Probably kitchens, laundry, maybe some storage rooms, though he wondered if there might be something left in them. It was probably unlikely. The upper levels would possibly be serviced by some sort of dumb waiter arrangement, popular in those earlier years when the hotel had been first constructed. He hadn't seen any sign of an elevator, but then it really wouldn't have been needed in a place like this.

He'd seen enough to satisfy his curiosity for now, anyway, and carefully, he retraced his steps and slipped out the back door. With a touch of conscience, he tried closing that rear door again, but for some reason, it now appeared to be wedged firmly in place. He put some weight against it, and was rewarded with a loud crack. A lengthy split had appeared the length of the door.

"Shit," he said below his breath, backing away from the door for a few steps and rubbing at his forehead with his fingers. He stood there looking at it for a couple of seconds, wondering what he should do and then turned to walk rapidly away around the side of the building.

On the way back to the house, along the coast road, and still muttering the occasional "Shit," to himself under his breath, Walter became aware, at first peripherally, of a solitary figure on the beach. Dressed in pale green shorts and a pale white top, boy or girl, Walter could not really tell from this distance, a child was crouched in the damp firm sand near the water's edge, inscribing figures with a long pointed stick.

Everything about the child's posture spoke of concentration, of studied action. Walter watched as he walked, more focussed now on the child's presence. The increasing angle of his viewpoint only served to obscure the carefully scratched lines in the sand and to further add to the androgyny of the child itself. He continued to observe for a while longer, before turning to cross the road and take the path back up to his house.

When he looked out the window, later, down to the beach, the child had gone and any evidence of the marks he or she had made in the sand had already been washed away, obliterated by the waves, a small section at a time.

-18-

Memory

The fragments of what we recall about our lives vary from individual to individual and manifest in vastly different ways. Some of us remember in pictures, those pictures blurring or fading with age, or even morphing with constant re-visitation into other, different shapes entirely. Others remember words or happenings as descriptive events rather than on the internal movie screen. Colour, black and white, or grainy sepia, it matters not which, there within lie the collected pieces of what we believe ourselves to be and to have done. Then, again, there's that which is referred to as selective memory. Sometimes, it's easier not to remember at all, and so we conveniently don't, even though, beneath the surface, in reality, whether we are consciously aware of it or not, we do. The mind's a funny thing in that respect. It can be made to perform tricks, tricks that alter space and time, change history, reconfigure faces and circumstances into other things entirely. In essence, it has the ability to adapt reality to our perceptions of how things should, or could have been, if only such and such had happened, even to shift the blame for how things turned out. If only you had chosen not to go to the beach that day. If only you had decided not get completely trashed that night. If only you hadn't slept with him that time. If only...

If you spend too much time dwelling on the what-might-have-beens, it only leads to regret. Somehow, deep within, perhaps the mind, clever thing that it is, knows that regret is not a healthy state and it takes steps to protect itself.

Sometimes it does not, with occasionally tragic consequences. Witness Angelica's grandfather. You can regret that which has not already come to pass as well as that which might have been. Wishes and dreams can still be constrained by time, but unlike memory, they are not bound to it. You cannot remember things future, only those things past. However, we all know the mind can play tricks.

Sometimes, however, we can simply and straightforwardly forget.

It has been known to happen.

Walter, for one, simply forgot about the child on the beach.

-19-

Angelica

When Angelica was growing up, before her father had performed his vanishing act, they would sometimes, on weekends or during school breaks visit her grandparents' holiday home down at the beach. It was a couple of hours drive from their home in Sandton, and they would pack the car with beach gear, towels, floats, casual clothing and coolers to take down to the seaside. Her grandfather didn't own any one particular holiday home; he owned a succession of them, one after the other, or sometimes simultaneously. All of it was driven by property speculation on his part. He would snap up bargains, maybe hold on to them for a few months or a year or so, and in the meantime, either rent them out, or take them for his own use, never investing in an iota of renovation along the way. He bought when the price was right, and he sold again when he adjudged the market would net him the greatest profit. Of course, he had very few legal fees associated with this string of transactions, as he was the one who did most of the legal work himself. Angelica, her mother and father, and her grandparents all benefited tangentially from this activity. Though firmly embedded in the country town where he had made most of his life, her grandfather loved the beach, loved the ocean and did everything he could, whether directly or indirectly, to be within its embrace.

During those short periods that they spent by the beach, like clockwork, every morning at 7:00 a.m. he would appear in his striped swimming trunks, towel across his shoulder, waiting impatiently for Angelica to be ready to head off for the required morning swim. Of course she was coming; don't be stupid. Rain or shine, the ritual would be the same. When they had the luxury of staying in separate houses, which they did from time to time when her grandfather had a surfeit, he would turn up at the front doorstep, regularly, 7:00 a.m. on the nose and stand around impatiently as the minutes ticked by and Angelica struggled into her one piece dark-blue bathing suit with the white flowers up one side. Her grandfather would drive her down to the beach and perform several laps of the salt-water pool that lay at one end, still looking fit for his age, despite the sagging breasts and expanse of white hair across his chest.

At first, Angelica struggled with the ritual. The cold seawater in the morning might have been bracing to someone like her grandfather, but to her, it was an unnecessary torture, especially when she was muzzy-headed, only half awake, and had not yet even had breakfast. Her grandfather, stickler for the regimen that he was, would brook no argument. It was Angelica's duty to accompany him to the beach each morning, and her parents certainly weren't going to stand up in her defence, despite her indignant stance. It was good for her, good for a growing girl. Yet never once, she managed to notice, did they perform the ritual themselves. Thinking back, it would have been unlikely that her grandfather would have let them.

The salt water pool itself was built at the edge of one of the rock platforms at the end of the beach, taking advantage of a quirk of the rock formation itself to form one side of the pool and extending it out into a square enclosure, retaining walls built from a mixture of cement and gravel, and over the years, covered at the bottom with sand and grown mossy around the edges with green weed. Angelica had lived in fear of the deeper end of the pool, so close to the ocean itself, and on rough days, tall waves would break over its end and send smaller rises and dips along its length. The water was always fresh and clean; the changing tides saw to that. Gradually, she became used to it, got over most of her fear, but she always stayed at the bottom half of the pool, what was the shallow end. When she gained some confidence, under her grandfather's critical eye, she would practice diving, receiving bobbing applause from her grandfather's hands as he trod water in the deep end, watching her. Looking back, these were some of the few gestures of encouragement or praise that she ever received from her grandfather. It was his belief that everyone had a duty to perform as well as they could, and no praise was needed. Achievement was its own reward.

After every morning's half an hour at the pool, they would head up and shower, bundle back into the car, beach towels draped around their necks and her grandfather would either drop her back home, where her parents were just staggering into the ritual of breakfast, or take her back to the house they were all sharing together. A little later, the morning exercise extended, and on days when the weather was not too rough, her grandfather took her into the water directly at the beach itself, into the open breakers where he body-surfed the waves while still keeping a close eye on Angelica who, in truth, was terrified of the waves, even the smaller ones that pushed against her legs, scooping the sand from beneath her feet and then sucking back to leave her uncertain in her footing, her arms outstretched for balance.

Although her parents didn't ever accompany them on the regular morning excursion, there were later times on the beach, her father's tanned brown body slicing through the waves, her mother careful to put a large hat on Angelica's head and slap on the sun cream, bedecked in a similar large straw hat herself and wearing sunglasses that seemed to cover half of her face. She guessed that ultimately, the morning swims were her grandfather's time, time in which he could engage in some quality bonding activities with his only grandchild and therefore something he would guard jealously. Much later, she would wonder whether it was something he did because he wanted to, or because it was something he felt he needed to do because it was right, a ritual duty, the sort of thing a grandfather was supposed to do. The clearest memory she had of his face though, was bobbing above the water, looking at her approvingly, his horn-rimmed glasses away, back up in the car, and his grey-white moustache bristling across his upper lip, his close cropped hair still grey at the sides but tending to white at the top, and the single gold tooth at the front of his mouth flashing in the sunlight. In that sense, the face she remembered most was the face that she didn't necessarily associate with him, because he swam without his glasses. The grandparent she went through those bonding rituals with every morning when at the beach was another man, someone else entirely.

Within a couple of years, her grandfather had decided that he would retire from his practice and move down to the seaside proper, so he could spend most of his retirement years at the beach. It seemed that part of the regular visits had been scouting activity as much as leisure. He made his own decision—her grandmother didn't enter into that process; hers was to accept the outcome, not that she would have argued anyway—and then proceeded to expand that decision to others. After some discussions, he managed to dangle a lure in front of her parents that was hard to resist. He had recently acquired a cheap house nearby, and if they wanted to, they could purchase it from him at cost. He would even lend them the money at no interest, so they could pay him back over time; that was, if they needed help with the financing, and of course, they did. Although Angelica wasn't really aware of what her father did at the time—she had a vague idea that it had something to do with printing—it seemed to be no impediment to them taking up her grandfather's offer. He was commuting to the city anyway, and in fact, the journey from their new town was likely to be shorter than the daily trip he had to make from Sandton. The decision was made and separately, the two parts of the family packed their belongings into trunks and boxes and shifted down to the coast. Her grandfather held on to his house in Sandton, until he had made up his mind what he was going to do with it.

In the same way that her grandfather had enforced his required morning seaside rituals upon Angelica, and there, by default, on her father and mother too, he had managed, quite subtly, to enforce his own choice of the proper environment on them as well. His family, his daughter and his granddaughter would be nearby within easy reach, just down the hill and across the town. Perhaps, despite his aloof nature, his closed-off removal, he really was attached to them and was afraid to have them somewhere else, distant and out of his reach, in the care of a man who ultimately he didn't trust and in the end, a man who he was right not to trust. Over the years, his commercial acumen in the property market and the experiences of his legal practice must have given him some sort of innate sense about people, of their reliability, their capacity to carry on and deliver. Something special about Angelica's father had tweaked a nerve, something unspoken, especially not with Angelica's mother, but something that had prompted her grandfather to take precautions, whether consciously or not.

-20-

The Corner Store

The small corner operation where Deepak and his two sons, Suraj and Latesh held fort did a passing trade at best during the cooler, winter months, but the thing that kept them going was the inherent laziness that people suffered. Deepak and his sons were not lazy. They opened in the morning and they stayed open till late at night, taking it in shifts. Deepak would hunt for bargains while the boys looked after the shop, buying six or eight of something that he thought people might want at knock down prices, then bring them back, calculate a decent mark-up for his trouble and then label whatever it was, scented candles, toothpicks, toilet freshener, sachets of various spices, paper plates, with the little pricing gun he kept for the purpose. Non-perishable goods were better, because he never knew when something might finally sell, or whether he had got it quite right. He would find a home for the newly labelled items and they would join the rows and stacks of previously acquired items in positions that might make sense to Deepak, or simply where there might be space. It was the consumables, those high turnover items that kept him going more than anything else, the milk, the bread, which he had delivered fresh, and similar items. Of course, he carried ice creams, drinks, packets of confectionary, those things that someone might purchase on a whim, especially if they had kids along with them. It was the night-time trade that kept his business running. Oh someone had forgotten to buy milk. Oh no, they'd run out of sugar. No matter, they could wander down to the corner shop and pick something up, and while they were down there, they might find something else that looked like a good idea, because most of his customers would have a browse amongst the stacked and jumbled shelves to see what they might discover. Long hours, careful planning and consideration allowed him to make a living and put enough aside to send back home. Of course, he didn't really have to pay his sons too much; they were family and what did they need for money anyway when they worked in the shop.

Deepak did not know his customers by name, but he could recognise a few of them by sight, the regulars. For the most part, he considered them to be single, unattached or in some other circumstance that indicated a lack of proper family. These were the people who browsed his shelves late in the night or in the middle of the day, regular, nameless faces and these were the ones that were likely to pick up one or another of his smart little purchases, spying something interesting as they negotiated their way sideways down the double rows of shelves. He had, on occasion, pictured himself as a furniture store for the newly separated, like that big chain that he had seen advertising on the small television. In the early evening, unless it was very late, parents would send their kids down to pick up something they had forgotten, and he would benefit, because mostly those children might buy a little extra with the change. He would watch them all in the round curved mirror sitting high up above the television and giving him a view of the entire shop apart from the little blind spot at the back of the central stack, but he had cleverly placed larger items back there, things like packets of paper towels of toilet paper that would be hard for people to shove into their pockets or inside their clothes. The children, for the most part, were the ones he had to watch, or the youths who wandered in pairs or threes during summer, but these were not his regulars. For a while, he had toyed with putting up a sign dictating that there were to be no more than two schoolchildren in the shop at any one time, but in the end, he'd decided against it. Ultimately, Deepak was a hard worker, but he was more than that; he was a student of human behaviour.

That afternoon, he had one of his regulars in. It was the blonde woman from up the hill. She was one of his favourite studies, not only because she seemed a little scattered, spending some time at one section of his shelves, moving on, and then coming back as if she had forgotten something, but also, usually, she would come away with one of his slower moving items, like the incense sticks or candles, or perhaps a small bottle of scented oil. She was crouching by the end of one of the shelves scanning when she called out to him.

"Hello. I am looking for tea lights. Have you got any tea lights?"

Deepak wasn't quite sure what tea lights were, but he waved his hand in the general direction of where she was positioned. If he had them, they would be down there somewhere. She nodded and went back to scanning the shelves. At that moment, another of his more regular visitors walked through the doorway, the man with the brown glasses and the greying dirty blond hair. It was not that his hair was dirty. It just looked dirty because of the colour. He started sidling down one of the rows, peering at the arrayed goods and looking thoughtful. That was the usual ritual, and he too was one of Deepak's favourites, because he could never quite predict what the man would come away with. He watched in the mirror as his sideways step took him closer to the rear of the row and of course, the blonde woman still crouched at the end of the other row. His man reached up, snagged a packet of coffee, and hesitated, his gaze running up and down the shelves and then he stepped around the corner.

"Oh sorry, I didn't see you there," he said.

The woman stood. "Oh hello," she said. "Can you see tea lights anywhere? I'm looking for tea lights and can't seem to find them."

"Tea lights?"

"Yes, you know. Those little candles in little silver cups. You know the ones I mean. You get them in boxes of twelve or sixteen."

So that's what they were, thought Deepak.

"Oh, right," said his man. He stood beside her, craning upwards, using his height to look at the upper slots. He reached up and pulled down a pack. "Is this what you want?"

She took the proffered packet and held them this way and that, as if she wasn't quite sure herself. "Yes, that's them. Thank you, so much."

His man nodded and sidled past her, continuing his survey of the shelves.

"Oh wait," she said. "I've seen you around, haven't I? If we're fellow locals, we really should be introduced. My name's Angelica."

His man cleared his throat and reached up to adjust his glasses. "Um, Walter," he said. "Walter Travis."

"Nice to meet you."

His man cleared his throat, nodded and then made a beeline for the counter, his browsing apparently at an end. He stood in front of Deepak, placed the packet of coffee down on the counter and pointed at the refrigeration cabinet behind. "This...and some milk please. One will do."

Deepak totalled up the purchases, accepted the money and handed over the change. While he did so, his man glanced nervously down the aisle towards the woman who had resumed her browsing. He took his change.

"Bag?" said Deepak.

"No, that's all right," said his man, and then he was gone.

A few moments later, the woman was in front of him, sliding the package of small candles across the counter towards him. As Deepak searched for the price label, he wondered what had caused his man to beat such a hasty retreat.

-21-

Moore Street

Deepak's corner store and its neighbours were not the only commercial enterprises in Woodford Park, though they occupied the prime piece of beach front real estate. If you travelled south and up the hill, another street led back up towards the mountain and the town's railway station and the terminus of the local bus service both. In the small strip leading up to the station's parking area lay a cluster of small shops, a veterinary clinic, a hairdresser and beautician, a shop selling bric-a-brac and second-hand clothing, run by the good Christian ladies of the local parish, a computer shop that specialised in setting up home networks and troubleshooting problems for the uninitiated as well as a single cafe and patisserie. Once upon a time, the patisserie had been a travel agency, but the call for exotic voyages in Woodford Park had been small, and it had soon closed its doors. The shop had lain vacant for a couple of years before some enterprising individual had decided it would be a good side-line business, family run and with a coffee machine, several varieties of tea available in multi-coloured packages and a selection of fresh baked cakes and pastries sitting under glass covers on cake-stands and arrayed invitingly along the counter . Simple round tables with neat white tablecloths stood surrounded by bentwood chairs painted in gloss black enamel. On the walls were arrayed a selection of paintings from local artists, small price tags attached. The shop did a trade with some of the visitors in the summer months, but for the most part, their clientele were locals, old ladies with their purses sitting together to discuss the local happenings, meeting up to sip tea and continue the conversations they had started in the hairdressers two doors up, or the young mothers, parking their strollers on either side of the outside tables, getting out of the house for some human contact. The paintings sat upon the walls, gathering dust and age, as the local wildlife chattered about them, never moving.

Angelica's house stood atop a small hill, looking down over the station on one side, the ocean on the opposite side, and to the front, down to Moore Street and its cluster of local shops. Her location was just a short stroll down the hill and with regularity, she would visit the ladies in the shop, greet their 'hello dears' with appropriate responses, and spend half an hour or so picking through the various wares, sliding hangers along rails, pulling out a dress or top to see it better, hanging them back in place and then moving on to the next. Though the stock varied little, relying for the most part on charitable donations from the local parishioners, from time to time, she would find a bargain. Her next stop along the way would be the patisserie, with or without a new plastic bag with a couple of garments folded and shoved inside. She would pick her usual spot by the window, dump her acquisition on the table and wander over to the counter to pore through the selection of teas and decide what she was going to indulge in that day — orange and ginger...chamomile and lemon, perhaps — and then order a pot, never simply a cup. That was one of the beauties of Angelica's life; she always had time for a full pot rather than a simple cup. Once she had made up her mind, she would stroll past the cake stands, finger resting on her bottom lip while she decided if she was going to indulge further. Generally, the answer would be yes.

Today, she had come away from the second-hand store empty handed and she'd already decided that it was an orange and ginger day. All that remained was to survey the range of cakes and pastries on offer. She had noticed, in passing, a black-forest gateau that looked particularly tempting and she didn't see why it couldn't be a chocolate day as well. She'd also noticed something else, while passing the hairdressers. Sitting inside, looking distinctly uncomfortable beside two old women , dwarfed beneath their vast metal and glass domes, sat the man she had stumbled across in the little corner store when she'd been in search of her tea lights. He had been sitting, legs crossed, a woman's magazine held protectively open across his lap, pretending to read. Sometime after she was settled comfortably at her table, sipping at her tea and just reaching with a fork for a piece of the cake, he appeared at the door, looking trimmed and obviously having survived his ordeal in the beautician. He stood for a couple of seconds outside the door before finally opening it and stepping inside. He wandered over to the counter and stood, scanning the chalked display, taking in the various cakes while the girl behind the counter wiped her hands on the front of her white apron.

"What would you like?" she said, when it seemed that he wasn't going to be able to make up his mind.

"Oh, listen, I'll just have a coffee for now."

"Do you want an espresso, or a regular coffee, or a plunger."

He paused, considering. "Um, a plunger."

"Anything else?"

He glanced up at the board. "Okay, yes. I'll have a grilled cheese on toast too."

"Just take a seat. I'll bring it right over to you."

He nodded and reached for his wallet.

"No, that's okay," said the girl. "You can pay when you leave."

He turned, scanned the tables, saw Angelica sitting there, gave a quick movement of his head in recognition and made for another table by the window, pulled out the chair with a loud scrape across the floor and positioned himself so that he looked straight out on to the street, and then proceeded to play with the salt and pepper containers, repositioning them then swapping their places, one after the other. She watched him for a little while, trying to remember his name. She supposed he was reasonably good looking in a straight up and down sort of way, conservative, particularly with the new haircut, close around the ears and back, a little bit more length on top. His big brown glasses gave him a studious, professional air, almost academic. He was starting to grey at the temples, and there were marks of silver in the brown-blond thatch that remained on top. He was wearing an old tweed jacket with a dark green sweater underneath and dark brown corduroy trousers. It all gave him even more of a professorial air. She wondered what it was he did. Academic might not be too far off the mark as she'd seen him a few times wandering around in the day, which spoke of some occupation allowing him plenty of free time. William? No, Walter. Walter, that was it. She shook her head. He'd told her the last name, but she couldn't remember what it was for the life of her. His coffee arrived, and he pushed the plunger down carefully, poured a cup and then topped it off with a brief tilting of the small white jug that had come with it.

Angelica watched Walter for a while longer, waiting until his grilled cheese had appeared, topped with little bacon bits that he poked at and then tilted his head in seeming approval. He cut off a corner with knife and fork and popped it in his mouth. She took another forkful of the rich cake, ate it and then holding her fork up in front of her face, cleaned off the tines with her tongue, one at a time. Finally, she leaned over towards him.

"Walter isn't it?" she said. "I remembered right, didn't I?"

He looked over, nodding and chewing.

"So, how long have you been in Woodford Park?"

She waited for a couple of moments while he finished chewing and then swallowed. "About seven months now."

"Visiting, sabbatical, something like that?" she asked hazarding a guess

He paused halfway through cutting another piece and turned to face her. "No. I live here. This is my home for now. Sorry, I don't remember your name."

"Oh, that's okay. I'm Angelica." Again, she took another piece of the cake and then licked the fork clean while she waited for something else. When it became clear that Walter was not going to continue without prompting, she spoke again. "Funny choice, Woodford Park," she said. "Why here?"

Walter lifted his cup, took a sip and then stared out the front window, thinking. "I don't know really. Something about the place I guess. It was almost as if I was drawn here. God knows, I needed a change of scene."

Ah, she thought. That spoke volumes by itself.

"What about you?" he continued.

Angelica considered her answer. "I had ties to the place before, you know, when I was growing up. It seemed like a nice place to end up. It's been about seven years now."

Walter looked thoughtful again. "End up. That's an interesting way of putting it."

He certainly was very serious. "So what is it you do, Walter?"

He placed his cup down and looked at her. "I'm an architect. Sort of freelance, though I'm attached to a company in the city. I get most of my work through them. I used to work for them directly, but then...well...things happened and it kind of suits me better this way. It's a nicer environment to work in." He shrugged. "Set my own pace. Make my own rules. It's nice. Woodford Park seemed like a good base. Maybe it's the light." He gave a little laugh. Obviously there was something in his last statement that had amused him. Seeing that the joke appeared to be lost on Angelica, he became serious again. "I don't know. Really, there's something about the place, almost as if I was meant to be here."

She nodded her understanding.

"And what about you, Angelica? What do you do?"

She suddenly realised that there was no real satisfactory answer she could give to someone like Walter. "Oh, you know. This and that. I'm thinking about something at the moment, but I haven't quite worked it out yet. There's time though."

He tilted his head a little, waiting for more, but really, Angelica didn't have any more to give him. It was her turn to look thoughtfully out the front window. To fill the space, she took another slice of cake and applied her attention to it instead. "Mmm, good cake. You should try some."

"Yes, it does look good, but not good *for* me, I think. Maybe I'll pass."

"You don't know what you're missing," she said.

In the meantime, Walter had managed to polish off his grilled cheese and swirled the remainder of his coffee before taking the final mouthful.

"Well, that's me done. I guess I'll see you around," he said, pushing back his chair and heading over to the counter to pay.

"Yes, I hope so," she said. "Nice to talk to you, Walter."

She watched as he pulled open the door, walked past the front window, gave her a brief wave, and then wandered down the street, his hands shoved back in his pockets. She watched him until he disappeared from sight. An architect. She didn't think she'd ever met an architect before.

It was only to be a couple of days before she saw him again, this time at her favourite spot sitting out on the stone bench at Ball's Point. Her conversation with Walter had left her thinking, and she needed to process, to watch the steady back and forth of the waves while she smoked one of her occasional cigarettes and let the breeze and currents work their magic to clear her mind. Of course she knew, though sometimes she didn't like to think about it, that her sense of self, what she was, had been as much defined by her Sweet Men, her Sweet Boys as it was by anything she did on her own. The only thing she really did on her own was to remember. That was an art, by itself, but it was hardly something that you could announce at a dinner party. It was a private and personal thing, not something for sharing and in that sense, her self-definition was something unavailable to the world at large. Johan Her Man had given her definition and identity. That was different. They were defined, identified by the fact that they were a couple, and after the accident, she was adrift again, formless, just Angelica on her own. When she had her conversation with Walter, he had his ready answer, a defining label that told her what he was: Architect. Yet Angelica, was simply Angelica. That's what and who she was. There was no convenient box that she might fit into. It was not as if she needed a generally understood label, but the conversation with Walter had shown her something else, if only the mere fact that she was so different, that her life was so very different.

"Hello," came a voice, a little behind her to one side, almost as if it had been conjured by her stream of thoughts..

Angelica jumped a little at the sound. She didn't expect to find anyone up here. She turned, and there stood Walter, breeze ruffling the top of his hair and flapping the ends of a tatty green coat around his thighs.

"Well, hello," she said, trying to mask her surprise, the uneasy feeling his appearance had invoked.

"Fancy meeting you up here," he said, looking both out to sea to the south and then back behind him to where the old hotel lay as if checking where she might have come from. The old bench had a broad stone back and Walter stepped forward to rest a hand on the top of one corner. With one of her hands, Angelica kept her cigarette down by the side of her leg; with the other, she pushed her hair out of her face and squinted up at him.

"I come up here sometimes," she said, "just when I want to be alone and think. It's a good spot for thinking."

"Yeah," he said. "I could see that. I was out here a couple of days ago to get a better look at The Bellevue, just another angle. It's a good vantage point, though the cliff looks a little treacherous at the edge over that way."

"Probably," said Angelica. "I tend not to look over that way much anyway."

"Why is that?"

"Well," she said standing and then pointing back behind the bench with her hand still holding the cigarette between her index and middle finger, her other hand holding her hair back from her face, waving the cigarette in the air to indicate the direction. "There's that old shell mouldering away there for one, but you see there, that other headland just beyond? You can just make out the top of it."

"Yeah, sure, I knew it was there. I saw it when I was up at The Bellevue the other day."

"Well out there on that second headland, there's an old cemetery."

"Really? You're kidding..."

"No, really," said Angelica. She stopped pointing, brought the hand back to her face and took a drag from her cigarette, blowing out the smoke, hard against the breeze. "I don't like looking at either of them too much. I don't particularly like being reminded of dead things, especially not dead people. Let them have their rest," she said, quietly.

She turned and sat again, crossing her legs beneath the bench and holding its edge with both hands, one on either side of her. Walter moved round the edge and sat down beside her, hands folded in his lap to and looked out to the horizon, his gaze focussed on the outline of the distant coastline to the south.

"I understand," he said. "Still, I'll have to check it out. I could see there was something up there, but I couldn't tell what it was." After a couple of moment's pause, he continued. "Yeah, nice view. This is certainly a great spot for a spot of thinking."

She looked sidelong at his face before turning back to share the view, lifting her cigarette again for one last drag before leaning down to crush the remains beneath one foot and then carefully picking it up and placing it back in her packet.

He glanced down to watch her action. "That's pretty good of you," he said.

Angelica shrugged. "I'll dump it on my way home. Why spoil one of my favourite spots?"

"Still..." said Walter, turning back to look at the waves.

Despite his greying hair, Walter still looked quite youthful, his face relatively smooth and unlined. He had quite a sharp nose, she saw, and here in profile, the conservative haircut, the large brown glasses he sort of reminded her of someone, though she couldn't quite put her finger on whom.

"Sometimes," she said, dismissing the thought, "in summer, I come up here at night. There's nothing quite like it, alone in the darkness in the warm air. You can smell the pines and the jasmine if the wind's in the right direction, and the water's all black, smashing against the rock down there.

Sometimes, when there's a moon, it traces a path across the water. A path to nowhere. My man, Johan, used to say it was a stairway to heaven."

"Ah, so you have a partner," said Walter, turning to look at her.

"No," said Angelica, the word barely spoken out loud, looking down and examining the tops of her feet. "Not anymore."

"Oh, I'm sorry."

"Nothing to be sorry about, Walter. It's just the way it is." She looked up at him again, seeing a touch of polite concern in his face. "It's okay, really. Don't worry about it."

She turned back to look at the waves rolling in against the beach. There were a few moments of silence while they were both surrounded by the sound of the waves below and the faint susurrus of the breeze through the grass at the edges of the cliff, blowing in small irregular gusts.

"I hope you'll enjoy your time here," said Angelica, without looking at him. "Woodford Park is special. It has its own special something."

"I think it does," he said, considering.

They sat for a couple of minutes more without saying anything, just listening to the sounds of the ocean and the wind. Finally, Angelica stood.

"Okay, Walter. Nice talking to you again. Oh, by the way, where do you live?"

He pointed back over the road. "Up there, a few houses in on the right hand side. You can just see it from here. The one with the dark brick garage."

"Oh right. That one. The old Simms place. Nice spot. I'm up above the station. You can probably see my place from up there. It's the white house on the hill. Anyway, perhaps we'll have a chance to have coffee together some time, properly. I'm sure we'll run into each other. I think the chances are pretty good."

"Sure," he said and smiled. His smile changed his face, cute, boyish, taking away some of the austere conservatism. She smiled back and turned, walking slowly back the length of the headland towards the road. As she reached the road and turned for home, she was humming lightly to herself, swinging her arms as she walked, the seriousness of her mood having dissipated entirely.

-22-

Walter

Walter's academic career, for the next few months in his second year, hovered and then slowly spiralled earthward, following the downdraft of his involvement with Dave, Greg and Rada. More and more time he spent in the company of the library lawn circle, the members never constant, but Dave, Greg and Rada generally a part of it, either individually or together. Greg and Rada, though he'd first assumed they were inseparable, were far from it, and after spending some time in both of their company, Walter was a little surprised to learn that each of them still attended classes, usually separately. He never learned, or at least could never remember what courses they were taking, but he had some idea that it was on the Sociology side of things, though he had never been given any hard evidence of that. Throughout their continued association, neither of them said very much, and inevitably, it was Dave who did most of the talking when they were together. Day after day followed, blurring one into the other as the hazy feelings of wellbeing (and occasionally paranoia) became the normal ritual. Walter would arrive, usually late in the morning, unless it was a follow-on from the night before, and inevitably head for the library lawn to seek out Dave first, as he was, by far, the easiest to spot. All through this period, Walter never wanted for anything, and the circle was bountiful in its supply, for Dave's grand benevolence extended well beyond Walter alone. Walter wondered, perhaps not without a touch of hidden malice, if Dave's father's wallet was aware of the charitable acts it was performing. Though that particular thought was there, along with several others, Walter had finally come to the conclusion that Dave simply bought people, bought their good will in the same way major countries sometimes negotiate the good will of their lesser neighbours and allies. It was something Walter decided he was not at all comfortable with.

Inevitably, Walter's grades suffered, he was skipping more and more classes, and he dropped out of a couple of the subjects because the writing was on the wall. There was a date by which you could do that with no penalty. Walter, ever-diligent in his preparatory research, had made very sure of that date so that he would be in time with his decision. Of course, it meant that it would take longer to finish his degree, but then, as Dave was fond of saying, it was all about the experience wasn't it? He could spare a thought for his parents, but it was all about the future, Walter's future, not theirs, and it was his choice to make. Much later, he would look back on those self-justificatory thoughts and wonder how he could have ever believed them. His parents got by, they did alright, but the burden of Walter's education was no small thing.

As Dave said, it was all about the experience, and the experiences grew. The painstakingly constructed cannabis cones on the lawn became other things; small blocks of hashish, crumbled in Dave's briar pipe and passed around the circle; the odd blotting paper squares that took him, for a few hours, to other places entirely, and the nature and quality of his mental state expanded and an underlying sense of drifting with it. He went home less and less, discussed none of it with his parents, of course, though once or twice, by the look on his mother's face, he suspected that they might have an inkling of what was happening to their son.

As for Greg and Rada, they lived in a shared house very close to the university grounds, had done for some years, and it gave them convenient access to everything that was

their life, everything that existed nowhere but in the
university itself. Why would they live anywhere else? Walter
had heard about the house, but had never been there,
although Dave claimed to have visited a couple of time for
'sessions.' One late morning, a steady rain drizzling from
above, Walter was standing on the library steps under cover,
watching the lawn get wetter and wetter and considering
whether he should go to the cafeteria or actually attend a
class. Dave was nowhere to be seen; he'd already checked the
cafeteria once, all steamy and filled with damp clothes and
wet hair, but there was no sign of him. He had almost decided
to go to the lecture room, when Rada appeared beside him,
silently, as if she'd simply materialised out of the air.

"Hi, Walter," she said to him, sharing his gaze out over
the lawn.

"Oh, hi," he'd responded. Of Greg there was no sign.

"Shit day, huh?"

Rada was not tall, coming up to about his shoulder, and
he turned to look down into dark eyes that were searching his
face. He nodded and turned back to the lawn.

"So what are you doing?"

"Not much, I guess."

"Why don't you come back with me? I'm more or less
finished for the day. It would be a lot more comfortable than
standing out here. We could have a coffee, a real coffee,
maybe something else."

"Sure," said Walter. She was right; it sounded a lot
more attractive than what he was doing at the moment.

"Okay," she said. She beckoned for him to follow and
headed off across the steps, walking with a languid, fluid step
as if she was merely floating along effortlessly as she went.
The impression was enhanced by the long, flowing Indian
print dresses she normally wore, clothes that naturally went
with her long dark hair and pale complexion. It gave her the

touch of something even more exotic, though Walter really
didn't know what her background was.

He followed as she led him through three or four
winding, tree-lined streets, walking casually through puddles
or under large accumulated drops that fell from the trees
above. By the time they got to the front of Rada's house, they
were wet, despite Walter having kept his bag above his head
to try and shield himself from at least some of the damp. Rada
just didn't seem to care — her hair hung in long damp strands
around her shoulders, and the ankle-length thin dress, dark
maroon with traces of gold thread running through it, stuck to
her body, making her full figured shape abundantly evident.
She turned back to him, giving him more of a view, as if
checking that he was still with her. He just stood there,
slightly stooped, ducking beneath the bag held above his head
and wary of large drops that threatened to spatter into his
face.

"This is it. Come on in," she said, giving a little smile,
then turning, unhurriedly climbing the front steps and onto a
wide wooden porch, slightly collapsed at one end, and pulling
open a faded screen door, and opening wide the front door
before stepping through. The front door had not been locked.
Rada turned again, unhurriedly as always, and beckoned him
forward. Inside, the house was all candles, batik wall
hangings, Indian prints, what was left uncovered of the walls
was a pale mustard yellow. Macramé lampshades or rice
paper balloons hung from the ceiling. Rada led him into the
kitchen where she put some water on to boil. Walter stood
awkwardly in the doorway.

"First some coffee," she said. "Dump your stuff
anywhere. It's okay."

Walter looked around, but not seeing anywhere that
was better than anywhere else particularly, he lowered his bag
to his feet.

"So, how long have you been here?" asked Walter, just as much to cut through the awkwardness he was feeling as he stood at the kitchen door, slowly dripping on the floor.

"Oh, about six years I guess. Greg and I weren't the first. This house had been around for a while, but we sort of inherited it. There's another guy and a girl here now too. Postgrads. Not together. Hey, you're wet. Let me see if I can find you a towel." She made no reference to the fact that she was still wet through as well. "Follow me."

She led him by the arm through the living area into a large high-ceilinged bedroom dominated by a huge wooden double wardrobe, an expansive double bed and more of the ever-present Indian prints.

"This is where Greg and I sleep," she said as she proceeded to open the wardrobe, stoop and rummage around in its bottom and then toss him a towel. "Here, use this." She turned back to the wardrobe, located another of the full-length dresses, this one grey with white stitched patters around the borders of the plunging neckline, and tossed it on the bed, as Walter tried to dry his hair and face ineffectually. His face was covered by the towel for a moment, but when he opened his eyes, Rada was pulling the wet dress up over her head revealing pale skin and nothing underneath. Walter froze. Her shape, which had before been clear enough to him outside in the rain, was unavoidably there before him, her round, full breasts, the slight curve of her pale belly, the dark curls of her pubic hair seen from the side. He tried to look away, but couldn't move at all. Rada tossed the wet garment over into the corner and leaned over to snag the new piece from the bed. Walter was still frozen in mid action, his hands up around his head, holding the damp towel. Unconcernedly, Rada turned to face him as she pulled the grey dress over her head. She stepped towards him.

"You're still wet," she said, relieving him of the towel and dropping it to the floor. A faint hint of amusement passed across her face. "Coffee first, and then we can see what we can do about that."

He followed her numbly as she moved back out to the kitchen, resting a hand on the flat of his stomach as she slipped past. He stood once more in the kitchen doorway, watching and just mumbling his responses to whether he wanted milk or sugar. Once the coffee was made, she offered him the mug in both hands and then turned, picked up her own and led him back into the bedroom. Putting her own mug down, she came back over to Walter, and gently prised his mug from his fingers to place it down beside her own.

"So," she said. "Still wet."

Walter somehow knew what was coming, but was struggling to believe that it was happening. He stood mute as she slowly started unbuttoning his shirt, pulled his arms free, dropped it on the floor and took a step back to look at him. She moved in close again, ran a finger down his thin, pale chest, and then reached for his belt. Walter felt powerless. His mind was tumbling with thoughts of whether this was really happening, what would happen if Greg should come back now, why him, and the erection in his pants. He didn't have to worry about that, Rada slid his jeans around his ankles, stooping with the action and took it slowly into her mouth. Walter looked heavenwards and closed his eyes.

"Mmm, good boy," said Rada, releasing his penis, standing and leaning past him to push the door shut. She turned, pulled her dress over her head again, tossed it in the corner, then led him to the bed with a firm grip on his achingly hard erection.

"I've been wanting to do this for a while," she said softly, stroking his chest with her fingers and letting them trace down his belly and further. It probably explained some of the looks she had been giving him over the last few weeks and months, but his mind was a long way away from analysis at the moment.

"But what about — ?"

"Shhh," she said, putting a finger to his lips and pushing him back down to the bed.

Walter had had a few experiences up to this point, awkward and hurried during school and once after when he'd returned home for the weekend with an old girlfriend, but it was all very traditional. What he experienced with Rada that afternoon was like nothing he had ever had happen. When, finally, he came for his third time, he collapsed back onto the bed, panting, his face wet, staring up at the ceiling and unable to say more than "God."

Rada lay beside him, running a finger through the sweat damp on his chest. "Well, we didn't exactly manage to get you dry," she said. "Never mind."

She rolled over and pulled out a drawer in the bedside table, and leaned over rummaging inside for a couple of seconds, allowing Walter the opportunity to turn his head and admire the curve of her hip, the roundness of her buttocks the small twin dimples at the base of her back and her pale white skin. She turned back with papers and small plastic bag and proceeded to roll them something to smoke. Walter's coffee was long cold and long forgotten. After the smoke, after the expenditure of all the energy, Walter pretty soon collapsed into a heavy, exhausted, but immensely contented sleep.

He was awoken later by voices, bringing him foggily to consciousness. Rada sat up beside him in the bed, her arms around her knees, no effort to cover herself. She was talking to Greg, who stood calmly leaning in the doorway.

Greg! Shit! Walter grabbed for the pillow and clutched it in front of his chest.

"Oh, hey man," said Greg, calmly. "I see you're awake. Sorry if I disturbed you. Okay, guess I'll leave you two to it." And then he was gone.

"But..." said Walter.

"Shit, Walter," said Rada with a slight laugh. "Do you think I would bring you home and fuck your brains out and in our bed if Greg wasn't okay with it? Silly boy."

After a little while longer, Walter awkwardly dressed and awkwardly left the dilapidated old house, sheepishly saying goodbye to Greg on the way out. He now had somewhat of a dilemma which he considered on his unhurried way back up the library steps--the rain had stopped by now. Walter was undeniably, irrefutably in love, he was sure. He just didn't know if they could cope with the circumstance.

As it was, Walter needn't have worried about his dilemma, although it had a similar aspect of choice to other events and even moral question Walter would find himself engaged in over the weeks to come. They would become a minor theme of his life during that period of the first couple of years of his studies; choices, paths, roads that he might have taken were it not for his upbringing and his presently dormant innate sense of morality and conservatism. The next time he saw Rada, a couple of days later, she merely acknowledged him with a friendly hi. Greg too just nodded amicably as if nothing at all had happened. Walter was crushed. He entertained thoughts of broaching the matter with Rada, drawing her aside and whispering to her in impassioned tones about his needs, his desires, the way he felt about her, but it was very clear to him that that was not going to happen. Inwardly, he sighed and kept it politely to himself. The gazes from Rada that had been a feature of their proximity previously, were gone, never to return. Walter decided that he had no choice but to turn his attentions elsewhere even though, sometimes, those attentions might still feature visions of an idealised Rada, remembered alone in his room late at night.

Towards the end of that second year, something happened that was to act as a watershed, something that would change the circling path of his life completely, although in reality, it was two. Another of the more recent circle members, a young blond guy called Albert who always went by his full name, Albert, never Al, started to spend more time in Walter's company. He was a gentle boy, always seemingly only half engaged with the world. Walter knew, as much by observation as by hearsay that Albert was far more heavily into the drugs than Walter had ever considered. As their association grew, Albert regaled him with tales of various chemical cocktails and their effects, about experiments with various forms of plant life that he'd read about in books. He made references to Blake and to Bosch, and about medieval witchcraft traditions, to Castaneda and so much more. He spoke of Huxley and of Leary. Really, Albert appeared to be on an urgent quest to remove himself from reality altogether, to break through those famed doors of perception that Huxley had written about. He carried an old silver, Zippo lighter that Walter was fascinated with, especially after the day that Albert proceeded to take it apart and dig inside to gradually draw out a line of small red tabs sealed inside a plastic strip of tape. He watched as Albert worked a single one free, careful not to drop it, and placed it under his tongue and then offered the strip to Walter too. Walter waved it away.

"Man, you really should try one of these. They're incredible," he said. "Twenty minutes and they're on. And I mean *on*."

When Walter shook his head, Albert merely shrugged, pushed the strip back in place and then reassembled the lighter, pocketing it and turning to gaze dreamily out over the lawn.

A couple of days later, he was there again but this time, what he had to say gave Walter a premonitory chill. "Oh, man. I just had a scare. I was in the library rest rooms you know. Wasn't ready for how good this stuff was. I just nodded off, then and there in the cubicle, the thing still in my arm. Must have been there for a couple of hours at least. Shit. Covered in stuff you know. I managed to get most of it off. But man..."

Albert shook his head ruefully and then turned his characteristic gaze back to the lawn.

That was the last time Albert was to speak to Walter. Two weeks later he was dead. His passing left barely a ripple upon the circle's members.

The other thing that happened, the other defining moment, was that Dave Whiteman dropped out, never to be seen again. Walter was suddenly cast adrift without any tangible chart to shore.

-23-

Resting Place

True to his word after his chance encounter with Angelica out at the end of Ball's Point , Walter decided that he really did want to check out the cemetery she'd spoken about. It was such a strange idea to him that people would be buried out on a headland, overlooking the ocean in the middle of nowhere. At the same time, it had a peculiar, poetic appeal. Did the graves face out to the ocean? Did anyone still use the place? Imagine consecrating ground out on a forbidding bluff, he could hardly imagine it.

As he wandered along the coast road, mission in mind, he walked right past the access road to The Bellevue, thinking about his conversation with Angelica. He had not, of course, made the connection between her and the woman in the town market that day, because, then she had seemed so different and really, that incident had barely touched him; it simply hadn't registered. He was still wondering what she did, how she survived. She'd been very vague about all that. In some ways, she reminded him a little bit of people he'd known at university, and now slightly out of her time, the age in which she truly belonged. The world had moved on since the days of essential oils and hippie clothes, although, judging from some of the stuff that he'd seen at the Woodford Park market, there was still a demand for it. Perhaps it never really went away. Things just moved in cycles. Perhaps, also, people carried their own past with them, like a set of clothes. Whatever she did, he suspected that below the surface, that light easy demeanour that he'd encountered at the patisserie that morning after his haircut, there were other things, just below the surface, that troubled her. She'd been pretty quick to cut off the conversation about her partner, abundantly clear that she didn't like to be reminded about death. The two facts made an uncomfortable equation in his mind. Anyway, that was none of his business and he wasn't likely to explore it any further unless it came up again. If she'd wanted to tell him, she would have.

As he reached the peak of the small hill over which the coast road curved, he was afforded a better view of the headland in question. It was long, low, sloping down towards the end and now, from here, he could see white shapes scattered across its grassy top. A small white wooden fence separated it from the road, before the road itself looped down and then made the winding ascent to the top of the cliffs above, appearing as a narrow blank grey patch as it wound in and out of the trees. Further up, he could see the dark mouth of the railway tunnel that climbed up and through the rock to the flat plain that extended back from the sea and led, further northward, to the city. From here, there were no houses, just overgrown grassy rises and falls leading up to where the tree line started. An old derelict shed sat on top of a small hill, wooden with a couple lichen covered slats having fallen sideways, angled across the front and allowing light through the structure. Apart from that there was nothing. Walter stood where he was at the top of the rise, scratching the back of his head. Why the hell would you put a cemetery out here? It was so...inaccessible. Jokes about the dead heart of such and such a town flitted through his head. This was simply the dead heart of nowhere stuck out in a forbidding shadowland.

Slowly he walked along the next section, keeping close to the single, fat metal barrier that separated the road from the edge. Along this patch of coast road, there was no beach, just a slope down to a tumble of rocks and marks where the land had, over time, started to fall away. It was a decent drop. He suspected they'd have to do something eventually to counter the erosion eating away at the earth and stone there, or the road would eventually crumble away entirely. As he got closer to the cemetery, details became more apparent — double metal gates, wrought iron, white paint flaking allowed access to the graveyard itself, a small white sign sitting above them. He guessed they were wide enough and high enough to take a vehicle. Across the road on the other side, there was a broader, earth and gravel covered verge, though it could hardly be called a parking space. Perhaps people just pulled off by the roadside, or maybe they parked back in the town and walked. He reached the gates and stood in front of them, looking up at the sign. *Woodford Park Cemetery*: that was it. The last word centred below the town name. The graves didn't start straight away. An open expanse of lawn separated the first line from the entrance. The grass was long, but it was not unmaintained. It was hardly the overgrown weed patch he had suspected. Who maintained the place? Perhaps it was someone attached to the local church. Well, at least one question that had first popped into his head had been answered. The graves all faced out to sea. If he was going to see who was buried here, he'd have to walk down amongst the graves themselves and turn to look at the headstones with his back to the ocean. He reached for the gate, lifted the latch and pushed it open, wincing as the hinges protested with a screech of metal on metal. Careful to swing it shut behind him, he entered.

There was another thing unusual about the cemetery; the graves were not in even rows, but almost looked as if they had planted haphazardly, randomly. One was further in than the one next to it. There was a larger gap between those two. Walter stood scanning them, taking it all in and then walked slowly down between the almost rows, before finally turning to look at one of the headstones. It was an old, old date and an old, old name. Interesting. The next couple of markers he read showed a similar pattern. Further in, towards the water side, he came across another grave with a faded bunch of flowers placed carefully against the headstone, held in place by a rock, the colours gone, the leaves brown. A few petals had fallen to scatter beside on the ground, but mostly, they were intact. Clearly, people still visited, made the pilgrimage to the graveside to spend some time with their departed loved ones. He stood looking down at the faded flowers, a little surprised that they were there and then squatted to read the date on the headstone. It was much more recent. Someone maintained the place, and someone clearly visited. He stood back up and scanned the remaining graves. All of the stones and borders were white, no black marble or brown granite. This was an old style cemetery, traditional. There were the words, the standard, expected words all around him: in loving memory, loving father, loving husband, loving everything. Why was it always loving? Ah, there was a 'devoted' over there. He wondered if he'd ever be depicted as 'loving' or 'devoted' not that he'd ever know. Words meant to give solace to those left behind rather than to the departed...

He turned and wandered down to the edge of the bluff, glancing at headstones here and there along the way, stopping when he reached the final row, and standing thoughtfully looking out into the ocean. So, here were the ones with the prime seats, the balcony box, the table by the window. Yes, there was some attraction to spending your final repose looking out over clear blue water. He crouched down again, resting on his haunches as he looked out to sea, the irregular lines of departed behind him. He plucked a few blades of grass with one hand, letting them fall, one by one and watching as they scattered slightly in the breeze. It was still strange to him, but he could see the attraction. He doubted though, whether it would have looked so appealing on a stormy winter day. As he stared out to sea, he could almost feel the weight of the dead behind him, as if they were…waiting? It was almost as if he was being observed himself, that sensation when you feel as if someone was watching you, that tautness between the shoulder blades. He turned slowly, looking over on shoulder back up the hill, his breath catching. Had that been a figure further up the rise? He swallowed and stood, turning completely to scan the graveyard and further up the hill, but if there had been someone there, they weren't there any longer. He was sure he'd seen someone. It was just his imagination. Cemeteries did strange things to your perceptions.

He'd seen what he had come to see and despite his brief flight of fancy, there really was nothing more to see. He wiped his palms one against the other a couple of times, and barely glancing at the graves any more, made his way to the gate, opened it and stepped back out onto the coast road, pulling the gate shut with a metallic clank as the latch fell into place. Just another of the peculiarities of Woodford Park, he thought. It simply added to the character. The place was special, the town that was. He was sure of it.

-24-

Woodford Park

Small towns *are* special in their own peculiar way, especially when isolated from others of their kind by geography or distance. In that, just like people, they develop personalities that react to the movements or events related to and initiated by their residents. Woodford Park was no different, with its community of artists, its crafty nature, its particular light and occasional visitors, Angelica and the town shared their similarities. With Walter, thriving on creative order, but at the same time withdrawn, one could draw similar parallels. Do owners and their pets look like each other? Do towns and their residents share dreams at night? Stranger things have happened.

Cities are different. They are made of clusters of microcosms, neighbourhoods, districts, precincts, whatever names you want to give them...ghettos even. Although a city functions as a large, multi-faceted entity, its microcosms remain, to an extent, self-contained. In many larger cities in the world, there are geographical boundaries that help define that difference as well, north or south of the river, east or west of the bay, and so on, but still we supply labels to particular areas—Little Italy, Chinatown, the East End, the South Side to give those characters meaning and context. It is far harder for a small town to separate the parts of itself, and so they tend to interact more generally. Unless you make a conscious effort to withdraw, stay locked inside, you will run into people, discuss the weather, interact, listen to your neighbours, pay attention to what the kids up the street are doing, know the business of people two streets over, catch the train or bus with the same person every morning and nod politely by way of greeting, and while all this is happening, you will share a bond. It is a bond forged of common knowledge and experience, of being and living (perhaps coincidentally, perhaps as a mere outcome of circumstance) within the boundaries of the same small place. That bond becomes a connecting bridge shaped by existing within those boundaries and functioning as parts of the same microcosm.

Human beings are tribal. Living in a place like Woodford Park, you become a part of a tribe, one that has its own characteristics; knowledge, history and folklore...even rituals. Each small town has its own. They may be similar, one to the other, but there will always be some peculiar difference that marks a place apart. The cemetery, the old hotel, the artist community, the stone memorial bench out in the headland as a place to be alone and sit in contemplation...take your pick. Woodford Park had a goodly share. Was it that which led members of its tribe to say there was something special about the place?

For some, that specialness was something different, because they belonged more comfortably to somewhere else, somewhere a little less tangible.

-25-

Angelica

After a couple of years of apparent contentment, for some reason that would always remain unknown to her, Angelica's grandfather decided that he would give up his house by the seaside and move back up the familiar environs of Sandton. He had never sold the old home back there, and it was a simple matter for him to pack everything up, including her grandmother and return to the old home town. Perhaps it was simply that very familiarity that comes with time; her grandfather had spent years building relationships within the Sandton community; people greeted him in the street, stopped for conversations, showed him the proper respect. Even though he had the beach and his family close by, even though he was supposed to be enjoying his retirement, clearly there was something missing that her grandmother's company and the ritual morning swims were not enough to provide. That left Angelica and her family alone in the small seaside community, her mother, her father, the beach, the local school, the school bus, the neighbours up the street, the old lady who used to sit on her front porch with her caged birds, all of it, just minus her grandparents and the ritual morning swims. Actually, that was fine with Angelica, and she settled in quite well to the new routine. Every couple of months, they would make the drive up to Sandton to have Sunday lunch with her grandparents. In the meantime, her grandparents had stopped coming to the beach at all. How does one assess the comparative value of rituals?

As a young girl, she had fit comfortably into the local community and the normalcy of their life had suited her. She mixed well at school, and the only time she really got into trouble was when she was found to be skipping classes to spend time with the old lady with the birds. Of course, the old woman must have known, must have realised that this child was meant to be somewhere else, but she was so glad of the company that she told no one and discretely refused to discuss it with Angelica herself. Her mother expected the worst, unable to guess what might be making her daughter skip school. She soon put a stop to those visits, even though Angelica was completely open about what she had been doing. Somewhere there was an unspoken, imagined threat there. Her father, as she remembered, was far more relaxed about the whole affair.

"It's not doing her any harm," he'd said. "Good social skills. The girl just likes talking to people. What's a bit of missed school?"

In some strange way it was an echo of her grandfather's opinion about education and females, but in a totally different way.

School progressed and evolved into high school as it does. Her life was stable, normal, and like many of the other children she attended classes with, like most of the local families. Her mother encouraged her to go to Church and to Sunday School, though she had no interest in it herself. It was important that a child received a proper religious education. Angelica, said her mother, could make up her own mind when she was old enough, but she couldn't make up her mind if she didn't know what she was deciding about. Throughout the period, her father remained as a shadow for her, there, but not there, leaving early in the morning to travel to his job in the city, and returning late at night on the train. She did remember, vaguely, that he had a small boat, and would venture out on it on the weekends, meaning he spent less time with them, although there were still the weekend excursions to the local beach when the weather was good. They would wander down as a family, picnic lunches of white bread sandwiches made that morning in the kitchen at home and drinks packed into a cooler and swung between Angelica and her father as they wandered down the hill. The grinding crunch of beach sand between her back teeth would stay with her for many years to come and she could still see her father's browned body slicing through the foam as he caught another wave into the beach.

It was not until a couple of years later that the late night arguments started in their long low family home. Angelica would hear both of their voices, the words muffled, the shouts, the bang of a door or something thrown. She would huddle under her covers and wait until the storm had passed, which eventually it would, but the raised voices, the noises from the living room or the bedroom increased in frequency. More than once, she stumbled in to find her mother at the kitchen table weeping, her face in her hands and her father nowhere to be seen. As she grew older, she became more aware of these periods, of the growing strain and tension in the house, teasing at the normality of their lives.

And then, one day, Angelica's father just wasn't there anymore.

Her mother said nothing for nearly a full week, and then, only when Angelica asked did she say anything.

"Where's Dad," she had asked.

"He's had to go away for a while, for work."

"Why didn't he say goodbye?"

"He had to leave too early, sweetheart. He didn't want to wake you."

"When's he going to be back?"

"I don't know, Angelica."

"Why don't you know?"

"That's enough!" and her mother had stormed from the room.

There were no further conversations about when her father was coming back, and as the months wore on, it became apparent to Angelica that he would not be. It was not till much later that she discovered the circumstances of his leaving—could it have been that her mother and grandparents were trying to shield her? She never found out the true details, but somehow, her father had managed to get into heavy debt, had no way of covering it, and finally, had simply skipped out, leaving Angelica and her mother to face the consequences. In the end, it had been her grandfather who had stepped in to cover what her father owed and pull his daughter out of harm's way. Angelica saw none of this, not until her mother moved to the city, took her job and sent Angelica back to live with her grandparents. The house that they had been living in reverted to her grandfather. After all, he had provided the funding and the house had been his to start with. He rented it for a while, and then sold it again when the time was right, just like the succession of other cottages he had owned, recovering a healthy chunk of the losses he had taken making good on his son-in-law's debts.

When Angelica did return from her grand adventure, she had no thought of the tiny seaside town she had spent most of her life growing up in. She made a beeline for the big city, the bright lights, rented a small apartment while she assessed her options and took up just about where she left off during her island-hopping indulgence. There were the bars and clubs, the succession of transitory bed mates and a gradual drifting into the periphery of the arts and culture scene of the city, though only the very edges. She was never truly, comfortably a part of the full-blown scene. Through contacts, parties, she managed to land herself a job at a gallery, but it was somehow unfulfilling. She went to the job — the gallery's opening hours were civilised — and filled her nights as she had filled nights before, in a blurred skein of lights, colours, glasses and faces. Angelica was on a slow spiral and its direction was certainly not heavenward. What was she going to do long term? She didn't care. Her resources were not unlimited, but they were enough to keep her going for some time.

For a while, she took up with the gallery owner, and that lasted for about six months, but it ended badly, and she left the gallery with the tatters of her relationship and the owner with his growing cocaine habit. At the time, coke was the drug of choice, and frankly, Angelica didn't like it. It didn't last. But then, nothing much lasted for very long in Angelica's life and when she'd had enough, she simply moved on. Perhaps the ephemeral cocaine rush was simple another reminder of the collage of her current life. Along the way, she might pick up a photograph, a letter, some keepsake or reminder of a brief period of happiness she had stumbled upon along that journey, more by accident than design. These were what she took with her every time she moved on.

There was nothing that prompted it, no event, no person that provoked the question, but one Sunday evening, alone in her bedroom, she had sat there, looking through the traces of what she'd done over the last few years, and she simply asked herself: "Angelica, what the fuck are you doing?"

And the answer was, she really didn't know. It seemed she had found her own special Road to Damascus.

-26-

Walter

Albert's death, the events that led to the end of that second year, but most importantly, the disappearance of Dave Whiteman, allowed Walter a period of reassessment. His discomfort level with what he was doing and what he had observed with members of the circle had already started him questioning, but with Dave out of the picture, it gave him breathing space. There was no more the continual stream of words urging him to this or that, no ready beacon to indicate his next stop on the map of his education and his path through university life. His experience with Greg and Rada meant that he no longer felt comfortable wandering over to the circle when they were the only major recognisable figures there. He still, even after all this time, felt awkward in their company. Ultimately, Dave's presence had, in essence, made it too easy for him. With Dave gone, so was the buffer of his big personality that subsumed all around it, and Walter was forced to make choices for himself.

At the start of what was supposed to be his final year at university, that in the end, turned out to be his penultimate, Walter laid the map of his academic career out in front of himself and found it wanting. He plotted out the courses and what he needed to manage, those subjects he'd withdrawn from, those that he'd never actually started, and realised that there was no way to manage all of it within the space of a single year.

For the first couple of weeks of that third year, he looked at the prospect bleakly, wondering, for a time, if there was any point at all, but then, if he considered the options, there was, actually, little else he wanted to do. He'd worked hard to get into Architecture; he'd applied himself, why did it need to be any different now? To do anything else would amount to throwing away all that invested time and energy, and, he thought, at the same time, a large proportion of his life.

On one such day, running those thoughts through his mind, he was a little shocked to realise that he was suddenly starting to sound very much like his parents. He withdrew from the lawn circle entirely, spent hours in the library proper, applying himself to his studies and broadening his research to cover other subjects that touched the edges of his interest and also helped to supplement some of the things he'd lost or missed along the way. Greg and Rada, Dave, all of them, began becoming mere memories, milestones along the way, marking the places where he had taken a wrong turn and been forced to retrace his steps. Little by little, Walter lost the lawn circle tan he'd acquired from sitting for hours lying back in the sun, and started to revert to the pale, bookish-looking young man that he had once been. At the same time, he started once more to achieve the sort of grades he had once been used to back when he was at school.

The routine of his study and his rediscovered diligence continued for the rest of that year, and for the next, broken only by visits home and in the middle part of that second year, by Pamela. Had fate taken a different turn, Walter might not have given her a second look.

She was the sort of young woman that merged easily into the bulk of the student population, and Walter had long since blanked them from his awareness. During his time with the library lawn circle, the mainstream student population became a faceless parade, something there in awareness, but only barely, a mere cipher. Mostly, they were irrelevant, and that attitude, one further encouraged by the circle, remained with him, even after his reversion. That was another thing that kept him focussed, less distracted. His social life remained limited, not necessarily by design, but as an outcome of his choices. The only people he knew, or associated with were fellow classmates, and they, as a whole, were also students who concentrated on their studies rather than the vast and changing circus that existed outside the lecture rooms and the library stacks and desks. By now, the numbers of those classmates were fewer, university already having worked its gradual process of attrition upon the student population as a whole. Just as not everyone made it into university, built into the numbers of freshman admissions was the subtle understanding that only a proportion of those would ever make it through to graduation. In effect, the entire system was built, unspoken, around the mechanisms that encouraged failure, rather than success or, at least, did not discourage it. Walter had almost, almost, fulfilled the system's inbuilt expectations of him.

Walter still visited the cafeteria, sitting alone with piles of books and notes open in front of him, always alone, sipping at his coffee and only peripherally aware of the noise and conversations that ebbed and flowed around him. It was a safe location; no traps for him there anymore, and it broke the monotony of the blank wall and lines of shelves that marked his personal corral on the library's third floor. It was on such a day pelting with rain outside, the cafeteria full to capacity and steamy that he was interrupted in his little private bubble. It came as a bit of a surprise, as he'd cultivated his can't-you-see-I'm-busy aura rather carefully.

"Um, excuse me. Is this place taken?"

He glanced up to look at the speaker, slim, jeans, plain pale pink top, stack of books clutched in front of her chest, short-cut brown hair, slightly retroussé nose, thin eyebrows and dark eyes, and then struggled for a moment to register what she had asked him.

"Um, no, fine," he said, waved his hand in the direction of the empty seat and returned his attention to his books.

She placed her stack down in the table in front of her, repositioned the chair and sat, sipping at a drink and scanning the other people in the room.

"Don't mind me," she said. "I'm just waiting for some friends."

"Mm-hmm," said Walter non-committally again glancing up, but only for a second. For some unexplained reason, his aura didn't seem to be working that afternoon. He didn't really think about it then, but later, he would wonder if some particular force had been at work to ambush him that day.

"Wow, that's a lot of stuff. Have you got an exam or something? You look like you're studying."

Walter suppressed a sigh and looked across the table. She had placed her drink down and was looking at him, her hands crossed neatly in her lap, her posture straight.

"No, no exam," he said. "Just working."

She nodded. "What are you doing? I'm Pamela by the way."

"Architecture. Walter." He said the two words, holding her gaze.

"Wow," she said giving a perky couple of nods. "I'm doing Social Work. I guess that's pretty different. I was thinking of doing Psychology at first, but then I decided that Social Work would let me help more people in the long run. I'm Pamela. Oh, I already said that, didn't I?"

He leaned back in his chair, reconciled to the fact that there was going to be no escape for the moment.

Just then, she lifted her arm and gave an animated wave across the room. "Oh, there are my friends." She scraped her books together and stood, once more holding them in front of her chest with both arms. "Well, thanks for letting me share your table. Nice to meet you. I guess I'll see you later." And she was gone, just like that.

Walter stared numbly at the spot where she'd been sitting, at the now empty drink container, a yellow straw poking out of its top, then shook his head and returned to his books, but it was a while before his concentration came back.

Naively, Walter thought that might be the end of it, but he was soon disabused of that particular notion. Early in the following week, he was sitting at his appointed desk in the library, working on a paper, when, once again, he was interrupted by a loud whisper.

"Hi! It's Walter isn't it?"

He looked up, dragging his attention from the paper in front of him. There she was again, stack of books and papers held with both arms across her chest. His heart sank as he nodded his response. At least they were in the library.

"Wow. Funny. I'm Pamela, remember?"

Again he nodded. She leaned in over his desk.

"Is this where you sit? Isn't that funny? I had a problem with where they put me. They gave me a new desk assignment. I'm going to be sitting right over there. That's my new desk."

He looked where she was pointing. It was against the wall that ran perpendicularly from his current position, three desks in, and if he lifted his gaze above the small, lockable wire bookshelf at the top of his own desk, it was directly in his line of sight.

"Wow," she said again in a stage whisper and looked quickly around as "Shhh," came from a desk further down the line.

She nodded her compliance to the invisible speaker and then leaned in closer, freeing one hand to place it gently on his shoulder. "Sorry," she whispered. "I'll talk to you later."

As she leaned in close, Walter caught her scent, clean, like soap, not perfume. Her breath was clean and sweet as well. She stood up again, gave him a little wave and headed for her desk. He couldn't help watching her as she walked over to her place, the slight sway of her hips, the slim waist, the tiny bounce to her step, probably from the plain white running shoes she wore. No, he thought, ridiculous. What the hell are you thinking? He watched as she arrayed her books and notebooks in neat piles, straightened the edges and then sat back to survey her handiwork before giving a little satisfied nod. She pulled a book from the top of the pile, placed it carefully in front of her, and then opened it. Before turning to the book, she gave a little glance around the room and caught Walter looking. She gave him a wave, moving her fingers rather than her hand, smiled and then turned back to the book in front of her. She was kind of cute in a perky sort of way. Walter shuddered to himself. Jesus, get a grip. He shrugged, shook his head and returned his attention to his paper, or tried to, though it was longer than he would have expected before he managed to get back into the flow.

It was all fairly innocent, and Walter didn't think much of it while it was happening. Pamela turned up often, and she was direct, maybe a bit too enthusiastic, and really, it wasn't a trial to look at her. Walter didn't think anything of it either, the first time she asked whether he'd like to accompany her to a movie, not that it had been anything he was expecting, either. He was surprised when she appeared dressed not in the usual jeans, simple top and the perpetual running shoes. She was in a very lovely, simple but lovely floral dress, with a white cardigan. She almost looked like something out of the '50s. Sitting next to her at the movie, he was more conscious of the subtle perfume she wore, rather than the film. Looking back, he'd be hard pressed to remember what the film was at all, though he remembered sitting there in the darkness watching her clean, fresh profile in the flickering light.

He learned quite a bit about Pamela over the next few weeks; how she was a farm girl, had three brothers, older than she was and that her parents still worked the farm. A few years separated her and her nearest sibling. She rode horses and liked dancing and going to the movies. All of this tumbled forth with Walter not having to volunteer very much himself. Pamela was a talker, that was for sure. He didn't think anything of it when she reached for his hand in the darkness during their third excursion to the cinema, nor of the goodnight kiss she leaned up to give him on their second dinner. He found himself watching her at her place in the library more and more, and the little wave evolved into a hastily blown kiss when she caught him watching. Pamela became his single and only main distraction during that final year of study, not because of anything Walter consciously planned. It just seemed to develop of its own accord and Walter rapidly became more of a passive spectator in the unfolding sequence rather than a conscious instigator.

Over time, they started to become more intimate. Pamela encouraged it and with it, she became more demonstrative in public too, reaching easily for his hand as they walked to the cafeteria, or leaning over to plant a kiss as she walked to her library table. The first time he invited her back to his room — she lived in shared dormitory accommodation — she came with him willingly, eager to see where he spent the rest of his time and chattering all the way. They only went so far though. Pamela brought proceedings to a halt very quickly.

"No, Walter, stop."

"But..."

"No, please. We're not ready for that."

She had left him aching and frustrated, but wanting for more. She left that night planting a kiss on his cheek rather than on the lips and patted him gently on the chest as if he were a good boy. Unfortunately, that didn't earn him a treat. The next morning, she'd smiled sweetly at him as if oblivious to how she'd left him and picked up a conversation from the night before.

Extended sessions of fondling in his room became a regular occurrence, and gradually, they become more intense. She would allow him to touch her breasts, fondle his erection; she would rub herself up against him, run her tongue across his stomach until he twisted with want. A few times, her ministrations were enough to bring him to orgasm and on those times, she would give a surprised little 'Oh' and then calmly reach for tissues to clean him up, concentrating with clinical efficiency. Despite all that, every time he reached down and tried to slip off her simple white cotton briefs, or move his hand inside them, she would take a hold and firmly move his hand away.

"No, Walter. No."

In bits and pieces, Walter finally managed to work out the Pamela did not believe in sex before marriage. The boundary of what defined sex seemed somewhat arbitrary to him, but he knew better than to push his protests too far. Pamela was a good girl. What was he thinking? He knew very well what he was thinking, and so, he thought did Pamela. Her denial of him merely served to heighten his desire, but there was no getting past it.

At the end of the year, Walter finished everything he needed to graduate. He moved away and back in with his parents, putting out applications for various reputable architectural firms. He was one of the top performers of the class, and he hoped, as a result to land a nice junior position at one of the major city-based firms. He could explain away the extra year it had taken him to complete, but really, it needed no explanation; his results spoke for themselves. In the meantime, he kept seeing Pamela, though now Walter was back with his parents, the opportunities for more advanced intimacy grew less. At the graduation ceremony a few months later, Pamela and his parents met for the first time. He had spoken about her to them, of course, and they were brimming with expectation. It was a big day, watching their son graduate and meeting the girlfriend at the same time. They told him later that they thought she was a lovely girl, so bright and polite, clearly well brought up. Yes, they approved. She seemed like a caring sort of young woman. And Social Work. Social workers were good people weren't they? They did a lot of good in the community and god knows you needed it in this day and age.

Walter had slipped into a routine of normality that was a far cry from the place he had been a couple of years previously. It was not too long before his parents asked Walter to invite Pamela over for lunch, and then she was in his home. The action granted her access, tumbling one of the final barriers of separation between their lives, though he was still a little afraid of where that might lead, to the inevitable visit to her parents' farm, the meeting of the brothers, the family, but it too, in time would come, and it was much as he imagined it would be. In the end, Walter was to get his treat for being a very good boy.

-27-

Woodford Park

What Angelica experienced in those couple of years prior to her move to Woodford Park was a sense of dissipation, of formlessness both about her life and everything that surrounded her. Relationships were transitory, people were transitory, where she was and who she saw shifted like the tides, and like the sand beneath the waves, there was no solid foundation upon which to base her sense of self. She tried, in a last ditch attempt to fix that, with another grand tour. This time, it was more traditional, Rome, Venice, Paris, Berlin, all the great and noble places echoing with culture and with history. All that really showed her was that her history was nothing more than a made up thing, fragments that drifted past in her memory like the shredded images of her father and the string of blurry faces that came and went with the days. She returned home, feeling, rather than healed, more in need of something to which she could anchor herself and her life. She spent a few weeks mulling over her choices. Money was still not an issue, thankfully. She had received a steady, though small income from the various jobs she'd engaged in; though not a grand amount, it had allowed her to live, and with the income from the estate, she hadn't really had to chip into the bulk of the savings anyway, only for extravagances like the big trip from which she'd just returned. So, putting aside the thought of cost and how she might live, she held her life up in front of herself and tested the episodes, the periods that made up the whole jigsaw. The only one that gave her a real sense of comfort was when she had lived with both her parents in that small seaside town — Woodford Park. She'd been content there, for a while, before the arguments had started, before her father had left late in the night, and there somehow, someway, she might be able to regain that feeling, give her a solid base from which to work out what she was doing. She began doing some online searches for property, rental accommodation, and it was thus that she first made contact with Bill Gundersen and his wife Doris.

When Angelica first spoke to someone, it was to Doris. Bill had been out and about somewhere. She'd assured Angelica that there were appropriate properties to look at, a few available at the moment as it was off season. She would have a word to her husband and confirm with him, but she was sure that they'd be able to help her out. Angelica wasted no time catching a train down to Woodford Park, and so it started — the next chapter of her existence.

As she re-entered the town for the first time, as the train swept out of the tunnel and the small community unfolded, spread out below her, she was full of conflicting emotions. At the same time, there were other things too; there was memory, the remembrance of times brimming with contentment and happiness. She walked down from the station, along Moore Street to the end, recognising things here and there, the bus terminus, the old wooden community hall where various meetings were held with its bare flagpole out the front, somewhat in need of paint, the old house across the street at the end that functioned as a boarding house in summer — so little had changed. She turned onto the coast road (she remembered it had a name, but just that everyone simply called it the coast road) past the shops, past the school, surprising herself that she'd forgotten it almost entirely, and up the hill again to the street where the Gundersen's home cum office was situated. She looked out at the headland, Ball's

Point, and the beach below and a feeling of rightness started flowering inside her.

She was met at the door by a deeply tanned, ebullient man, shorter than she was with a pronounced belly wearing pale slacks and a white striped polo shirt. A thick gold watch sat upon the wrist attached to the hand that reached out to shake hers. At the back of the house, she could hear the yapping of small dogs.

"Miss Cooper, is it? Yes? Come right in. We've been expecting you. Bill Gundersen." He stood aside to let her enter a wide front room that doubled as an office. "My wife's out the back, attending to the dogs, but I believe you two have spoken on the phone. Sit, sit. Please."

Bill Gundersen took up a chair opposite and steepled his hands in front, elbows resting on the desk. "So, Miss Cooper, how can we help you? My wife gave me some idea of what you are after, but you never know do you? We've a lot of potential here in Woodford Park, and sometimes it helps to explore the boundaries, don't you think?"

"Please, call me Angelica," she said. "Well, I'm looking for something to rent for a few months, three or four, while I get a feel for the place. Maybe I might think about buying something if I like it enough, but I want to feel comfortable at first. You know, better safe than sorry, before taking a plunge." She almost didn't believe that the words had issued from her own mouth.

At the mention of a purchase, Bill Gundersen leaned forward, nodded gravely. "Wonderful town, Woodford Park. I can't recommend it highly enough. Just wonderful." He gave a little laugh and spread his hands expansively. Angelica noted his hand, the foreshortened fingers and blinked. "Look at me and the wife; we landed here a few years ago and the place stuck. They say it can draw you back, that there's something special. At least the local artists think so, and they

152

should know, right? There's a real community of them here. They hold exhibitions up in the old hall on Moore Street from time to time and you can often see their works in the regular market day they hold down at the school. Not exactly my cup of tea, but they seem to do alright."

He sat across the desk, smiling at her, urging some sort of a response with a little nodding of his head.

"Yes, I do know a little bit about Woodford Park," said Angelica.

"Oh really? How's that?"

"I spent some time growing up here as a child."

"Ah, I see," said Bill Gundersen. "So, you know what I'm talking about then. Ah, here's Doris," he said, looking past Angelica to a doorway that led further into the house. Angelica was forced to look back over her shoulder. In the doorway stood a plumpish woman, tight mauve slacks that ended halfway up her calves, a purple zip-fronted top and a pile of heavily curled and shaped dyed-mahogany hair that surrounded her head like a deep fiery halo.

"This is Miss Cooper, Doris. You know," said Bill.

"Please...Angelica." She didn't want to complicate the memories with the name thing. When she'd been here, her name had been Sparks, but after her father left, her mother had reverted to using her maiden name, and Angelica had been using it ever since.

"Would you like coffee, tea, something? How long have you got?" asked Bill.

"Hello, dear," said Doris.

Angelica was forced to look from one to the other, turning to face almost opposite directions.

"No, no, thanks, Mr Gundersen. I only really have a couple of hours. Perhaps we can see the properties."

"Yes, yes, of course. Doris, Miss Cooper...um, Angelica here was just telling me that she grew up right here in

Woodford Park. Can you imagine that? Maybe what they say is true, about the place drawing you back."

"Are you sure you don't want anything?" said Doris. "It's no trouble."

"No, I'm fine, really."

"Okay, dear, then I'll leave you two to it." She disappeared into the shadowed interior of the house. Angelica got an impression of mirrors and glass shelves, perhaps porcelain figures behind her as she disappeared.

Bill reached for a folder on his desk, flipped it open and slid it across to Angelica.

"I've put together a few options for you. Being out of season, and because you might want something for longer, we can do you a reasonable deal on the rent. Some of the owners would be happy to have someone renting at this time. Anyway, have a look at what's there, and if you see anything you like, we can pop out and have a look at them." He sat back, watching her as she flipped through the copied sheets and photographs.

"So how long ago were you here?" he asked as she scanned through the offerings, pausing to look closer and read the details of one or two of the apartments and cottages.

Angelica gave a short laugh. "Oh, about twenty-three years ago was the last time," she said without looking up.

"Really, you're kidding me," said Bill.

Angelica glanced up to see a look of mock surprise on his face.

"I would have guessed it to be a lot less," he said, grinning.

"No, not at all," said Angelica, returning to the folder.

"I guess a few things have changed."

"Actually, you know, not that much," she said. "It's pretty much the same as I remember it. Oh, a few things here and there, but not as much as you might expect. It's a bit like going back in time."

"Really," said Bill.

"Yes, funny really... Anyway, I think I'd like to look at these three," she said, jiggling them out of the pile one by one.

"No sooner said than done," said Bill, standing, glancing down at her choices and reaching for a small wooden cupboard up above him to one side and pulling down three sets of keys. "Follow me. Let's go for a little drive."

Bill led her to the door, opened it to let her pass and then called back inside the house. "Doris, we're going to look at a couple of places. Be back in a while."

"Alright, Dear. Take your time." came from inside the house.

Bill drove her to her selected properties in his big old Mercedes that had been parked in the driveway, plush interior, big padded leather seats, talking all the way, Angelica only half paying attention to the flow of words as she tried to pick out familiar landmarks along the way. The first couple of places they saw were properties subdivided into small holiday apartments, but the third, a tiny solitary cottage further up the hill was more to her liking. It was semi-furnished, just the basics, but she thought it would be comfortable enough with a few home touches. She stood at the bedroom window looking out. There was a large tree taking up most of the view, but off to one side, she could just see a sliver of ocean. It would do for now.

"Yes, Mr Gundersen," she said. "I like it. I think I'll take it."

"Wonderful," he said. "Wonderful. Let's head back to the office and sort out the paperwork."

Angelica had made up her mind.

On the way back, they passed the old empty shell of The Bellevue, sitting out there all alone in front of the ocean.

She turned her head to follow it as they drove past, still looking at it as they slowed to take the turn. As the Mercedes turned into Bill's street, the noise of the indicator signal was ticking as if counting down the years in Angela's mind.

"I'd forgotten all about that old place," she said, as much to herself as to her driver.

"Yeah, the old place is still empty. Think it'll sit that way until it falls apart," he said. "Now, about your desire to purchase."

As they pulled into his driveway, she said. "Oh, I think there's plenty time for that, don't you, Mr Gundersen. Plenty of time. Let's sort out this part first."

He nodded his acquiescence, for the moment, and led her inside, after skipping around to open her door. Angelica had a feeling that Bill Gundersen wasn't simply going to let it rest.

-28-

The Move

Once she'd made the decision, it was easy, easier than she'd thought, and Angelica was a little surprised at how little uncertainty she felt. It was the right choice. Of course, since she'd moved into the small cottage, Bill Gundersen had been bombarding her with suggestions and choices. He would turn up on her front doorstep and knock, a small folder held in one hand, full of papers and photographs, his sunglasses shielding his eyes and professional smile firmly in place. She began to wonder, in fact, how many times he'd dropped in when she'd been out wandering or taking a trip to the library, or to the towns further afield. She certainly had to give him points for enthusiasm and persistence. It had probably been a mistake when he'd asked if she needed assistance arranging finance that she'd told him that she had no real need. He had almost taken a step backward when she'd told him.

When she had first moved down from the city, she had left much of what she'd had their behind, donated it to charities, given it away. They were only things, after all and they cluttered where she wanted to be. Ultimately, she didn't want them around to remind her of the mental space she had been in before. Woodford Park was a fresh start. The simply furnished cottage helped create a sense of that in her mind and it was a deliberate choice, one of the many Angelica was starting to make. The first couple of weeks she'd spent exploring the town itself, remembering things, noting where the changes were and discovering things that she never knew existed, or perhaps she had, and they had less significance back then when she'd been growing up. It was funny how your perspective changed at different stages of your life. She remembered that period of growing up more and more, and as a result, couldn't help dwelling on her father's disappearance. That night, so many years ago when he'd first left had taken place only a few streets over. She'd been past the old house a couple of times since she'd been here—it was a different colour now, and whomever had been in it during the intervening years had completely remodelled the garden. Her parents had invested great time and effort into turning the front yard into a rockery, very popular at the time, but all that was gone, the black plastic sheeting, the stones, the desert plants and had been replaced with neatly manicured lawn and shrubs, and there was something different about the windows too. The second time she'd wandered down that way, she had stood in front for several minutes, debating with herself, biting her lower lip. Should she go up to the front door and knock? Would they mind if she asked to come inside and see the place, see how it had changed? In the end, she decided that she didn't need it. She had her memories of the place, and that was enough. She had, instead, simply turned and walked away, heading for the beach.

After Angelica had been in the rented cottage for two and half months, she had a real feel for what Woodford Park had become. It wasn't that different in essence, but the feeling of the place was different. She wondered if that was the perspective thing too, seeing the town through different eyes. A lot of the things she noticed now she naturally saw in other ways.

Around the same time, Bill Gundersen turned up on her front doorstep with a gem.

"Angelica, hi. It's me again," standing on the front doorstep with sunglasses, a short-sleeved shirt and the patent grin. "You really have to see this one. If you'd asked me, I would have said this one would never have come up in a million years. Apparently there's been some stuff in the family and they've decided to move as a result. Luckily they came to see me, and here I am. Hot off the presses, if you like." He slapped the folder with his other hand.

"You'd better come in, Mr Gundersen," Angelica said, not quite convinced.

"Actually, listen," he said. "Are you doing anything right now? I'm telling you, I think this place is perfect for you." He leaned in close and said mock slyly, "That is of course if you've decided to stick around...."

Angelica put a hand on his bronzed forearm. "Okay," she said. "Convince me Mr Gundersen. "

"Ah, you won't be sorry, Angelica," he said and with a wave of his finger-challenged hand motioned for her to follow him out to the Mercedes parked out in front on the road. "And please, Bill. I don't know how many times I have to say it. Really, call me Bill."

"Just a minute while I lock up," she said, processing again what he'd said to her, but not quite sure she wanted to cross those bounds of familiarity. She popped back inside, found the keys and slipped on a pair of sandals, and then headed down to join him in the car.

Uncharacteristically, Bill said virtually not a word all the way there, just humming and smiling to himself, tapping gently on the top of the steering wheel as he drove. He took the tree-lined road that ran up the side of the railway line, and the dappled light flickered across the shining front of the car, reflecting dark green shadow and blue sky between the breaks. He turned over the railway bridge, around a corner, up a slight hill and then almost immediately pulled into a steep drive and killed the engine.

"Well, here we are," he said and turned to give her a big smile. Sometimes, it was unnerving that she hardly ever got to see his eyes. He looked up at the house and placed his hand down on the folder beside him, patted it again as if considering. "No," he said. "I think we'll let the property speak for itself."

Angelica turned to look where he appeared to be looking. The steep driveway led up to a small garage, bounded by a line of short trees that ran all the way up from the start of the drive to the rear of the garage. A small path led between the garage and the house and disappeared around the corner, sealed by a trellis gate. The house itself, more another cottage than a house, but larger than the one she was staying in now was angled on the plot meaning that the front windows all faced down towards the sea.

Bill followed where she was looking and said, "True, it's not right on the beach, but that has its advantages as well, especially in the silly season. You still get the view though. There's a porch out front there, and the front door, but it's just as easy to get in through the back way. Shall we go and take a look?"

Angelica nodded. As always, Bill was out of the car in an instant, leaving his door wide open while he skipped around the front of the car to open her door before she had a chance to fumble with the handle and open it herself. He led her up the side path twirling a key ring as he went. The white-painted wooden house seemed to be well maintained, few cracks or flakes on the exterior. Bill opened the trellis gate and held it wide for Angelica to step through first. The path led around the back, past some rose bushes and to a set of three steps leading up to a door. A small patch of lawn was bounded by a tall wooden fence at the rear.

"Plenty of privacy here," said Bill, gesturing towards the fence. "The owners are away for a couple of days while they are getting things in order." He headed for the back door, went through the keys till he found the one he wanted, pulled open a screen door and fitted the key to the lock. "It's got two bedrooms, kitchen of course, dining room, living room, bathroom. There are built in wardrobes, but nicely done, discrete, not like some of those glass and aluminium monstrosities you see, and of course, there's the front porch. Bedrooms are a decent size, but you could use the second one however you wanted I guess…turn it into an office or a studio or anything else you might want. Anyway, let's let the place speak for itself." He stood back to let Angelica climb the steps and enter. The back door led straight into the kitchen, which was a decent size and had all fairly up-to-date fittings.

From the kitchen, there were two doorways, one leading straight into the dining room and from there to the living room, and the other, opening into a short hallway that had two doors set on one side and an open archway that also led to the living area. It turned a corner at the end.

"Second bedroom there, bathroom, main bedroom is around there."

Bill led her through the house, pointing out this and that, opening and closing doors as they went. The style inside was neo-modern conservative, not particularly to Angelica's taste, but it was functional. She noted everything Bill directed her attention to, but she was only half listening, thinking instead what she would have done if she'd owned the place herself. All those thoughts disappeared as he led her into the main bedroom. Twin, wood framed windows sat at the front of the room, to one side, was a large walk in wardrobe a standard double bed against one wall with tastefully framed prints above it, but it was the windows that held her attention. The current owners had a large curtain rail above them both with heavy drapes, but they were pulled back with a single white gauze drop curtain running the entire length. The windows were long and wide.

"Mr Gundersen, can we pull that curtain back?" asked Angelica.

"Sure, sure," he said, jumping to comply. With a touch of difficulty, he managed to pull the curtains out of the way, giving Angelica an unrestricted view of what the windows revealed. Through the revealed panes of glass, was an uninterrupted line of sight, over the tops of the roofs of Woodford Park, straight out to the horizon, blue ocean and the headland there below. She could just see the end of the beach on one side.

"My god," she said, "That's gorgeous. Why the hell would they want to cover it? At least not like that."

Bill shrugged. "No idea. But there's no accounting for taste, right?" He stood there, holding back the curtain and watching her reaction carefully. "So, a bit early for first impressions?"

"No, no, I like the place. I really do."

"So…," he said slowly.

"It's a bit early yet, Mr Gundersen. I want some time to think about it. Perhaps if you could show me the details. You know, price…that sort of thing." She didn't want to appear too eager about it, but despite her words, Angelica had already made up her mind. She couldn't imagine that the price would be prohibitive.

"Well, just saying," said Bill. "It's not really even on the market yet officially. Although I'm sure the sellers would be interested in a quick sale. Point is, as soon as I put it out there for real, I'm sure there will be interest."

"I understand, but I still want some time to consider. Why don't you show me what you have, and then I'll think it over? I don't think I'll take too long about it." Angelica could almost feel him sniffing the air.

"Okay, then," said Bill, dropping the curtain back into place and smoothing the way it hung. "Let's go have a look."

He led her back out to the car, via the front this time, so she could have a look at the front porch, the neatly tended garden, the front door and the paved path leading up from the street. Once back inside his car, he flipped open the folder and pointed at a figure with one of his stumps.

"That's the asking price. But you know…what I said before…." He let the statement hang.

Within the very short space of four weeks, Angelica had moved in for good.

-29-

Bikes

For a while, Angelica spent time settling into the new house, decorating, finding and purchasing a big old Victorian brass bed, getting rid of the inappropriate curtains, browsing through the local second-hand store and others in nearby towns, looking at antique and old furniture stores. All that kept her busy, but then she decided she had reached the place where to spend any more time on it would have been too much. She was happy with her furnishings, happy with the bits and pieces she had collected around herself. In one of the antique stores, she had found an old box, decorated with shells and other pieces, constructed of found materials, she would have guessed. She fell in love with it immediately. It too became an acquisition. All of her photographs, letters and everything that she'd been carting around in large manila envelopes, she transferred to the box, which took pride of place on the top of a heavy wooden chest of drawers beside her bed. The box was like a finishing touch. She looked around her house and she saw that it was good. Eventually, she decided, she would have to get it painted. She could, of course, do it herself, but probably it was better to have it done professionally. She couldn't see herself in old stained overalls with paint smudges on her nose and matting her hair.

Right about then, she was at a bit of a loss. She didn't have anything to do and so, just as much out of habit as anything else, she started checking out the local bars, clubs and cafes, not that there were too many. Within a five town radius, there were maybe a dozen or so. A brief trip down the coast took her to one spot where an enterprising proprietor had taken advantage of an impressive cliff top location as a draw and it worked; people came from miles around, especially on the weekend. There was a small restaurant, a bar, and a rear deck hanging precariously out over the cliff and ocean, stacked with tables and bench seats where, on a fine day, or even a so-so day, you could sit and watch the view with your drinks and snacks. To further add to his patronage, the proprietor provided live music on a Saturday, probably the only local venue that did so. Angelica started spending most of her weekends at the Clifftop Inn. She met people, both local and visitors. She was soon known by name by the bar staff who would nod as she entered and already start to fix her first drink. She ate in the restaurant, at first alone, and then with others as she accumulated various acquaintances and casual friends. When the band was playing, she would be out the front dancing, with whoever wanted to or even alone, but generally, by the time the band started up, Angelica had usually been there for a while.

There were other places she tried, but apart from the odd brief encounter which usually ended up in a bed somewhere, rarely at her place, they didn't really provide anything like the familiar comfort that the Clifftop Inn had grown to provide. She cut them from her list and every couple of days would instead catch a bus—the local service ran right outside the Clifftop Inn and there was a stop right across the road—and spend the bulk of her evening.

One Saturday, Angelica was there, turning up early. When she arrived, she was a little surprised to see a line of motorcycles standing to one side at the front. She gave a little frown, but only because it was an unusual sight, and entered, receiving her usual greeting from the bar staff. She always liked to have her first drink sitting at the bar, so she could check out the room, see who was around and she headed straight for the bar, exchanged pleasantries with Jack the barman as he slid her Gin and Tonic across towards her. She pulled up a stool, placed her bag on the floor in front of her, concentrating first on the drink, stirring the ice and the slice of lemon with the clear plastic stick that came in the tall glass. When she'd had a couple of sips, she turned her attention to the rest of the room. Over to one side, in a cluster of three tables sat a bunch of leather clad and hairy men. Helmets were positioned on tables and on the floor nearby and large beers sat in front of them. There was a couple out by the door to the deck, not a part of the biker group and she could see someone outside, but apart from that, the place was empty. That was unusual in itself.

She leaned across the bar and motioned Jack closer.

"Is this something special?" she asked, leaning in and gesturing towards the corner with a slight movement of her head.

Jack shrugged. "Not really. They turn up this way every couple of months or so. They're okay. Decent boys, I guess. Just some of the others don't like to come when they're here. They see the line of bikes out front and the place goes quiet. They come in, they spend their money, they don't generally make trouble, so that's the way it is."

Angelica nodded. "What are they a club?"

Jack nodded. "Yeah, you see the back of the jacket there? Red Devils. That's them."

For the first time, Angelica noticed that they all wore similar denim jackets with a cartoon devil tossing a pair of dice, surrounded by the words *Red Devils Motorcycle Club*. She had never had anything to do with bikers before.

"You say they're okay, Jack?"

"Sure," he said, wiping the bar with a cloth. "Not unless someone gives them trouble, then...well..."

"But what about the band? Are they playing?"

He stopped his wiping and fixed her with a look. "Sure, why not? Bikers like music too."

Angelica went back to her Gin and Tonic, stealing the occasional glance at the leather and denim clad group in the corner. A few more semi-regulars trickled in, but the numbers remained low. Eventually the band arrived and started to set up, one of the usual groups who played at the inn and specialised in old rock covers. Angelica, tired of sitting at the bar, and with none of her usual conversation partners present, took her drink over to a solitary table that gave her a good view of the small stage and made herself at home. She sipped, the band started testing their instruments, and the bikers continued drinking and talking and laughing. Outside on the deck, the weather was intermittently sunny, and a breeze pushed along the cliff top, bringing the taste of ocean spray to mix with the smell of beer, polish and snacks inside. After a while, the band started playing.

That probably would have been the rest of Angelica's afternoon and evening, but instead, something happened that would change her visit and a number of things to come. The band was into their third piece, an old Dire Straits number, when a tall black leather-clad figure connected with the edge of her table as he tried to negotiate the small gap, clutching an armful of beers, sending her own drink tumbling over and splashing on the table and floor in front.

"Ah shit," he said. "Hang on..." He deposited his load of drinks, unspilled back at his table, said something to his companions, and was right back a moment later.

"I'm sorry, little lady," he said. "Stupid. My fault. Let me replace that for you. What are you drinking?"

Angelica looked up into his face. He was tall, long dark hair, a scrabbly dark beard and blue, blue eyes with the crinkle of laughter around their edges. He was smiling down at her, his hands outstretched as if in supplication. Angelica might have objected to being called 'little lady,' but from this smiling half giant, not only was it accurate, it sounded kind of right.

"Um, Gin and Tonic," she said.

He nodded once, and was back at the bar, returning with a cloth and wiping up the spill, keeping his attention on her face. "Drink will be right here," he said and then he was back at the bar not with one, but two drinks in his hands. He placed hers down in front of her carefully and straightened, holding a large beer in one hand. "And there, sorry about that."

This tall, dark, stranger — what a cliché, she thought to herself — was quite good looking beneath the mass of dark hair, beard and black leather and he seemed to have an easy way about him.

"Don't think I've seen you before," he said. "I'm Johan. Is it okay if I sit?"

"Hi," said Angelica. "Sure. I'm Angelica."

He pulled out a chair and arranged his lanky frame, leaning back, legs stretched out in front of him, crossing black boots at the ankles, placing his beer down in easy reach of one hand, then turned to study her face.

"Well," he said. "It's probably not that strange that I haven't seen you before. I only join the boys here now and again to catch up when they're in town. It's kind of a semi-regular thing, but that semi-regular can turn into months in between."

"You're not with them?"

Johan shrugged, and then leaned forward to show her his back. "No colours. I ride with them now and again. I'm local. They all know me and I'm kind of part of the family, you know. I build bikes. I fix bikes." He sat back again. "What about you?"

168

Angelica considered before answering. The band started on another number and she had to lean forward to make herself heard. "I'm sort of between things at the moment, making up my mind about what I want to do. I guess you could say I'm killing time for a little while."

He seemed to accept that for what it was, nodding. He leaned in again. "And you, are you local?"

"Yes," she said, realising with the word that she did feel exactly that, local. "I'm up in Woodford Park."

"Ah, right. Just a couple of towns up from me. I'm over in Banham"

They both sat back listening to the band for a couple of minutes, waiting for the next break in the music. Johan concentrated, sipping slowly at his drink one foot tapping in time to the music while Angelica studied his face. He was different, different from anyone she'd ever really associated with and he seemed to exude an aura of easy-going comfort. He seemed settled in place, barely glancing over at his companions, only once tossing his head in recognition of some gesture or word that was passed in his direction, and then turning his attention back to the band.

During breaks and between numbers, Angelica and Johan exchanged further snippets of information. Johan took his time with his drinks, while Angelica maintained her normal pace. By the time the band had finished, the rest of the bikers had already left, Johan waving them a quick goodbye and telling one of them that he was staying. The band members were carting their gear out to the van when Johan turned to her.

"Well," he said.

"Hmmm," said Angelica in reply.

"Can I give you a ride home?"

Angelica considered. The only real experience she'd had of bikes had been those little motorised death traps back on the Greek Islands and in Italy, but by now, after the evening and a number of drinks, she thought, why not.

"Come and see my beast then," said Johan, standing and stepping back while Angelica got herself together. "I've got a spare helmet, so don't worry. And just take my lead. It's easy." Somehow, he had measured her hesitation.

He led her out to the front, and there, standing alone now was a low-slung yellow bike, big, all shining chrome picked out in the front lights of the Clifftop Inn. Johan carried a simple black helmet in one hand. There was another perched at the back of the bike.

"That's my baby," he said. "Leaks oil like shit, but she's a beautiful machine. You've gotta take the good with the bad, right? She's a Norton. What can I say? I've got a thing for British bikes."

All of that meant absolutely nothing to Angelica, but it sounded impressive. Johan straddled the bike, and then kicked it into life. A deep throaty rumble surrounded her and fed through her deep inside. He handed her the helmet and put on his own.

"Climb aboard. Hold on to me. When we hit a corner, lean with me, into the turn, not against it. I can get us to Woodford Park. You can direct me once we're there."

Angelica had a bit of trouble with all her hair trying to manage donning the helmet, and once she did, she felt as if she was in another place, the sound muffled, her vision partially obscured. There was a strange smell inside the helmet, like rubber or something. She climbed on, putting her arms around Johan's leather-covered torso. He turned the bike and then kicked it into gear, slowly at first, and then accelerating. The throb of the engine pulsed through her and as the acceleration took hold, she clung tightly to Johan's frame.

They were back in Woodford Park in no time at all, and with an awkward combination of shouts and gestures, her head leaning forward over his shoulder and their helmets touching, Angelica directed them to her place. Johan pulled up outside and stood there, holding the bike upright while she climbed off and struggled to remove the helmet. She handed it to him.

"Thanks," she said.

He pushed up his visor and smiled at her. "No problem. Guess I'll see you round." And with that, he clicked the visor down and was gone, leaving Angelica standing watching after him. That was it? She swayed a little, standing where she was, coming down from the adrenaline of the ride and feeling the effects of perhaps a couple too many Gin and Tonics, then she shook her head and fumbling for her keys, made her way up to the back door. The evening had certainly not ended as she might have expected, in more ways than one.

Four days later, she had a visitor at her front door. Tall, grinning, and holding a helmet in one hand he stood gauging her surprise.

"Hi there."

"Um, hi," said Angelica.

"So," said Johan. "I felt like going out for a ride. I wondered if you'd like to come."

Angelica smiled back. She didn't really have to think about it. "Sure. Just let me lock up." She looked down at her flowing, patterned dress. She hadn't even really finished getting herself together for the day. "Um, am I okay like this?"

"Sure," he replied, his gaze going from head to toe. "Why not?" His grin got wider.

"Oh," said Angelica. "Do you want to come in for a coffee or something first?"

"Nah. Let's just go."

She nodded, left him standing there while she ducked back inside, found what she needed and locked the house before following him back out to the road. She felt like a little girl again, excited, her heart beating, a not unpleasant lightness in her stomach.

They rode for miles, around bends, along open highways, along the edge of the cliffs, stopping once at the top of the escarpment to look out to the ocean and take in the view. Johan brought her back to the house and parked in front again, letting her off.

"That was fantastic," said Angelica.

"Good. Let's do it again sometime soon."

And then he was gone once more, leaving her out in front of her house, watching him as he disappeared up the road, the deep throaty rumble of his bike trailing after him, and lingering in the distance, long after he had disappeared from view. What was with this guy?

Three more times, he turned up unannounced, and only after that third time did he wait around long enough to be invited inside. They had coffee and talked and then had more coffee and talked some more. Later, they wandered down to the beach to pick up something to eat. Over those few hours together, though she hadn't really meant them to, bits and pieces of Angelica's life came out one by one. Johan listened, absorbed, noted, not seeming to judge, just taking it all in and accepting.

It was two more weeks before Angelica first took Johan to her bed and it was easy and natural. It wasn't a performance, a little one-act play; it just seemed to happen as a logical order of events and it was good.

One afternoon, they were lying in that bed, her bed, Johan tracing patterns on her shoulder with one finger and he leaned in close to her.

"You know, Angelica," he said. "You've had a lot of shit you've been through. You hold it at a distance. I guess you're protecting yourself. That's fine. I just want you to know; I just want to be there for you. That's all."

She made to reply, but he turned her over and held a finger to her lips. "That's all," he said.

She looked up at his face, his long hair hanging down beside her head, draping both of them like a curtain, his eyes gentle and the barest smile on his face.

They couldn't have been more different — him with his leather and grease-stains, she with her pastels and lace, but there was something. She thought about it later and then she thought about it more. She had space. She also had a garage that wasn't being used for anything. It might even work. He made her feel...secure. It was only two months later, that Angelica took the plunge and suggested he move in with her.

-30-

Walter

With Pamela, eventually, as he'd known it would, the inevitable happened. Walter was not sure in the end whether it was merely social pressure or circumstance itself that drove him to the act, but unwilling to fight against the world at large, he found himself complying. Though it always remained unspoken, he had been aware for some time that there was an assumption, an expectation that Pamela and he were heading down the path to marriage. There were no specific plans, no discussions, but Walter knew in the back of his mind that he would ask Pamela to marry him, and he knew too, roughly when that was supposed to happen. After she graduated, after she had finished her studies, then they would be in the proper position for a young couple starting out, and Pamela herself would not have any distractions to interfere with her studies in the meantime. She would be able to concentrate on finishing her degree, and only then would they be in a position to really make proper plans together. The week of her graduation ceremony, he organised dinner at a flashy restaurant, on the surface, a private celebration of her achievement, just the two of them, and there, right time, right place, he had asked, feeling awkward and uncomfortable, but at the same time, knowing she would say yes. She had punctuated the excited flow of words confirming her acceptance with the characteristic 'Wow!'s that he had become so used to in the last year or so.

Pamela's parents were pleased, as were his own. Walter was doing quite well at the city architectural firm he worked at, his prospects were good, and he was a nice young man. Pamela was a nice girl, uncomplicated, clearly with a strong social conscience, and the sort of girl who was likely to be a good mother and homemaker, guaranteed to grace them with grandchildren. Clearly, there were no impediments to them proceeding, and both sets of parents contributed to the arrangements for the wedding that was to be held at a country church within striking distance of Pamela's parents' farm. (No, to have it in the city was too far to travel. We have the relatives to consider.) The parents also helped contribute to the starter home in the suburbs and their path was set. Pamela managed to secure a job with a local government agency and commenced her program of good works, changing the world one inner-city underprivileged family at a time. Meanwhile, Walter was working on shopping malls and office blocks, large, corporate glass and steel structures that were destined to house the machinery of the city's commercial enterprise. Two-thirds of the way through their first year, Pamela became pregnant, as, naturally, now that they were married, Walter had been able to gain access to that last hidden bastion that had lain hidden for so long beneath Pamela's practical white cotton briefs. It was only a surprise that it took so long for his renewed enthusiasm to produce results. When Pamela announced her pregnancy to him, Walter absorbed, processed and showed, outwardly, the appropriate level of enthusiasm, but underneath, it was tinged with the same feeling of inevitability that had led to his proposal and the road that had followed thereafter. Roughly nine months later, their son, Andrew John was born late in the evening on the 24th December. Pamela was, although she joked about it afterwards, a little disappointed that Andrew, who would become Drew, couldn't have waited a few hours more for his arrival and pushed it over to the morning of the 25th. That, to her mind, would have been just perfect.

The grandparents, on both sides, doted on the grandson. As the sleepless nights and the strain of a new child in their little first home began to pass, Pamela started to talk about her return to work. She had performed her first, primary duty as wife and mother, and now wanted to get back to changing the world. That meant childcare — her parents were too far away — and, inevitably, more space as the child got older. They had to think about private school as well, because the boy had to have the proper education and the appropriate start in life. The local schools would not provide the sort of standard required. Walter considered where he was, his prospects at his current firm, and decided he needed to make a step. He didn't have a choice. He put feelers out into the marketplace and started looking for another job, one that would pay more and give him better prospects of advancement. He received an enthusiastic response from another, smaller firm, and quickly accepted their offer and moved. It meant longer hours, a less protected environment, but for the potential rewards it was worth it. Additionally, it was a young, dynamic outfit, with a variety of clients and projects that would give him the opportunity to expand, to start to play with some of his own ideas rather than those dictated by the needs of large corporate structures. Some nights, Walter thought about how he had moved from one extreme to the other, from his couple of years of dissipation and freedom into a life where he could almost predict step by step what was to come next. It was almost as if he had taken it too far. He needed an escape, an outlet where he could express his creativity, and this new firm promised to provide at least a part of that and promised at least a sort of mitigation to the predictability of his domestic regimen.

Walter fit in well with the new firm. He provided an ordered balance to the mix and provided some focus and direction to some of the more maverick projects they undertook. Walter didn't mind holding that lynchpin role at all; it gave him more of a sense of ownership and contribution, and he quickly found himself liking the environment and the company he worked with.

For the next few years, Walter's life progressed with a similar aura of inevitability. There were the steps that came naturally and in logical order, one after the other, and just as the rest of his life, Walter was almost able to predict their emergence. Drew grew larger, as did their house. Predictably, Pamela's waistline grew along with her hair. The mortgage payments grew as did the niceness of their neighbourhood. Walter's position within the firm expanded, along with his responsibilities. Pets came and went, along with the attendant little tragedies and Drew developed into a serious young man who started attending high school and with the same level of seriousness attached himself to his mother's religious beliefs. That was the only thing, really, that Walter hadn't been able to predict; the fervour with which Pamela threw herself into the local church community, their charitable works, the Sundays she and Drew would spend, dressed in their best clothes off with the rest of the believing local masses. Walter refused to attend. He didn't begrudge Pamela her beliefs, but he didn't expect her to thrust them down his throat either. Prayers at the dinner table, prayers at night, and prayers first thing in the morning, his wife and his son sitting together at the kitchen table clasping hands with bowed heads before she sent him off to school. For a while, he tried to ignore it, pretend it was just one of those things, but that didn't last very long. When he left every morning, Pamela would lean up, peck him on the cheek and say: "God bless you, Walter," not "Have a good day, dear," or "See you tonight, honey." It was always "God bless you." Gradually, Pamela's little "Wow!"s mutated into "Praise God!"s but worse, as time went on, she became not only truly righteous, but self-righteous with it. She started to see things in black and white lines of Christian or un-Christian and it became very clear to Walter into which side of the divide he ultimately fell.

Pamela started ambushing him at the dinner table, telling him how disappointed she was that he had not accepted Jesus Christ the Lord and Saviour into his life, how he was setting such a poor example for his son, that he was a bad father. Stoically, Walter accepted these harangues for a while, but tolerance only goes so far. He started searching for references to inconsistencies in the Bible, unexplainable anomalies, thrusting them in front of her in response to her arguments and sitting back in disbelief as she just talked around them or refused to listen. With increasing frequency, she would leap up from the dinner table, hands clapped over her ears and rush off to the bedroom crying, "May God forgive you, Walter."

He didn't want anyone to forgive him.

Walter began spending more and more time at the office, eating out in town, light meals and takeaways in order to avoid the evening family dinners. He would come home to find a plate warming in the oven, which he would scrape clean and rinse before going to bed. In the bedroom, there was an uncrossable gap between them, no a chasm, with Pamela dressed in prim nightie and stiffening at every shift of his weight on the bed as if it might threaten the unspeakable, though he was sure she would see that, too, as he Christian, wifely duty.

Late at night, when he had finished with the plate in the kitchen, he would pour himself a drink and sit in the semi-darkness, slowly sipping and looking into nothing. That was, until Pamela threw out all his whisky bottles.

When he discovered that she was trying to force Creationist dogma down his son's throat, he was close to having a fit. He had rounded on her in the kitchen.

"Jesus Christ, Pamela, what are you thinking?

"Don't blaspheme Walter."

"Are you serious? We aren't living in the Dark Ages. What the fuck are you thinking?"

"Walter, if you're going to talk to me, you will respect my beliefs. Now, please…."

He stood there, fists balled at his sides, fury building. "Christ. I will not have you filling our son's head with superstitious bullshit. If he wants to believe in that crap, that's his choice, but you are not going to force it down his throat either."

Her hands went to her ears and he reached up and pulled them down. "Listen to me dammit! Do you hear me?"

And then Drew was behind him, pounding on his back with his fists.

"Leave her alone! Leave her alone!"

He threw up his hands in exasperation and left the house only to come back much later and sleep on the couch.

Later, during the legal proceedings, that was one of the incidents trotted out. Walter had been trying to harm his good Christian wife and their son had been forced to leap in to try to defend her.

The final straw, for Walter, was when Pamela had copied down all of his email addresses, personal and private and sent each of them a lengthy email, over a page long, explaining the evils of the world and that accepting their personal saviour, Jesus Christ, into their lives, was the only path to fixing everything that was wrong. Of course, seeing who the sender was, every single one of them read it. It would weeks before he got over the public embarrassment at work and with his friends. It was enough, however, for Walter to take a decision.

"I'm leaving," he told her at the dinner table. "You're going to have to find some other poor soul to convert. I can't take it anymore. Maybe I'll think about coming back when you've got yourself together."

Pamela nodded slowly without saying anything. Drew looked at his mother. Walter looked at both of them, understanding that there was no other choice for him to make. At least she hadn't said: "Praise God."

Gently, he put down his fork and went to pack, reconciled to the fact that this too was marked with the traces of inevitability.

Add desertion to the list of things he would eventually be guilty of.

-31-

Angelica

At first, it simply started with coffee. The previous chance encounter in the Moore Street shop, the incident out on Ball's Point, they were immaterial and tangential. This third chance encounter, though Angelica only considered it the third — she was unaware of the previous potential encounter at the Woodford Park market — was to be touched with something else, something new. By then, she had already performed the requisite rummage through the second-hand store, exchanged morning pleasantries with the pair of old ladies who pottered around inside. This morning, she had settled on orange and ginger tea and a healthy slice of passionfruit cheesecake when Walter appeared at the door. He spotted her sitting there, blinked a couple of times as if in confusion, and then nodded once. He was dressed in old corduroys and a waxed jacket. After pulling open the door and stepping inside, he hesitated in the entrance, scanning first the board above the counter, and then looking once more in her direction. She smiled.

Lowering his head, he took the few steps over to her table.

"Well, hello, again," he said. "Haven't we been here before?"

Again Angelica smiled, meeting his eyes. "I think that might just be possible," she said.

Walter nodded once, then after a slight awkward pause, gestured at the vacant chair at her table. "Do you mind?"

"No, of course not," she said, her smile growing wider.

"Well, it seems kind of silly not to, after all we know each other now, don't we?"

She had no idea why he seemed to be looking for justification. She said nothing.

"Um, okay," said Walter. "I'll just get something and be back."

She watched him as he went to the counter, scanned the boards again and finally made an order. At last, he returned with a cappuccino, a healthy sprinkling of chocolate over the top, and placed it down awkwardly on the table in front of the vacant chair, before pulling out the chair itself and sitting.

"Well," he said, turning the saucer and cup around and around on the table, not meeting her eyes. Such shyness....

"It is Walter, isn't it?" she asked.

He continued gazing out the front window, taking a second before answering. "Yes, that's right."

"Oh," she said. "I'm glad I didn't get that wrong."

He cleared his throat. "You know, I went up and had a look at that old cemetery you were talking about."

"Really?" she said.

"Yeah. It's kind of strange, sitting out there, looking out over the sea. But you know, thinking about it, it's not a bad place to end up, I guess. Hmm, do you know where you are after you're dead? I wonder...."

Angelica lifted her cup and watched him over the rim as she sipped.

"Have you been up there?" he asked her.

She carefully placed her cup down. "No, Walter. Not my sort of thing. I've passed it a few times of course, but really, I don't like to spend a lot of time thinking about death, cemeteries, that sort of thing."

He met her eyes for the first time. "No, I guess not," he said. "Nor me really. Not normally. It was just unusual. Fascinating in its own way, you know."

A few seconds of awkward silence followed while Walter played with his spoon and Angelica sipped at her tea.

Angelica broke the silence finally. "So what are you up to, Walter?"

He nodded. "Just waiting for the next project, really. I just finished a plan for a client. The firm's going to oversee the building, so my part is done. I guess I'm just waiting for the next one to come along."

It wasn't so different from what Angelica herself was doing.

"So what about you?" he continued. "I know we started to talk about it last time, but I can't quite remember where we got to."

Angelica shrugged. It was a real question, one that she didn't necessarily want to face in the clear light of day right at the moment. There was the proposed jewellery adventure, if that was going to turn into anything at all, but apart from that....

"Well, you know..." she said, realising straight away that it was an unsatisfactory answer. "I guess I'm waiting for the next thing to come along too, just like you. I've been thinking about a couple of things but..." She looked down into her half empty cup. "Nothing has really struck me yet. Nothing that really inspires me, anyway. You know Woodford Park is a little like that. It's its own little bubble. Easy enough to float along, you know."

"Yes, I guess I can see that," he said.

"Listen," she said on a whim. "Are you doing anything tonight?"

He gave a little frown. "No, not really."

"Well, why don't you come up to my place for dinner? Nothing fancy. I'll put a few things together. Do you like Italian?"

"Sure," he said. "Why not? I'll grab a bottle of wine. Red's okay, yes?"

"Yes," she said. "Now, let me explain to you how to get there." She pulled out a paper napkin from the small silver rack on the table and smoothed it flat. Reaching down for her bag, she rummaged around, finally coming up with a pen, smoothed the napkin once more with her hands and then proceeded to draw a small map. "Not that you really need instructions. It's easy enough."

-32-

The Child

The young girl with the sun-streaked blonde hair stood at the edge of the headland tugging at her pigtail on one side with a delicate little hand. The wind stirred the edges of her pale blue dress, but she seemed not to notice it, her attention focused on the beach below. She stopped tugging at her hair and moved to the stone bench to sit. Down on the sand in the middle of the beach, an old man in red and black swimming trunks stood at the water's edge, the waves lapping around his ankles, his hands on his hips as he stared out to the horizon as if considering, his short peppered hair barely moved by the breeze. The girl's attention never strayed from the solitary figure on the beach. She leaned forward a little, her palms flat against the edge of the seat, her legs crossed beneath her, intent.

The old man lifted one hand, shielding his eyes against the light to look out across the waves. His head turned, first one way, then the other, as if seeking something or someone along the beach. He lowered his hand and shook his head slowly. Up on the headland, the small girl drew in a slow breath and held it.

As if having come to a decision, the old man shook his head again, then giving one more look up and down the beach, and then once up at the sky, he lowered his head and took a step forward, and then another. Within moments, the waves were up to his waist, and then to his chest. He stopped there for a few moments, considering, and then took another step forward, and another.

Slowly, the child let out her breath. She stood, smoothed her dress into place and turned away from the beach. Unhurriedly, she walked away from the stone bench and back towards the coast road and the town.

She had seen what she'd come to see.

-33-

Bill

"Doris? Doris? Where are you, my love?"

"Here I am, Bill. What is it?" Doris had emerged from the kitchen, wiping hands down the front of an apron decorated with brown and black dogs all over the front of it. She stood in the archway leading into the office space, having attended to the drying, now rubbing her hands as if testing that she had truly removed all traces of moisture.

"Doris, you won't believe it. I just got off the phone." He rocked back in his chair and clasping his hands behind his head, stared up at the ceiling. He could barely believe it himself.

"Yes...?" she said. "What, Bill? You just got off the phone."

"Yeah, yeah, sorry." He rocked forward again in the chair. "It was this guy from the city. There's a bunch of them. According to this guy, they've got some sort of plan for the old hotel."

"Noooo," she said. "Really?"

Outside, the dogs were yapping, and Doris glanced in that direction with a little frown.

"Yeah," Bill told her. "So it seems. Though it isn't firm yet, and this guy wanted to keep it pretty quiet. Early stages yet."

"So what was his name? What did he say?" Doris moved over to the desk now and sat, perching on the edge of one of the chairs that sat in front, watching him attentively, her hands held together in her lap.

"Black. Terrence Black. Here look." He spun around the pad on which he had written the name, so she could see. Bill had learned long ago that he was far better off if he wrote things down. "He was saying that the old place was a perfect location for an exclusive health spa, or something like that. Members of their group were looking to make an investment. They have a bunch of natural doctors working for them. You know, all kinds of herbs and stuff like that. Massage, I dunno. That sort of thing. You know what I'm talking about."

"Uh-huh." Doris nodded. "So come on, Bill. What else?"

He shook his head and pressed his lips together, struggling a little. "Of course they want to look the place over, or that's what he said, but it was kind of strange. Said he wanted it to be discrete."

Doris frowned in turn. "Whatever that means. Did he say anything else?"

Bill nodded. "Talked about looking at a preliminary proposal."

"Proposal? What does that mean?"

Bill scratched his head. "Sketches, I guess. Drawings. That sort of thing. Or that's what it sounded like, anyway."

"Ahhh," said Doris. "Yes, I know. So, did he say anything about timing?"

Again he nodded. "A bunch of them want to come down and look at the place next week. I guess he will want to talk about the proposal then."

"You've still got the keys, right?"

Bill frowned at her. Of course he had. Not that he'd been anywhere near the old place in months. He reached up and flipped open the cupboard where he kept the keys. "Up there. See?"

She gave a satisfied nod. She settled herself further back into the chair, crossing her legs and leaning forward. Bill knew that stance of old. Doris was entering into business mode.

"Okay, so you've got his number, good. Did you settle on a day for the viewing?"

Bill nodded. "Wednesday."

"All right. That gives us a few days. Now, this proposal thing. It wouldn't hurt to do a bit of up front work on that. Have they got someone lined up?"

Bill was having trouble keeping up already. It was always like this when Doris got this way. "Hang on. Let me think what he said. Oh that's right. Yeah. This Black guy said he wanted to keep things pretty low profile for the moment. Asked if there was anyone local he could use. If he farmed it out to a city firm, then word would be sure to get around. Yes. He asked if we knew anyone."

"And what did you say, baby?"

"Said I'd do a bit of thinking and let him know."

"Good boy. That's not bad, letting him wait a little bit. Of course, we have just the guy."

Bill tilted his head to one side and looked at her. "We do?"

"Yes, baby. Think about it. That Walter Whatsisname. He's an architect isn't he?

"Ahhh." Bill leaned back in his chair again. "Why didn't I think of that? Of course he is."

"So," said Doris. "This is what we do. You pop over to see this Walter and make him a proposition. Feel him out. See if he would be interested, but I can't see why he wouldn't be. Once you've done that, you get back in touch with this Terrence Black and confirm the meeting. Tell him you're firming up details or something. When you're talking to him, you mention that you might have someone for the job, but you want to talk to him about it in person. At the moment we have no idea what he's prepared to pay. You'll know more once you've met them. Of course, there's no point if our architect isn't interested, but we'll cross that bridge once we come to it. As I said, I don't think it's going to be a problem. You take them around to look at the old place, get a feel for them, then we'll know where we stand."

Doris reached up and patted at her hair on one side, a good signal that the torrent of words had finished for the moment.

"Okay, got it," he said. Sometimes he was reminded how lucky he was to have her. "So when should I go and see Mr. Travis?"

"Well, there's no time like the present, is there, baby?"

"Hmmph," he said. As usual, Doris was right.

"All right," she said. "You go over and see him. Meanwhile, I need to go and see what's upsetting the babies."

-34-

Walter

Walter was pacing, measuring the length of the front room with his strides, not consciously, but back and forth he walked with a mug of coffee in his hand. Outside, down the slope and across the road, the sea was grey, like his mood. He was at a strange loose end, restless. He needed something to do, but for the life of him, he couldn't work out what it was he wanted. The next assignment from the firm wasn't due for about three weeks yet, and there was no real motivation to start. He was in mid-pace when a noise from the other end of the house interrupted his internal muttering and brought him up short. Had he heard something? He stopped where he was, listening. Yes, it was a knock. He gave a slight frown and placed the mug down on the table. He'd be forced to traipse through the entire length of the house, and who the hell would be knocking at his door anyway? Walter didn't get visitors. Maybe it was the Jehovahs. They'd been here once before, all neat haircuts, scrubbed faces and boring suits. Walter, of course, had had enough of religion to last him a lifetime. He was about to dismiss it entirely when the knock came again.

There was a sudden thought. Perhaps it was Angelica. She knew where he lived, didn't she? With a slight nod to himself, he headed down the hallway to the official front door and opened it, smiling. Standing there, rocking back and forth on his heels was someone, but certainly not Angelica.

"Mr. Travis. Hello. A very good day to you." A suntanned smile and a hand thrust out in front of him. "I was afraid you might not be in."

Walter couldn't remember the man's name for the life of him. Gundersen, he knew. He could hardly have forgotten it with the big sign further down the street announcing it to the world, but what was his first name. Bob? Pete?

"Um, hello," he said reaching out and taking the proffered hand.

The stocky character saved Walter the trouble. "Bill Gundersen. You remember Mr. Travis. I fixed you up in this place when you first came down."

"Yes, yes, of course," said Walter, still at a loss. "Is there something I can do for you? Is there a problem with the house?"

"No, no. Nothing like that," said Bill. He craned to look over Walter's shoulder, an effort in itself with their relative heights, finally releasing his hand. "Perhaps if I could come in… There's a little thing a wanted to talk to you about."

Walter was completely adrift now. "Um, okay," he said and gave a brief shake of his head. "Down this way, but then I guess you'd know that already."

As he turned, Gundersen gave a laugh and slapped him lightly on the shoulder. "Yes, I guess I do, hey?"

Walter led the way down the length of the house and back to the front room. "Can I offer you something? A coffee maybe?"

"No, no, I'm fine," he said, standing bang in the centre of the room and peering at the furniture and the room's set up. "Nice," he said. "Good use of the space. Yes, I can see why you'd want to set yourself up here. If I remember correctly, it was the view that sold you in the first place, right?"

"Mmm hmm," said Walter, watching and waiting for Bill to come out with whatever he was here for.

Bill clasped his hands behind his back and stepped forward to the window, staring out across the beach and the ocean. "Yes," he said, almost to himself. "Golden view. Simply golden."

Walter had reached for his mug again, and took a sip. "So what can I do for you Mr. Gundersen?"

Bill turned to look back over his shoulder. "Bill, Bill. No need for formality." He turned back to the window. "Well, it's kind of about the view that I'm here."

Okay, now Walter really was confused.

Bill lifted one hand and indicated the headland across the beach. "See that old place up there?" he said.

"Sure," said Walter. "I could hardly miss it." Walter felt a sudden hint of unease. Had someone seen him? Did Bill Gundersen know about his little explorations? Oh, shit, he'd forgotten about the back door in the place. Perhaps that was it.

"A lot of potential, that old place."

"Yes, I guess so," Walter answered, trying to suppress the guilt he was starting to feel. "A lot of work though." He took another sip of his coffee.

Bill nodded sagely. "Yes, a lot of work. A lot of work." He stared out the window, as if lost in thought. Suddenly he turned away from the view. "In fact, Walter...I can call you Walter, right....good. Well, in fact, Walter, that's really why I'm here."

Okay, Walter thought. Here it comes.

"You're an architect, right?"

"Sure."

"Place like that has to be interesting to you. Big old buildings."

Walter was sure now that he'd been found out.

"Well, yes, certainly," said Walter carefully. "But, it's not as if I—"

"No, hear me out," said Bill raising a hand. Walter had completely forgotten about the missing fingers. "First, this has got to remain between the two of us for now."

Walter nodded, with a little frown, cradling his mug in front of him as if it was an act of protection.

"Good. Well, like I said, that old place has potential. I've thought so for a long time. Well now, it seems, there's a bunch of people in the city who think the same thing, or might think the same thing with the proper encouragement."

Walter shook his head. "I don't see..."

"Sure you do, Walter," said Bill. "You're an architect." He waved at the drafting table. "You draw buildings and things. Well, here's the thing. These city guys have some ideas about turning The Bellevue into something, but they want to have some preliminary ideas to start with. Or that's what they said, anyway. You're sure this will remain between just the two of us?"

Walter gave a quick nod.

"Good, good," continued Bill. "Now, they said something about some sort of health spa or something. I don't really understand those things, but you being an architect and all.... Anyway, they want some preliminary ideas. Asked me if I could come up with someone local, because they want to keep it pretty low profile, for now. So...what do you say, Walter?" Bill crossed the space between them and placed a hand on Walter's arm.

Walter carefully placed the nearly empty coffee mug down on the breakfast bar, looked down at the hand resting on his arm and then back at Bill's well-tanned face, smiling expectantly up at him.

"Bill, I still don't know what you're asking. Really."

"Simple, Walter. I want to hire you."

"Oh."

He hadn't expected that at all. What with his remaining traces of guilt and the confused bombardment of words that Gundersen had thrown at him, he hadn't seen it coming at all.

"Um," he said, extricating himself from Bill's hand and crossing to the window to stare out. The hotel stared across the beach at him, not giving any answers. The idea was interesting, for sure. He didn't suppose that it would get in the way of the official project. Something truly freelance...

Bill hadn't moved, just standing there waiting while Walter processed. He must be used to it, standing around while people made up their minds. It seemed that Bill decided that Walter had had enough time because he started in again.

"Now I don't know what you get paid, Walter, but like I said, this would be between us. Nothing fancy to start with. A few sketches. Some ideas what you could do with the place. Nothing major. Of course, it could turn into something bigger if they like what you do, but no guarantees, right? The important thing is that it remains quiet. Like I said, between us. Oh and of course the wife, Doris. You know Doris, right? My wife."

"Uh-huh," said Walter, still thinking.

"Well," said Bill. "I don't know if you need more time to think about it. Maybe I should leave you alone to..."

No, no," said Walter, waving with one hand behind him. "I like the idea. I've been sort of interested in the old place anyway." He turned to face Bill. "We can talk about terms later, exactly what you need. But you're right; I want to think about it a little bit. Generally, though, I like the idea." He looked back out the window at what he could see of The Bellevue. "I'd have to get access of course. Need to see the state of the place, what would need to be done. Walk the floors, if you like, get a feel for the place. Come up with some ideas. Yeah. Actually...I think I like it, Bill."

He turned back, and Bill Gundersen had a wide grin plastered across his face. "You know, Walter," he said. "I think we're in business."

Walter nodded slowly. "Yes, I think perhaps we are," he said. "So, when do we start, Bill?"

"No time like the present, eh? Strike while the iron's hot."

Walter glanced back through the window and over at the hotel. "Sure." The idea was becoming more and more attractive as he thought about it. Already some ideas were starting to form on his inner landscape.

"Look," said Bill. "Why don't you come back with me now and we'll get you a spare set of keys? That is unless you've got something else to do…"

"No, not at all," said Walter. "Let's do that. Perhaps we can discuss terms on the way."

Bill cleared his throat. "Yes, of course. We can, um, let Doris know too. Yes."

"All right, Bill. Lead the way."

Bill had one more look around the front room, nodded to himself, and then turned back and nodded again at Walter. The wide grin was gone now. "Yes," he said quietly and headed for the hallway, pausing for a moment to check that Walter was in fact going to follow, and then walking back towards the front door. At that moment, strangely, he sort of reminded Walter of a pet dog.

"Wait a moment, Bill," he said. "I need to find my keys."

"Sure, sure," came Bill's voice from up the corridor.

The keys were still in his coat pocket where he usually left them, and instead of bothering to dig them out, Walter lifted the coat from its peg by the door and shrugged it on. He followed Bill down the corridor and found him standing facing the blankness of the front door, not moving, simply waiting.

"Okay," said Walter.

Bill reached for the handle, opened the door and stepped outside, waiting until Walter had emerged, had closed the door behind him and checked that it was firmly shut.

It only took them a couple of minutes to walk down the street to the Gundersen's place. During the walk, Bill was uncharacteristically silent. He opened up, led Walter into his office space and gestured to a chair in front of the desk.

"Is that you, Bill?" a voice came from inside. "How did you…? Oh." The question trailed off as Doris Gundersen appeared in the doorway from inside. "Well, hello, Mr. Travis," she said, wiping her hands and then crossing to where Walter sat, extending one of them for him to shake lightly. "I see Bill's told you about our little proposition."

Bill cleared his throat again.

"Yes, he has, Mrs. Gundersen. How are you?"

"Call me Doris, love," she said. "Especially as we're all going to be friends now." She pulled out one of the spare chairs and sat beside him, peering into his face and then looking over at Bill as she asked her next question. "So, how much has Bill told you?"

"Enough, I would say," said Walter. "We've just come back to get a set of keys, so I can have a proper look."

"And have we talked about terms?" she asked, still looking at Bill.

Bill answered her this time. "No, my love, not yet. We thought we'd wait till we could have that conversation with you."

"Good, then," she said, breaking her gaze with Bill and turning back to look at Walter. She rubbed her hands across the top of her thighs. "All right. Well, Bill should have told you that this is just a speculative thing at the moment, right?"

Walter nodded.

"Okay. Now I don't know what you would normally charge for this sort of thing." She left the statement hanging, waiting for Walter to fill in the information.

"It's hard to say," said Walter. "Usually we charge for a project overall, depending on the size and then—"

"We?" she interrupted with a slight frown.

"Oh, don't worry," said Walter. "Bill's already said that this is between us. I only used the term because normally I work with a firm. That's why the 'we.'"

She seemed satisfied. "All right. Sorry, please go on."

Walter continued, and they talked back and forth for a little and then agreed on a not unreasonable flat fee. When they were done, in turn, both Bill and Doris extended a hand for him to shake.

"Get him the keys, Bill."

"Yes, yes. Of course," said Gundersen, reaching up to a cabinet above his desk and hooked a heavy bunch of keys with one finger, then passed them over to Walter.

"Fell free to go up and look over the place," said Bill. "But try not to do so next Wednesday. That's when the city guys are coming down to look at the place. I'd prefer to pull you out of my back pocket, as it were. We can have another chat about what we're going to do once they've been down."

"Is that okay for you, Walter?" said Doris.

Walter had been looking through the keys while they talked. Now he shoved them deep into his coat pocket. "Yes, fine," he said, looking up to meet her gaze. He couldn't help feeling that he was still being assessed. "I might just head over that way now and take a look," he said.

"No time like the present, eh Walter?" said Bill. "Do you want me to run you up there?"

"No, no, that's fine," said Walter. "I'll just walk over. It's not too far, and It'll probably be better off I do this on my own."

Doris stood and again extended a hand and Walter took her cue. "I guess we'll be talking soon," he said.

Bill accompanied him to the door, one hand resting on Walter's shoulder as if steering him. "You need anything else," he said. "You just let me know."

"Thanks, I'll do that," said Walter. He waited for the door to close behind him and stood for a couple of minutes, fingering the large bunch of keys in his pocket, thinking about what they'd just agreed. Funny how things turned around. Here he stood now with the keys to the old hotel firmly in his possession when before he'd been so worried about it. He gave a little smile and then he strolled unhurriedly down towards the end of the street and the coast road that would lead him around to the hotel's entrance.

-35-

The Child

Down on the beach, a small figure stood, hands clasped behind her back. One by one the waves rolled into the beach, the sand flat, shining and damp at the water's edge. Slowly, slowly, she turned her head, tracking the solitary man as he walked along the beachside path, heading towards the hotel. She watched him for a while, her face expressionless, and with all the time in the world, turned her gaze back to the incoming waves and the distant grey horizon beyond.

-36-

Mary

It had been a slow day in the snack bar, nothing going on and Mary had spent most of the day in front of the small portable television or flicking through magazines at the counter. It was a life, she guessed, though what sort of life she wasn't sure. When she compared her circumstance, a shop, an apartment, the smell of cooking grease, to the pictures in the glossy magazines she read, there was no real comparison. That sort of stuff was fantasy anyway. It wasn't meant for someone like her. Mary didn't have dreams of her own any more. She bought her dreams from a magazine rack.

The afternoon soap had just finished, and she was just thinking about making herself something to eat when the phone rang. With an effort, she heaved herself up from the chair and moved across to the doorway where the phone was attached to the wall and picked up the receiver.

"Hello?"

"Yeah, Ma, it's John." It was unlikely to have been someone else really. Who else was going to call her?

"Hi, Johnny. You okay?"

"Sure, Ma. I just thought you ought to know...Charlie's out."

"What do you mean?" she asked.

"Just what I say. He's out. They released him early. Time off for good behaviour or something."

Mary felt a cold knot growing in the pit of her stomach. She held the receiver away from her face, looking at it while she bit her bottom lip.

She bought the phone back to her ear and spoke. "How do you know, Johnny? How can you be sure?"

"He called me this morning, Ma. He called me at work."

"What did he say?"

"He said he was coming down here."

"When?" she asked.

"He didn't say. But that's what he said."

Mary thought. She didn't want to see him, but it was not as if she could really avoid it. Maybe he'd changed. Maybe the time inside had done him some good.

"Did he say anything else? Did he say what he wanted to do?"

"Just that he needed to catch up with a couple of friends, had to sort out some cash and then he'd be down."

"Okay, okay," she said, still thinking. "Listen, Johnny, you call me if he gets in touch again. Call me if you see him."

"Sure. Sure I will. Bye."

Mary replaced the receiver slowly, staring at the phone. So Charlie was out. It could mean no good, no good at all. Charlie was out, and he'd said he was coming to see them. She grimaced. It didn't matter what he'd done; he was still her son. She had a duty. Despite everything, he was still her son, her flesh and blood.

She moved back to stand above the small table, not sitting. She reached down to flick through the pages of one of her magazines, turning each page slowly, scanning, but not really seeing the glossy photos, looking in vain for something to distract her mind from the thoughts now running through her head.

After a while, she sighed and turned to look out the front at the ocean, watching the waves as they rolled in and crashed against the beach.

-37-

Walter

For some reason, Walter was feeling more than a little nervous about the dinner engagement with Angelica. Had he simply accepted the invitation to bolster that sense of disconnectedness he'd been cultivating since the divorce and the move to Woodford Park? The town's constructed isolation, his distance from the city, his removal from the social contacts and network that had evolved as part of his past life all contributed to that detachment, but perhaps it was something he simply constructed as a reaction against his circumstance, something designed by default. He didn't know. Now there was this unexpected liaison, this get together that on the surface was innocent, but beneath, held other possibilities, the sort of possibilities that always came when a man and a woman got together in a potentially intimate setting. He wondered, briefly, whether it was mere circumstance, action by default, or something else that was driving it. He mulled it over for a while and then ended up berating himself for overthinking. What could be the harm, anyway?

He'd spent some time browsing the shelves at the corner store, seeing if he could pick up something worthy of a dinner with someone new. He didn't want to turn up with a completely undrinkable bottle, and he'd finally settled on a mid-priced Chianti, though nothing in the little shop was truly reasonable with their mark-up on top. Chianti was acceptable though; Angelica had said Italian was the order of the day, so it fit. When at the store, he had considered picking up a bunch of cellophane-wrapped flowers from the bucket that sat out the front, but then changed his mind. Not only did it seem slightly tacky, he decided that he didn't want to deliver too much of a message.

Around six-thirty, wearing his good sports jacket and a decent pair of trousers, he grabbed the bottle and headed out, stifling his trepidation and determined to enjoy the evening. It had been too long since he'd engaged in something truly social. It would do him good to get out of the solitary existence he'd been leading, at least for a change. He had no idea what the evening was likely to deliver, but it was something to break the routine, or so he told himself. Angelica, as a woman, per se, was not unattractive, that was for sure, but he wasn't going to think about that, because until it was revealed to be anything else, the evening was nothing more than a spot of simple companionship. Two lost souls and all that. He had something to talk about anyway, after Bill's visit. Sure, he'd agreed to keep it quiet, but it was Angelica who he'd talked to about the old hotel in the first place, and in a way, it was she who had sparked his deeper curiosity and encouraged him to get involved. What harm could it do?

He was humming slightly as he reached her place. She was right; it was easy enough to find perched up on the top of the hill there. A steep path rose up toward the front porch, across a sloping lawn after leading in through a short white fence. Sunset had come and gone on his way up, and now the light yellow blue glow of the twilight sky placed the cottage in half silhouette. Lights were on in a couple of rooms, and Walter stood there, still considering, before he swallowed, took a deep breath and climbed the path. He stood on the porch for a couple of seconds, just listening, before he reached for the bell. She had probably seen or heard him on his way in, so he'd just look like an idiot if he waited any longer. He rang. The smell of cooking drifted to him through the front windows, steaming water and garlic and something else.

Angelica answered the door a few moments later, and Walter waited, grinning a little stupidly, the wine bottle held behind his back.

"So, you found it I see," said Angelica.

He nodded. "Hi."

"Come on in," she said, stepping back, one hand still on the doorframe, holding it wide for him.

Walter did as he was instructed. Stepping into a short hallway, a room leading off to the right and meeting up with another in front of him, Walter stood where he was, waiting for instructions.

"Um, here, I hope this is okay," he said, proffering the bottle of wine. "It was all I could find at this short notice. Next time I'll try a bit harder."

Next time. What was he thinking?

She took the wine. "I'm sure it will be fine," she said, barely looking at it. "Come through."

She led him into a living room with comfortable chairs and windows all around, looking out onto the ocean on one side and the darkness of the cliffs on the other. He peered through the window, and out, off in the distance, there was a ship, far out to sea, lights blazing.

"Yes, it's a nice view from here, but you must get a pretty good line of sight from where you are too," she said.

Walter nodded. "Yes, it's pretty good. Especially in my work room. It helps me concentrate, when it's not distracting me," he said, and smiled again. When the hell had he turned into smiley boy?

"Here, sit down," she said and gestured to an old overstuffed sofa. "Can I get you something to drink, or are you happy to start with the wine first?" She had already retreated in the direction of what he presumed was the kitchen.

"Whatever you want," he said.

"Okay, the wine it is. Give me a moment," she called out.

As he waited, he looked around the room. It was simply but tastefully decorated, a predominance of pastels, and a few touches of lace and velvet. A batik print sat on one wall and what he guessed were Thai temple dancers in pictures on another. There were bits and pieces on shelves, the sorts of things you might pick up as a tourist.

Angelica reappeared with two glasses, one in each hand. She handed one to Walter and sipped at her own, not bothering to sit, but standing there clearly assessing him over the top of her glass.

Walter cleared his throat. "You've travelled a bit, I guess," he said.

"Sure," said Angelica, following his gaze to a couple of the items arrayed around the room. "But not for a while now. There was a time when I travelled a <u>lot</u>. Just couldn't get enough of it. After a while, it became a little samey. Everywhere began to look like everywhere else." She gave a short laugh. "Then it was time for me to stop running away," she said. "Give me a minute." She placed her wine glass down and retreated back into the kitchen.

Funny way of putting it, he thought. Running away from what? Was that what he was doing too? He took a contemplative sip from his glass. The Chianti wasn't too bad. It was drinkable at least.

"Just as well you did bring the wine," Angelica yelled from the kitchen. "If I'm making spaghetti, I always use up nearly a bottle in the sauce. I'm afraid I've nearly run out of what I had. I'm afraid once we've finished your bottle, that we're just going to have to move onto something else. Okay," she said, reappearing in the doorway. "Just a couple of more minutes. Here's to us." She raised her glass and tilted it in his direction.

"Yes, cheers," he said, following her gesture and tilting his own glass and taking another sip.

"Good to have you here, Walter," she said with a smile, then placed down the glass once more, and disappeared back in the direction of the kitchen.

He occupied himself with looking at the little trinkets and keepsakes collected around the room, picking them up carefully and replacing them with just as much care as Angelica clattered away in the kitchen. He carried his wineglass with him on his trek around the room. Angelica appeared once or twice, took a hurried sip from her glass and then retreated back to the kitchen. Next to the living room, a separate dining room sat with table, two place settings and a floral arrangement at the centre. Having exhausted the contents of the current room, he moved into the dining room, wandering around the edges and peering up at more oddments and collections arrayed along the top of a sideboard and a set of corner shelves. It seemed that Angelica had a passion for collecting things, although there didn't seem to be any particular pattern to them. Some people collected owls, or bears or something like that, but the collection ranged from tiny teapots to buildings in miniature. Walter turned to look out of the window, out to the darkened ocean. The ship had moved on a bit and was just nearing the dark on dark of the headland where it would disappear from view.

Angelica appeared behind him and carefully placed a large salad bowl in the table's centre.

"Here," she said. "Make yourself useful, Walter, and give this a toss."

He placed down the wineglass and did as he was instructed while Angelica went back to the kitchen. She reappeared a couple of seconds later with a wooden board, foil wrapped garlic bread on it, placed it down without ceremony and then returned with a large bowl of spaghetti and a pot of sauce which she placed down on a broad ceramic tile.

"Nothing fancy," she said. "But I hope it's okay."

"Smells great," he said.

"Well, come on. Sit. Sit. No standing on ceremony here," she said and laughed.

-38-

Angelica

The sauce was pretty good, she thought, even if she did say so herself, and the wine wasn't bad either. Over the salad and garlic bread, Angelica and Walter had traded bits of history with each other, memories of their lives, things that she could taste and roll through her mind. Of course she glossed several of the incidents and the whole latter part of the story with Johan Her Man. She told him about how Johan and she had met, how they had come to move in together, and the several years they had spent together before he had gone, before her great loss, but about the loss she said nothing. That belonged in her memory and wasn't up for public discussion just yet, at least not with Walter. Compared to her own existence, Walter's life had been pretty normal really. He was a little awkward and conservative, but it lent him a kind of clumsy charm. She was starting to think about the possibilities.

They finished off the spaghetti, cleared away the plates and moved on to a rich chocolate cake she had brought just down the road, and then coffee and liqueur. In keeping with the evening's theme, she'd managed to find a not half-bad grappa secreted in one of the top kitchen cupboards, though she couldn't for the life of her remember where it had come from. She relocated them to the living room for their coffee, sitting on the big comfortable couch, bottle of grappa and coffee pot on the table in front of them. In bits and pieces, they'd been through the past, their respective moves to Woodford Park, and now it was time for the present.

"So, Walter," she said. "Have you thought about how long you might stay in Woodford Park?"

He sipped at his coffee and looked thoughtful. "I don't know really. It's a nice enough place to end up, certainly. I guess it depends upon all sorts of things that I have no control over really." He shrugged. "Perhaps I'll end up staying, perhaps not. Who knows? What about you?"

"Oh, I think I'm here for good now," she said. "I can't see much happening that would change that. I like this house. I like the town. I like the people. One of the things that appeals to me is its simplicity and its consistency, I suppose. Woodford Park doesn't change very much. It's reliable. You can depend on it."

Walter gave a little frown.

"What?" she asked.

"Mmmm. I don't know. What would happen if the place changed? Would that change your mind?"

Angelica frowned in turn. "I don't know. Why would it? People change. I guess places change over time, but I don't see that happening here."

He put down his coffee cup. "But let's say it did. What then?"

"I don't know. I guess so. It depends. What makes you think it might anyway?" She peered into his face, looking for some clue as to what he was thinking. He gave a little secret grin to himself and took another sip of grappa, then turned to look at her.

"It's supposed to be a secret, but I guess it won't do any harm."

"What, Walter?"

"Well...I'm kind of working on something at the moment. You know we've talked about the old hotel, right. Well, I'm working on a project right at the moment that will transform the old place. It will be a real injection of life for

Woodford Park, or so Bill Gundersen and his wife seem to think."

He looked at her, waiting for her reaction, seeming like he was waiting for nothing more than for her to be impressed by what he'd just told her.

He had another thing coming. "I don't quite know, Walter. What is it you're saying?" She looked at him steadily, waiting for him to fill in some more details.

"Well, there's this consortium, an investment company of some sort. They want to make over the old place, turn it into some sort of upmarket spa. They've engaged me to do the design work. It's a big project, or at least could turn into one. I guess what they are thinking of doing will take a year or so. There will need to be permissions and everything, but I can't see that being a problem. It's not too far off what the old place used to be after all. Exclusive hotel, exclusive spa…not much difference really is there?"

Angelica stared at him. "You're kidding me, right?"

"No. Not at all." He smiled and shook his head slowly, proudly. "Not at all. And it looks like I'm going to wind up being the one that changes the face of Woodford Park."

"Huh," said Angelica, putting her glass down on the table with a loud clunk. "Not if I've got anything to do with it."

Walter looked confused. "What…?"

"Just what I said, Walter Travis. Not if I've got anything to do with it." She gave him a hard look with her jaw set. "Woodford Park is just fine as it is, Walter. It doesn't need any group of businessmen from outside changing what it is. I suggest you drop these ideas of yours pretty damned quickly."

Walter looked a little surprised, almost disbelieving. "What?" he said. "I'm just the architect. It doesn't matter what I do. I just design what it's going to look like, make sure it works. It doesn't matter if it's me or someone else. If they don't like what they see, they can just as easily hire another architect. That won't stop them going ahead."

"That doesn't matter," said Angelica, her jaw becoming more firmly set. "We don't want it. You should simply tell them that you're not going to do the work and they should leave us alone."

"Oh, come on," he said, an exasperated tone creeping into his voice. "You're being unreasonable. Angelica. You've got to see that. I thought you'd be interested. Well, if you're not, then fine. Let's talk about something else."

She gave a short laugh. "No," she told him. "And I'm not being unreasonable. I care about this place. You can't just change the subject."

"I'm sorry, Angelica," he told her. "I shouldn't have brought it up in the first place. Too much wine, too much grappa, maybe that. I don't know. Stupidly I thought it was something that might impress you. Let's talk about something else."

"No," she told him. "You just can't squirm out of it like that, Walter. I'm serious. You need to tell them you're not going ahead."

He looked at her in clear disbelief. "I'm sorry."

"I think I'm being pretty clear."

Walter shook his head. "Yes, I think you are. Maybe it would be better if I went home now," he said and got to his feet. He stood there, expectantly, as if waiting for her to change the subject and ask him to sit, but that wasn't something Angelica was likely to do in a hurry. She stared up at him saying nothing.

"All right then," he said. "Thank you for dinner. Thank you for a…pleasant…evening."

"You should think very hard about what I said, Walter," she told him.

Walter shook his head. "All right. Good night, Angelica," he said and headed for the door.

She watched the place where he had stood, mulling over the conversation, long after the front door had closed. In fact, she decided, she knew exactly what she was going to do.

-39-

The Meeting

Walter tried to put the whole sorry incident from his mind, and managed to do so, for at least a couple of days. He still didn't know what he'd been thinking, but what was done was done, or so he thought. The events of the other night were brought back to him in sharp relief prompted by a knock on his back door. Walter peered through the window of his workroom, to see Bill Gundersen standing at the door, rocking back and forth on his heels. Walter stepped quickly over to open the door for him.

"Bill, hello."

"Walter. Who's been a naughty boy then?" said Bill.

"What? You'd better come in."

Bill stepped past him and wandered over to stand at the drafting table, looking down at the currently-in-progress sketches that Walter had been working on.

"So," he said. "This was supposed to be between us, between you me and Doris, but it appears that someone has been a bit talkative, eh Walter?" He looked up at Walter, still standing by the door.

"How do you mean? I mean…"

"Well, damage is done," said Bill. "There's going to be a town meeting tonight."

"What?" said Walter, slowly closing the door and then stepping back to join Bill in front of the table. "What town meeting?"

"I knew if this got out we'd have trouble," said Bill. "You've gone and told someone about The Bellevue, haven't you? It wasn't Doris or me."

Walter thought quickly. Oh no. Angelica.

"Well, yes, I suppose I did. But I didn't see how it could do any harm. It was pretty innocent really."

Bill stared out of the window at the edge of the hotel across the beach. "Maybe so, but this is the way Woodford Park works. A word here, a whisper there. It doesn't take long. So, whoever it was you told has been busy flapping, stirring up opposition to the project. Means we have some work to do you and I."

"But…"

"Like I said, town meeting tonight. You better come along, front and centre. We're going to have to put the case for how this is going to be a benefit to Woodford Park, and I'm going to need you to help me. We want to quieten down the noise a bit. Don't want to scare off the investors if you know what I mean. They're due back in a couple of days to have a look at what you've done and talk through the plans. You think about what you might tell the rest of our Woodford Park residents to shut them up. Meanwhile, Doris and me will do our bit in the background, okay? I'll come over and pick you up around 6:45. Meeting's up in the old Moore Street hall. It will take us about ten minutes to get there. Don't want to drive; it would make too much of a statement according to Doris and she's usually right about these things. Anyway, I'll see you then."

Bill clapped him on the arm, and then made his way to the door and let himself out. He gave Walter a brief wave as he crossed the back windows and headed back around the side of the house.

Walter stood in front of the window, looking out across the beach and thinking. Even more, now, he was regretting the little incident with Angelica. Stupid. And what the hell was he going to say to a bunch of the town residents. He'd need to think about that. It wasn't as if he wasn't used to standing up in front of groups of people to make a pitch, but this was going to be different. He wasn't selling a bunch of drawings and plans this time. It was a whole different prospect.

He spent the rest of the day riffling through his sketches and phrasing sentences and speeches, discarding them one by one, all the time staring intermittently at the old hotel, trying to think of appropriate things to say.

Fifteen minutes before the appointed hour, right on time, Bill turned up at the back door again. Walter took a last sip from the mug of coffee he was drinking, put it down beside the drafting table and patted his pockets to make sure he had his keys. He already had his coat on in preparation.

"You ready, Walter?" asked Bill as Walter pulled the door shut.

"As ready as I'll ever be, I guess," he replied.

"Good, good. Doris is out front." Bill led the way around the side of the house. "You're not bringing anything with you?"

"No, I think it's better if I don't," said Walter. "Don't want to give them too much ammunition right?"

"Yes, good thinking," Bill replied.

Doris was standing by the front gate. "Hello, love," she said as Bill and Walter approached. "When we get there," she said, "we'll sit up near the back. Don't want to appear too eager."

"Right," said Walter.

"Anyway," she said as the headed down towards the corner. "I've been chatting to a few of the girls. I guess we'll just have to see how we go."

They walked together in silence, down past the shops and up the hill to Moore Street. When they got to the small wooden hall, the doors were already open, and Walter could see chairs arranged in rows inside, most of them occupied. One or two faces that he half recognised stood outside still, but they started to make their way inside as he, Bill and Doris made their way up the front steps and inside to the back row.

At the front of the hall was a small raised stage and on it sat a table with three chairs. On one side sat a woman Walter didn't recognise, and on the other, an older gentleman that he thought he recognised from the beach. In the centre sat Angelica, decked out in a knitted shawl and floral dress, her hair piled up on top of her head. A slow buzz of conversation murmured through the hall, until the woman on the left cleared her throat and spoke in a clear loud voice that cut above the noise.

"Right. I think we're all here, or enough to get started anyway. Gerry, if you could close the door? Thank you."

Walter scanned the faces, some familiar, some not. There was the little Indian man from the corner shop and the woman who ran the snack bar. Over at one corner towards the front sat the old lady who regularly walked her dog on the small beach leading across to the hotel. One or two others were also faces he knew.

The woman at front continued. "As you all know, it has been brought to our attention that a group of people are planning a reconstruction of The Bellevue. As far as we know, they plan to turn it into some sort of spa resort. That's correct, Angelica, isn't it?" She turned to face Angelica and received a nod. "Some of you may ask how we know this, but let's just say that we do."

"No," said Angelica, interrupting. "I can tell you for a fact exactly how we know." She pointed across the assembled heads directly at Walter. "Sitting back there is Walter Travis.

For those of you who don't know him, he's an architect and he told me all about the plans."

A few heads turned to look in Walter's direction.

"What we need to decide," she continued, "is if that's something we want in Woodford Park, and I for one am pretty sure that it's not." The heads turned back. "Why would we want some group of businessmen from the city deciding they're going to make over our town? Because that's what will happen. Put some rich people's resort right in the middle of our lives and just think of the effect it will have."

Bill stood then and the woman at the front nodded at him. "I'll tell you what effect it will have," said Bill. "It will revitalise the town; that's what it will do. There'll be an injection of money, commerce. Any one of us here who runs businesses will know how much we depend on the tourist trade. Deepak there. Carl. Mary. I bet every one of you could do with the extra business."

There were scattered murmurs of assent.

"Yes, Mr. Gundersen," said Angelica from the front. "That may be so, but we've seen those resorts from further down the coast. All of us have seen them. The sort of people they attract. What they do to the coastline. What they do to people's way of life. Do we want to turn our town into an extension of the hotel services? Our town, Mr. Gundersen. Because that's what will happen."

"You can't know that, love," said Doris from beside Walter.

And so it went. Voices came from the front and from the middle and the back, one by one stating arguments for and against. Walter watched Angelica and with every exchange, her mouth seemed to take on a firmer set. In the end, nobody called on him to say anything and Walter was quite relieved about that much. Bill and Doris seemed to be handling things quite comfortably on their own. In the end, there was no real resolution, but it was clear that Woodford Park's residents were divided in their opinion.

"So, what now, Grace?" said someone from a couple of rows in front. Walter learned later that she had been a town council member at some stage of her life before moving to Woodford Park.

"Well," she said from her place at the front table. "We will have to see how things develop. There will be plans, I imagine, and they will become available for viewing and appropriate commentary. Perhaps nothing will go ahead at all, but until there is a firm proposal, we will need to keep an eye on developments. Clearly, Bill, you're involved. It will be up to you to keep us informed. And Doris…you make sure he does. I will take it on myself to make sure that I keep abreast of things as they eventuate, and I'll be sure to let you know if anything starts moving ahead. I'm not sure that we can do anything at this stage, and I don't think we have a clear opinion one way or another. Let's just make sure we are prepared, for now. And that, I think, is that."

Walter got to his feet and turned to walk up to the end of the row, but not before he had caught Angelica gracing him with a pointed, narrowed-eye look. He let it slide off him, turning his attention to the people shuffling out of the row in front of him. So much for a quiet life. Angelica had made pretty sure he was going to be well known in Woodford Park from now on.

Outside the hall, Bill and Doris had stopped to chat with a few people, but Walter tapped Bill on the shoulder and gestured that he was going to leave them and go back home. It was Doris who nodded to him in understanding.

He left the front of the hall and headed down the street alone, his hands shoved into his pockets and his head slightly bowed. He still didn't get it. What had he done to Angelica anyway? It was just one of those things, he guessed.

-40-

Walter

The representatives of the city consortium had come and gone. Walter had walked them through some initial sketches in Bill's front office, with Bill hovering nervously in the background while Doris watched from the doorway leading into the back of the house. As he had explained what he was thinking to what were now his clients, Bill had made to add comments a couple of times, but Doris had rapidly shushed him with a gesture and a frown. Bill had stood there, clearing his throat and clasping his hands behind his back, dutifully keeping his words to himself.

The meeting had gone quite well, from what Walter could tell. The men from the city had both seemed enthusiastic about what he was proposing, and they left with firm handshakes and smiles and encouragement to continue on the path he was heading down. After they had climbed into their big black car parked out in front of the Gundersen's house and headed off back to the city, Bill turned to him with a broad smile on his face.

"They looked as if they liked where you were going," he said. "So what now, Walter?"

Walter looked out toward the ocean while he thought. "Well, I need to do up some more detailed plans. I need to think about a couple of things, and I'm a little unsure what to do about the kitchen facilities, that whole basement thing is a little awkward. I need to think it through."

"How do you mean?" said Bill.

"Well, you know…it depends what they want to do about providing service to the clientele. I am pretty sure with what they're proposing, there are going to be strict dietary requirements, that sort of thing. I need to make sure we can plan the facilities accordingly, but make proper use of the way the place is laid out. I don't think we should undertake an extensive remodelling, just try to use the existing configuration as much as possible."

"Ah, I see…." Bill didn't sound very convinced, but Doris nodded from her spot at the doorway and Walter had already determined where the true decision-making power lay.

"Let me get you a cup of tea," said Doris. "We can talk about next steps."

"Sure."

Bill led him back inside and they each took a seat around Bill's desk as Doris disappeared to attend to the tea.

"Really we should be cracking a beer to celebrate, don't you think, Walter?" said Bill. "But you know, Doris doesn't like me drinking during the day."

"I heard that, Bill," she called out from inside. "And for good reason too, my love."

Bill humphed, his gaze sliding away from Walter's face and down to the plans, still spread out on the desk.

"What about the meeting?" said Walter.

"I think we can handle them," said Bill, his enthusiasm quickly returning. "You know. This is a small town, a community. They don't like change that much, but in the end they're going to see what's good for them."

"You're sure?"

"Of course," said Bill. "Don't you worry about that. Doris and me, we've been here long enough to know what's what."

At that moment, Doris reappeared with a tray, teapot, milk jug, bowl of sugar and three cups, which she placed on the desk, shuffling Walter's sketches to one side.

"Yes, Bill's right," she said, as she started to pour. "We know the people in this town. Of course there are a couple of hotheads among them, but for the most part, they aren't the ones with true influence in Woodford Park. It's the long-term residents who really decide what's what, not these newcomers, if you know what I mean."

"I guess I'm one of those newcomers," said Walter as he accepted his cup of tea.

Doris sat and sipped at her own cup. "Sure, love, but not in the same way. There are newcomers and there are newcomers. It's a state of mind. We get our fair share of people who just turn up, like what they see and stay around for a while. It doesn't matter if you've been here for two years or twenty though, in the end. It's all about what's good for our little community here. That's what matters."

"So don't you worry about that bit of brouhaha," said Bill. "We can take care of that. You just need to concentrate on doing the work."

"Yes, I guess so," said Walter and took another sip of his tea, then placed his cup back down on the desk, and slid his sketches around in front of him. "You know, I am still a bit worried about this," he said, pointing at the area where the kitchen lay. "I haven't had a real look at it. I probably need to go up to the place again and stand up there for a while and think about it. I'll get more of feel for the space and the dynamics that way. Pity the power's not on up there. It's awfully dark."

"Well," said Bill. "Now that we're getting closer, I might be able to do something about that. Why don't you go up and have a look and I'll sort that out in the meantime? It might take a couple of days, but you can still get something done while we're waiting for the power guys to get their act together, right?"

"Yes, sure," said Walter. "In fact I'll head up there in a couple of hours and see what I can do."

"Okay, well you let me know how you get on, Walter," said Bill.

Walter reached for his sketches and scraped them together before slipping them inside the black folder he had carried them in. "In fact, I think I'll just drop these off and head up there now," he said. "Thanks for the tea, Doris."

"You take care, love," she said. "You did good today. Bill will be in touch with you later on, after he's had a chance to sort out getting the power turned on and also had a chance to talk to the city boys, see if they've had any other thoughts. We want to keep them warm you know, but that's our job, Walter."

"Right," he said, clutching the sketches beneath one arm as he stood and turned for the door. Bill ushered him out and gave him a gentle slap on the back as he opened the door. "Good job," he said. "Good job."

Walter nodded to himself as he wandered across the street and back to his place. It was a good job, so far and it was more than that. The project, the old hotel, they were capturing his imagination. So what if the town was up in arms about what he was doing. Doris was probably right. She and Bill knew the ins and outs of the residents and he was sure that they could take care of the resistance. What was important now was to capitalise on the progress they'd already made.

He'd spent some time thinking about the minor disaster that the association with Angelica had turned into. In a way, he'd been fooling himself anyway. Any port in a storm. She was so unlike anyone he'd usually been drawn to, and in retrospect, it had probably been little more than a combination of circumstance and convenience or opportunity. What had he been thinking anyway?

He reached his place, wandered into the back room and dumped the folder on top of his drafting table, standing for a few moments and looking up at The Bellevue. No, despite her protests, despite the noise from the other vocal residents, this was something worth doing, if not for Woodford Park, then at least for himself. He tapped the folder a couple of times with his fingers and then turned to find where he'd put the hefty flashlight that would give him some light in the subterranean kitchen and service complex that lay beneath the old hotel. What he needed to do was exactly what he'd explained to Bill and Doris. He needed to stand in the space, get a feel for it, understand, almost sense how it would function when the work had finally been done.

He located the flashlight, the keys to The Bellevue and shrugged on his coat before heading up to do just that, pictures of his sketches made real wandering through his head. There was a stiff breeze blowing along the coast road and the ocean was steel grey, the waves crashing hard against the base of the cliffs. He could taste the salt spray in the air and the wind whipped his hair around his head. A chill from the air made his fingers ache within the looped handle of the flashlight. There was no traffic along the road, but as he looked up towards the end of Ball's Point, he could see a solitary figure sitting out there on the bench, watching the beach below, snakes of blonde hair lifting in the air. She was facing the other direction, away from him, but he quickened his pace, almost guiltily, but then admonished himself for the action. What did he care if she saw what he was up to? It harked back to the feelings he had in the latter days of his marriage to Pamela, that sense of guilt, whether he had done anything wrong or not, and that wasn't something he wanted to be reminded of really. It wasn't something he wanted to feel and there wasn't any reason why he should. He sniffed and turned his attention to the old hotel. That was what he needed to be thinking about. Past glories were better than past failures.

At the top of the bluff in front of the hotel, the wind was stronger, and Walter could feel it pushing against him, almost as if urging him onwards. The clouds raced above, smudged and dirty with threatened rain. The ocean below showed patches of darker grey, stirring blackness in the depths. He walked around the cliff side of the hotel, around to the rear, feeling in one pocket for the pencil and notebook he'd slipped into his coat before leaving the house. He reached the still split door at the rear. The door gave him a bit of trouble today, as if in the meantime the old hotel had shifted its weight, wedging the door further in position. Finally he managed it and slipped inside, grateful for the respite from the outside wind, though he could hear it, whistling around the edges of the old structure and pushing fingers through the numerous chinks and cracks in windows, doors and walls, whistling on and off when there was a particularly powerful gust. He headed up the corridor, slowly, feeling the walls and the spaces, confirming the work he had done. It felt right. He knew he was on the right path.

In the main lobby, he paused for a couple of minutes in the semi-gloom, listening to the wind and the shift of old dried leaves, scraping across tiled floors. The smell of damp and dust was strong today and the dim light heavy with the outside greyness. Walter closed his eyes and felt, felt the presence of the old building and the ghosts of memory that walked the vast space around him. He could do something for this place, he knew, make it live again. Memory was just memory, after all.

A deep scraping noise came from somewhere behind and he opened his eyes and looked back over his shoulder, still, holding his breath. No, it was just his imagination, or the wind shifting a window in its ancient frame. He let out his breath again and reached down to turn on the torch. He shone it around the wide open space sending reflections back from the darkened windows, silver black in the pool of light. Turning the beam back towards the rear of the space, he walked toward the darkened staircase sitting at the back and leading down to the lower level. He really needed to understand the space and how it would work. It would be far better once Bill had managed to get the power back on, and who knew if any of the light fixtures down there actually still worked, but for now, he could make a start.

The staircase led down to a corridor, and Walter picked his way carefully, conscious that although unlikely, there might be some deterioration of the structure down here. He didn't want one of the stairs to suddenly crumble beneath his feet and send him tumbling to the lower depths. Who knew, he could lie down her for days without being found. The staircase was definitely too narrow, and he'd have to think about widening the space to turn it into something more practical. At the bottom, a broader corridor led off around a corner. He shone the light, but there was nothing there but blank wall, stained with watermarks and yellow in the oval beam. To the right was darkness.

There was a noise from up ahead, and Walter froze. This was crazy. There couldn't be anything down here, unless some animal had managed to find its way inside and had decided to make its home here. He didn't want to come face to face with some wild dog or something. He swallowed and took the few steps to where the corridor turned. Carefully, slowly, he peered around the corner, shining the torch. There was light. How could there be light? And then suddenly there wasn't. Double doors, faded red sat at the end of a short passageway with round glass windows at the top of each. There had definitely been light.

Walter was feeling nervous now. No, more than nervous. "Um, hello?" he called.

There was a bang of something against metal in the darkness beyond the doors.

"Hello? Is there someone there?" he said.

Nothing.

Tentatively, Walter took a step towards the double doors, holding the flashlight in front of him like a weapon. He took another step, and then another.

"Hello?"

Still nothing.

Using his shoulder, he pushed at the leftmost door, easing it open, wincing and gritting his teeth as it creaked with the pressure. Peering through the narrow opening, he shone the light through, trying to make out things in the darkness. A wide room ran back, low ceiling, the light reflecting faintly from rusting metal. There was another smell down here, something other than must and dirt and old buildings.

He took a step inside, continuing to shine the light in a broad arc across the floor. Towards the corner of the room there was something blue and bundled and the edge of something else, metallic.

"You stay where you are," came a voice from the shadows.

Walter, without even thinking about it, lifted the flashlight in the direction of the voice. The beam dazzled the speaker, forcing him to screw up his eyes in a big heavy face, teeth bared.

"Argh, fuck!" said the voice. "I told you. You'd better get away now. You've been warned."

Walter lifted his hand, took a step forward. He was confused. What was this guy doing here?

Then there was a loud noise that echoed deafeningly from rusting metal and the low ceiling, a flash, more yellow in the darkness than the whiteness of the torch, and something slammed against him.

The flashlight fell from his hands, smashing against the floor, and everything was black, apart from the sudden redness of pain bursting somewhere in his chest and behind his eyes.

Moments later and there was only blackness, nothing else.

-41-

Discovery

"Doris? Where are you, my love?" Bill called through the house. As far as he was concerned, the meeting had turned out quite well, but he wanted to reassure himself that his impression was right. Doris emerged at the back door, wiping her hands down her front. She'd been out with the dogs, of course.

"What is it, Bill?"

"We're all right, aren't we? I mean the other night went okay, right?"

Doris reached up and poked at her hair. She had her thinking face on. "I think so, Bill, but you know, we can't settle back yet. There's still work to do. Your man Walter didn't help us blabbing away to that Angelica woman. We're going to have to keep an eye on things. If I were you, love, I'd pop over to Walter's place and see how he's getting on with the plans. We need to keep these city guys warm."

She headed into the kitchen. It looked like a cup of tea was in order. He heard the sound of water, the kettle being filled.

"Why don't you go and do that now?" she said from the kitchen.

"Right you are, then," said Bill, and headed for the door.

It took him only a couple of minutes to cross the street, walk up the block a little and pass down the driveway at the side of Walter's place. He knew, now, that Walter would be most likely to be found in the back room, particularly if he was working. He climbed the back steps and peered in through the wide window, but the back room was empty. He frowned and then knocked. Silence.

"Walter, you in there?" he called and then knocked again. Still nothing. He was probably down at the shops or something. Scratching his head, Bill turned around and made his way back home.

When he got there, Doris was sitting in the living room, sipping at her cup of tea and watching something on the television, a daytime talk show.

"That was quick, love. So, how's he doing?"

"No sign. He's not there. Maybe he's gone out shopping or something. I'll try in a couple of hours."

Doris nodded and turned her attention back to the show.

Bill waited for a couple of hours before heading over to Walter's again. Once more, the place was silent. He scratched his head and wandered back.

"No sign of him," he said. "I wonder where he is."

"Perhaps he's gone up to The Bellevue, Bill. Why don't you jump into the car and go see? He's probably working up there."

Bill nodded, went into the front room and opened the wall cabinet holding the sets of keys for the various properties they managed. He grabbed the other set for The Bellevue, shoved them into his pocket, snagged his car keys from on top of the desk and went out to the car. It didn't hurt to have a look at the old place anyway even if Walter wasn't up there. True to his word, over the last couple of days, he'd managed to have the power reconnected and he might as well check if it was working properly.

It was only a short drive, down the hill and up the other side to the access road and then into the bare earth parking area out front. He got out of the car, locked it and stood for a few moments, hands on his hips staring at the old building, trying to imagine what it would look like. Of course he'd seen Walter's preliminary sketches, but they weren't really enough to give Bill a vision of how The Bellevue might look. It would take some good, artistic representations to give him a real idea. Still, that sort of stuff was up to Walter. It didn't matter what Bill thought; what mattered was whether the city guys liked what they saw. So far, it seemed to be working. Let Walter attend to the artistic side of the business; Bill could worry about the negotiation.

He pulled the bunch of keys out of his pocket and wandered across the empty parking lot, climbed over the low wooden railing, not bothering to walk around and headed up to the front entrance. The old place still looked the same as it had last time he'd been up here. The thick chain was still in place, looped through the large metal doors at the front, the heavy padlock still closed. Bill grunted to himself. Walter had probably just used the back entrance rather than fiddling about with the chain, but Bill was here now, and he couldn't be bothered walking around the back. He undid the padlock, pulled the chain free and threaded it back through the holes in the metalwork, opening the door finally with the loud protesting screech of rusted hinges. A few flakes of rust and paint fell to the ground and wound up patterning one sleeve. He brushed them off, muttering to himself.

Just inside the metal doors was a set of switches to the left of the entranceway. He flipped one, looked around, but nothing appeared to have happened. He flipped another. Still muttering, he pushed through the double wooden doors into the reception area. As he did so, a cloud of dust floated down to surround him, shafts of light from the front windows cutting through with regular lines. He coughed, patted at his body and shook his head.

"Walter?" he called. "You here?" His voice echoed around the lobby. Somewhere further in at the back of the building came the sound if wings beating. He'd disturbed a pigeon or something. "Walter?"

No answering voice came, just the echoes of his own.

"Hmph," he grunted to himself. Where was he?

He looked around the lobby and finally located the main switches over by where the reception desk had originally stood. One by one, he flipped them, and was finally rewarded as a couple of bulbs in one of the old dusty chandeliers burned yellowly into life. One of them immediately burned out with a flash and a sizzling pop.

"Walter, you in here?" Bill called again. Still nothing. If he was here, he would have answered by now. Jingling the keys in one hand, he wandered towards the back staircase that led down to the bowels of the place. That was the problem area, according to Walter, if Bill remembered correctly, so it wouldn't hurt to have a look down there. A light switch sat on the wall just inside the doorway to the staircase leading down, and this time, Bill was rewarded with a glow of whiter light than the old bulbs in the chandelier. The stairs were dusty, showing the marks of footprints leading down and up. Okay, so it looked like Walter had been down here, but if he was down here now, surely he would have tried the lights. Bill took a step down.

"Walter, you down here?" Nothing.

Still fondling the big bunch of keys, jingling them together, Bill walked down the rest of the staircase. Twin doors at the end of the passageway led to the kitchen area. Bill headed straight for them, pushed his way through, and in the light filtering through the rounded glass windows at the top of each door, located the light switches and turned them on. Fluorescent tubes lined the ceiling. One of them flickered on and off, failing to light. Another sat with grey and white bands running down its length, but two of them lit properly bathing what was the kitchen area in a dusty white glow. There was a smell down here, and Bill wrinkled his nose. Large metal fixtures were set around the walls, cupboards, stoves and a big central fitting, tarnished and blackened with age. Across in the corner, was a pile of stuff. It looked like an old blue sleeping bag, and there were bits and pieces of food containers, drink cans scattered about. How the hell had that happened? Towards the rear of the room were doors leading off to other spaces beyond. He continued his survey of the room, looking at the ceiling, the walls and...

"Jesus!" said Bill.

Half propped against the wall on one side of the door lay a figure. Bill knew straight away it was Walter. A massive darkened stain marked his chest. Pieces of a broken flashlight lay scattered on the floor beside him.

Bill swallowed.

"Shit," he said. He leaned over, peering at Walter, making sure. There was no doubt—Walter Travis was definitely dead. There was a dark pool on the floor around him too, that spread to one side.

"Jesus," said Bill again, backing out through the double doors and swallowing.

He didn't think about what might have happened here. He couldn't think about it. All he could see was Walter's body half-propped against the wall. He climbed the back stairs as quickly as he could, his heart beating, his mouth gone dry. Doris would know what to do. He had to tell Doris.

He didn't even bother with the chain on the front doors of the hotel. It simply didn't seem to matter.

– 42 –

Aftermath

Doris did know what to do. She knew exactly what to do. She called the police, but not before sitting Bill down and handing him a stiff whiskey.

"You're sure he was dead, love?" she asked him.

"Yes, Doris, I'm sure he was dead."

Bill still looked shaken, and she tut-tutted and fussed about him, making sure he took a healthy swallow from his glass before questioning him further.

"So how could it happen?"

"I don't know. It looked like someone had been living down there. Whoever it was had a gun; that much is pretty clear. Well, I guess it was a gun."

Doris frowned. None of it was making real sense. Why would someone want to shoot Walter Travis? Her mind went to unlikely places, ticking off the town residents. Nobody in Woodford Park was hot-headed enough to do something stupid like that. Of course there had been the town meeting, the opposition to the plans for The Bellevue, but again, it was just too unlikely. If Bill said that it looked like someone had been living in the old hotel, then it seemed as if it was just a very unfortunate set of events. She sat down and looked at Bill who was hunched over, clasping his whiskey glass in both hands.

"Don't you worry, love; the police will sort it out."

The knock on their door came about twenty minutes later. It took the local law enforcement that long to get over from the next town. Two uniformed officers stood at the front door as Doris opened it. One of them wore sunglasses and he reached up to remove them just before he spoke.

"Mrs Gundersen?"

"Yes, that's me. But call me Doris."

"It was you who made the call?"

"Yes, that was me. Why don't you boys come inside?" She led them into the living room where they stood awkwardly just inside the doorway.

"This is Bill," she said. "It was him who found the body."

Bill placed his glass down and stood, extending a hand to each of the officers. "Bill," he said. "Bill Gundersen."

"So what can you tell us, Mr. Gundersen? Where is this body?"

Bill wiped his palms on the tops of his trouser legs. "Yeah. It's up at the old hotel, The Bellevue. Downstairs. He's been shot by the looks of things. Or at least I think so. His name's Walter Travis."

"So you know the victim…"

"Yes," said Doris. "Bill and he were working on a project with the old place. Walter is an….was an architect."

"I see," said one of the officers. "Well, Mr. Gundersen…Bill. You'd better take us to look at this body, show us where it is. Is that okay with you?"

Bill nodded.

Doris led them out to the front and watched from the door as Bill climbed into the back of the police car, still looking shaky. She stayed there in the doorway, one hand up on the frame watching as the police car turned the corner and disappeared from view. The police would sort things out now. Whatever had happened to Walter, well, that was their business now. Bill could show them what was what, and then the both of them could back off. There were bound to be a few questions, but nothing she couldn't handle. She and Bill would tell them everything they could and leave the rest up to them. Whatever had happened to Walter was terrible of course, but there was nothing she could do about it.

Meanwhile, she wondered what the heck they were going to do about the project. Bill was clearly in no state to think about it and probably wouldn't be. She doubted that there was any way they could keep this whole thing quiet — not in Woodford Park. And what about the plans? It would be a real pity to let them go to waste, wouldn't it? She sighed and shook her head as she gently closed the door. Somehow, she was going to have to work out what to do. It looked like she was going to have to worry about what would happen with Walter too.

-43-

A Funeral

It was a grey day, grey and cold. The wind blew steadily across the small, fenced plot of land, causing people to reach for their hats and hold them in place. Below, the waves crashed against the cliffs, throwing salt spray high into the air where it was seized by the wind and whipped higher above, sprinkling everyone with a fine cold mist. Most of them wore black, though Angelica, as loath as she was to wear the darker colours, tempered it with a deep satin purple, worked with darker flowers. She wore no hat. Across the street from the cemetery sat a line of cars, parked along the small siding, including the hearse. The local minister stood at the head of the plot, the pages of his book fluttering in the wind, his longer strands of grey hair whipping back and forth wildly like pieces of thin dirty string. Many of the town's people had turned out. The Gundersens of course, Bill and Doris both looking sombre and serious as well they might. Off to one side, standing back a little apart, was Mary, from the snack bar by the beach. She looked awkward, shifting her bulk from time to time. Beside her stood her son, the mechanic. Last she had heard, the other son, the one who everyone suspected had done this, was still at large, still roaming free with a weapon and a spirit of violence. They would catch him eventually, she supposed, but that was something beyond her power to predict. Whether they caught him or not, whether it had really been him, it would not change the fact of Walter's death. Angelica scanned the faces for others. There, closer to the head of the gravesite stood a shorter, dumpy woman, dressed all in black, her straight silver brown hair pulled back severely from her face and tied with a black ribbon. Beside her, holding her hand, was a pale young man, short curly dark hair and a long narrow face. He stared fixedly at the gravesite and at the coffin, resting on the green and gold bands ready to lower it into the ground, his jaw set. This must be the son, she thought, and the ex-wife. Now that she looked, she could see a faint resemblance around the young man's eyes. She remembered, the wife's name was Pamela. The woman's lips were moving slightly, silently, not that Angelica would have been able to hear in this wind, but it looked like she might be praying. Closer to Angelica stood another stranger to Woodford Park, a heavyset man with shaved head and large designer sunglasses, a soul patch gracing his lower lip. That would be Walter's partner from the firm he worked for in the city. He stood with his hands clasped behind his back, pushing out the designer suit and emphasising his evident bulk.

Looking around the assembled faces, the minister began to talk. Half of his words were swept away on the wind, the pages of his book riffling back and forth as he struggled to control them and at least an essence of dignity in the circumstance, though Angelica thought it was a little hard with his ridiculous comb-over flapping about above his head. It was not as if she was going to listen to the words anyway. They were formula, ritual and some people needed that. Not Angelica.

Even though Bill had insisted, Angelica was the one who had taken over, throwing herself into the arrangements, dedicating herself to them, despite the fact that she hated everything to do with funerals, even more so, anything that reminded her of death in such a pointed way. After all, she thought, it was the least she could do. In various ways, Woodford Park as an entire community had rallied behind the cause, all of them conscious of the fact that, in some way, it was their responsibility to see that Walter Travis was properly served, along with his memory. His time in the town hadn't been very long, but it had been long enough to embed him forever, though by no design of his own, into the town's history. Walter Travis was a part of Woodford Park now, and would remain so forever. He was as much of a part of the town now as The Bellevue. In the same way, Walter Travis was a part of Angelica's own history, however she wanted to look at it. Perhaps it was that, as much as anything else, that had urged her to take such an active role in the preparations for today, for Walter Travis's final resting place. It would have been unthinkable now that Walter could have been laid to rest anywhere else, and Angelica knew it as soon as she had recalled the conversation she'd had with him about the old graveyard. As soon as she had realised, she had made sure that it would happen that way, though there were no real protests from the residents...none at all.

As the minister finished his words, as he pressed the small device that caused the electronic motors to whirr into motion, haltingly lowering the plain wooden coffin into the depths of the earth, the woman Pamela crossed herself, and the son followed suit. Doris and Bill each stepped forward, took a sprinkle of earth and tossed it into the grave on top of the coffin. Not so the ex-wife and the son. As Angelica watched, they looked at each other, she gave a slight nod, and both of them simply turned and walked back up the rise towards their car parked over the other side of the road. Apparently, they had done their duty. Walter's old partner was an earth-tosser, and so too were a couple of others. The surprise, for Angelica, was Mary. Hesitantly, waiting for more of the assembled people to drift off, the big woman approached the graveside, clutching something before her. Her son stood back. As Mary neared, Angelica could see what it was she was holding—a single white flower. She stood there at the grave's edge for a moment or two, as if considering, and then tossed the flower into the grave. She glanced across to Angelica, then closed her eyes, bowed her head and stood that way for a couple of moments, and then finally turned back to join her son. As soon as she reached him, the son stretched out an arm, put it around her shoulders, and led her back up the slope towards the gate. Strange. Angelica watched them till the rising lawn had hidden them from view.

One by one, the attendees started to drift off up the hill, all except for Bill Gundersen and his wife Doris. Angelica watched them across the rectangular opening of the grave itself. Bill was unable to hold her gaze, and he looked down to the grave itself and then out to sea. Doris met her eyes unflinchingly across the space between them, a fixed set to her jaw, as if daring Angelica. In the end, it was Angelica who broke the contact, turning her own attention, first to the grave, and then out to the churning ocean beyond them.

There you go, Walter, she thought. At least you will know if you can tell where you are after you're dead. You'll have the ocean. You'll have the waves. Maybe, just maybe, that will be enough for you.

She turned away, refusing to meet Doris's eyes, though there was no reason she shouldn't, and made her way up the hill towards the gate.

-44-

The Bellevue

What had happened with Walter, the town, everything else, the city consortium decided in the end that it was all too much for them. Much to Bill and Doris's disappointment, they made excuses and backed off entirely, despite Bill's arguments to the contrary. He just couldn't convince them anymore that it was a good idea. The Bellevue was destined to remain as the old mouldering hunk of memory that it had been for years, an icon in the background of Woodford Park's memory. In some way, Walter had been drawn to a set of circumstances that manoeuvred him into becoming a sacrifice for the continuity of Woodford Park's memory. He had no volition. He had no choice. In some respects, fate conspired against Walter Travis, but in the end, it served the town and what it was and what it was destined to remain. Deep within the guts of The Bellevue, lay the impression of Walter, his memory, impressed upon the building and the echoes of our pasts that lie within the places that we move within.

Angelica understood that, somewhere deep within, that voluntarily or not, Walter had made a sacrifice, and it was because of him that Woodford Park would continue on as it had done before, her sanctuary, her place of personal retreat. Despite the original hostility at their first exploratory dinner, despite the way things had turned out between them, she started, gradually, step by step, to view Walter in a different light. Because of him, the place she called home would remain home, unsullied by the outside intrusions that had been threatened.

Enquiries by the local police led to Mary and it was not long before she told them about Charlie, about his release, about his visit to Woodford Park, and all that she knew about what he had done, or might have done. Much of it was speculation on her part, but she knew her son, and she knew, despite her vain hopes for her boy, what he was truly capable of. The Bellevue was a great place to hole up, local, accessible, but untroubled by random visitors. In that respect, after the armed robbery, Charlie had been smart. How was he to know that some local architect would be wandering the halls and corridors looking for inspiration? How was he to know that some group of city businessmen had tentative plans for the place? How could he? The Bellevue had lain deserted for years, for as long as he could remember, and it seemed ideal as a place to hide, secure, while the heat died down — somewhere familiar and safe. He simply could not account for the possibility that The Bellevue, that Woodford Park might have other plans for him.

A town has its own energy, and it shapes the memory and the possibilities within it. Charlie remembered The Bellevue and he remembered it as it was, as a part of something that was there when he was growing up, but the reality changes over time, and if we are not a part of that reality, then from time to time, our memories can fail to keep pace with what is really there. Did The Bellevue have plans of its own? Did the town have plans of its own? Perhaps. Perhaps Walter was only a tool within a grander design, or perhaps it was merely circumstance and a collaboration of coincidence that Walter walked into by unfortunate chance.

Whatever the real answer was, it served to change Angelica's memory of Walter, her perception of him, and finally, all of the things that he had done.

- 45 -

Angelica

They never found Charlie, or if they did, no one in Woodford Park was any the wiser. Certainly Angelica heard nothing. There was no trial, no arrest; there were no big headlines to grace the front pages of the local rag or the television news. In that sense, there was a lack of closure and it niggled in the back of Angelica's consciousness. Walter remained a half-fulfilled memory, along with the vague recollections of the town meeting and plans for The Bellevue. Perhaps Mary had heard something, or her other son, the mechanic, but if they had, they weren't letting on. Little by little, Walter became little more than a shadow. Life in Woodford Park went on and Angelica settled down to her plans. After a few weeks had passed, she got back into her jewellery, attended the local market and actually managed to sell a few pieces, one or two to locals, and the rest to the passing tourist trade. Things picked up in Summer and so, gradually did the town's mood. The warmer weather brought a flock of sun-seekers to the beaches and the holiday cottages — new faces to observe and chatter about in the coffee shop and behind the market stalls.

Angelica still made her pilgrimage to the end of Ball's Point, sitting up on the bench, smoking the occasional cigarette and watching the waves slide in across the bay and dissipate along the beach, leaving shiny wetness in their wake. Although she liked the top of the bluff in the colder months, the warmer season filled her with something else. The breeze was rich, and the smell of salt and the pines lay heavier in the air. The sound of children playing in the surf would drift up to her on her vantage point, tugging at memories that were half hidden from view, but still lying nestled securely, quiet in their presence, memories of solidity and stability and a stern older man who ultimately cared for her deeply but would never show it. From time to time, she would venture out to the headland at night, the evening air warm and full of the sweet scents of roses and jasmine and on nights such as that, she would feel sadness, but a rich sadness. She was never quite sure what prompted those feelings, but she did not begrudge them. They belonged, poignant, with the rest of her sensations about the place.

After a few attempts, she expanded her enterprise, taking up her friend's offer to share space at some of the other regional fairs. Little by little, over the Summer months, she started to become a regular, a familiar face at these events, and though it wasn't very deep, there came with it a sense of belonging. Woodford Park was becoming something more to her now, and she wondered whether Walter, The Bellevue, everything that had taken place had bonded her in some way with the town and the community. From time to time, she still had a longing, not for a Sweet Boy, not even for a Sweet Man. Somehow she had moved beyond that need, but still there was something…missing. She started to suspect that that was the natural state of existence, that her self-reliance was what really mattered. It had taken time, but finally, she had reached a place where she was confident in herself; she needed no one else to define her, and anyway, anyone she ever relied on had simple gone, or died, or disappeared. People were ephemeral. People were transitory. They were simply phases in your life, and eventually you moved beyond them.

Perhaps, after all, it was the places that defined what you were, and you grew to become a part of a dynamic that was larger and more powerful than any of the people that were a part of it. In the end, each individual is tied with ribbon and placed within a box of memories that makes the history of a town or a city. In some strange way, Angelica felt quite comfortable with that thought.

-46-

Johan Her Man

A few more weeks passed, gently fading with the warmth of summer and moving to the browns and oranges of autumn. There was a chill in the air that evening, and Angelica pulled a warm knitted shawl around her shoulders. She'd just come in from the garage where she'd set up her jewellery making equipment on one of the benches at the side. There was still the clutter of old pieces of bike and tools occupying most of the space, and she supposed that really she should set about having them cleared, making the space truly her own. She would need to put a heater in there soon if she was going to continue working out there when it got truly colder in the winter months. There was time for that though. She made herself a cup of tea and stood looking out of the front window down to the beach, to the fading oranges and the slight tinges of purple and green darkening at the edges of the horizon. She turned to her music collection and riffled through, looking for something that would carry her away for a while. She finally settled on an album of baroque choral music.

The voices were growing and swelling about her, as the sky grew darker, when there was a knock at the kitchen door, not at the front, and she gave a little frown. She hadn't been expecting anybody. She placed her cup of tea down, reached over and turned down the music. Pulling her shawl tighter around her shoulders, she headed back through to the kitchen and opened the door. There in the semi-shadow stood a tall figure, dressed all in black. She couldn't see his face.

"Hey, babe," he said. "It's been a while."

"Johan?" It couldn't be. "Johan?"

"Yeah. Are you going to invite me in or leave me standing out here in the dark and cold?"

"But...."

"Shhh," he said, reaching out with one hand and putting a finger to her lips. In the other hand he held gloves and helmet.

She was still confused, scrambling to readjust to this turn of events. He slid his tall leather-clad frame past her and walked straight through the kitchen and into the living room, leaving her to close the door.

"Place hasn't changed much," he said.

Angelica walked back into the living room and stood staring at him.

"Johan," she said, then paused, unsure what to say next. "Where have you been?"

He laughed lightly and placed his helmet down on the coffee table before sitting arraying his long legs out in front of him. "You wouldn't believe some of the places I've seen," he said. "I feel like I've been everywhere."

Angelica sat down across from him, a little unsteadily, staring across.

"Well," he said. "You don't seem very pleased to see me."

"I'm...just...I didn't..."

"Or maybe I'm interrupting something," he said. "Maybe you've moved on. I wouldn't blame you." He leaned forward in his chair, looking at her intently, studying her face. "Did you miss me, babe? I missed you."

She felt lost for words. She didn't know what to say to him.

"Listen, Angelica, I'll understand if you want nothing to do with me, but I've missed you. There were times I thought about you every day on the road. I told you back then it was something I had to do, but I guess it's out of my system now and no matter how I tried, you were the only thing I wasn't able to get out of my system."

Still she had now words.

"Will you have me back, babe?" he said. "Do you want me back here in your life? I'll understand if you say no. I will."

"Johan, I…"

"Well…"

"Of course I want you back," she said.

The tears were starting to come now, welling in her eyes and running down her cheeks. She reached up to wipe them away. She stood.

"Come here, you big stupid man," she said and held out her arms. "I've missed you so much.

He stood and in turn stepped forward, wrapping his big strong arms around her, the smell of leather and oil wrapping about her along with his grip.

"Me too, Angelica," he said. "Me too, babe."

As Angelica stood there, wrapped in the security of his arms, she thought once more to herself: memory is a funny thing sometimes.

-47-

The Memory Box

Angelica lay on her bed, windows firmly closed against the winter chill, wind buffeting the glass and rattling them in their frames. Breakers were rolling in against the beach below, dark, gun-metal grey and churning with brown foam. There was too much energy, directed force there, reminding her of all the uncontrollable things at work in the world, too much there to even think about. Johan, fool that he was in this weather, had taken the bike out despite her protests, but regardless of the wind whistling around the edges of the house, the leaves slapping against the walls, and Johan's absence, with the fire in the next room, Angelica felt secure and quite safe. Johan would be okay. He knew what he was doing and just sometimes he liked to pit himself against those elements. It gave him a sense of freedom, he said. Johan Her Man, simply being a man was what it was. She stared down at her memory box for a few seconds, not thinking about anything in particular, but hesitating. Somehow, some way, there was a touch of reluctance, but then, finally, after a moment's pause, with a slight sigh she forced herself past the hesitation, reached down slowly, carefully and stroked the lid before easing it back to reveal all those bits and pieces, the fragments she had collected to make up the memories of her life.

One by one, she lifted items from the box and arrayed them on the floor, choosing which ones she wanted to look at, and which ones she would leave for today. This was reflection, this was understanding, and somehow, in its own way, it was catharsis. More than that, it was coming to grips with her own identity, communing with what she was now and what she had been. There, the photo of that Sweet Boy, there that little poem she'd written and there, carefully sealed in an envelope, that first flower that Johan had given her. She lifted another couple of letters and then paused, hesitating, her hand hovering over the box's contents. No, she wasn't ready for this, or was she? It had been nine months now. Nine months was perhaps time enough. Nine months was, after all, a period of gestation. This time, perhaps, rebirth instead of birth. Long enough. Time was subjective anyway.

Slowly, carefully, with the fingers of both hands lightly holding the edges, she lifted the newspaper clipping out of the box. Instead of placing it on the floor with the rest of the items she'd chosen, she placed it carefully down on the edge of the bed cover in front of her, and then propped herself up on her elbows to study it more closely. Gently, delicately, she traced the fingers of one hand across the paper's surface, marking the outline of his face, though blurred with the dots of newsprint, gently biting her lower lip as she did so, almost as if she might damage the picture, or the memory that went with it.

"Walter," she whispered. "Oh, Walter."

All she remembered then was his presence, their brief time together. It had been far too short. She tried not to think about the details of what had happened, though she knew, perhaps, that it was because of those events that she felt the way she did, that hollow of loss that remained. Their time together would not have lasted, she knew, but it was shared being together for that brief duration and that, that was enough.

"Oh, Walter," she said and with a small shake of her head, she carefully returned the clipping to the box. She did not feel like tears, though there was sadness. The ache was poignant, dreadful, but it didn't need tears. She had done her weeping already.

Just then, she noticed a corner of something poking out from beneath the others. It was old, she could tell that. For some reason, she didn't quite remember it being there. She leaned down and juggled the old black and white photograph from beneath the other piled pictures and papers. Frowning, she lifted it to peer at the faded detail, a man and a child standing on a beach. Behind them stood a row of thick-trunked pines, a few cars and sky. She remembered the photograph now; it had been ages since she'd actually looked at it, even years. Angelica and her grandfather standing on the beach, hand in hand, so many years ago. Angelica as a child. It wasn't a particularly good picture, a little blurry and the passage of time had taken its toll. There was her grandfather, his stern face staring fixedly at whoever was taking the picture, and Angelica herself, so young, her arm slightly raised with her hand held in the much larger hand of her grandfather. She didn't remember the little bathing suit she wore, but it was some colour and white, with flowers, probably blue. She could just make out the marks of the sun, streaking her blonde hair. She had been so young then. In the photograph, the image of herself looked happy. She closed her eyes for a moment, and then opened them, and taking a deep breath, she slipped the old photograph back between the piles of other memories, deep within the box.

Suddenly, she had no appetite for the other things, for the bits and pieces of memory that lay neatly laid out across her floor. One by one, she picked them up in turn and placed them back in the box, finally covering Walter's picture from view. She didn't need a photograph to remember him, but despite that, she was glad the clipping was there, that she had the short newspaper article as a prompt. Memory was a funny thing, anyway.

Slowly, thoughtfully, as if having reached a decision, she nodded to herself. With a shallow sigh, catching her lower lip between her teeth, she reached down and gently closed the lid. That was enough for today.

It would be enough for that particular day and then, after, for a long time to come.

oOo

About the Author

Jay Caselberg is an Australian author currently based in Germany. His works, both short fiction and novels have appeared in many places worldwide and in several languages. He is currently working on a couple of new novels and some more short fiction. More can be found at his home page, http://www.caselberg.net

Printed in Great Britain
by Amazon

16380182R00148